A C

ROOM FOR
MURDER

Lois Lamanna

Manufactured in the United States of America

This book is a work of fiction. Names, characters, and incidents are the product of the author's imagination. Any resemblance to actual events, places, or persons, living or dead, is entirely coincidental.

Cover design by Right Brain Press, LLC.
www.rightbraingraphicdesign.weebly.com

ROOM FOR
MURDER

A Grant House Mystery

Lois Lamanna

Enjoy!

Lois Lamanna

CHAPTER 1

EVEN THOUGH I had travelled along the manicured gravel driveway thousands of times and the gates were open, this time was different. I stopped the SUV at the entrance to the estate and read the brass nameplate attached to the pillar, Grant, one simple word. Shivers of excitement raced up and down my spine. Less than an hour earlier I met with the family attorney and signed the necessary papers. I was now the proud, fourth generation owner of the hundred year old, ten bedroom structure known by the locals as Grant House. My cheeks hurt from smiling. I admired the twin turrets, the stately columns of the port cochere, and the stained glass window arching grandly over the front entrance.

I knew the five people currently living in the red brick mansion, they were my relatives and not one of them had the surname Grant. Following family tradition Grant was somewhere in their names; first name, middle name, or hyphenated along with a different last name. Respectfully, I called the residents Aunt and Uncle and the part of their name that wasn't Grant. They were: Uncle Norman, Uncle Stewart, Aunt Dorothy, Aunt Mildred, and Aunt Helen. The true genetic lines were blurred.

I also had Grant tucked into my name. Unfortunately, my parents couldn't decide which part of my name or which ancestor I should be named after, as a consequence my given name is Grant Grant Grant. Fortunately everyone calls me Gi-Gi (no last name, like Madonna or Cher).

The attorney had joked that having three Grants in my name was the reason the house had been deeded to me. In reality it is because I am the only member of my generation. I don't have any siblings or cousins.

My name was not the only reason why the house was deeded to me. My recently acquired nursing degree held an attraction to the five residents. I represented a live in, able bodied professional who could look after their aches and pains, distribute their medications, and supervise their diets without the benefit of a paycheck.

Shifting the car into gear, I slowly drove up the driveway to the double doors at the front of the house. I hurried to lift the suitcase out of the trunk and carried it to the entrance. I wasn't anxious to enter the house, but I was afraid Harold, the butler, in his eagerness to fulfill his role, would attempt to carry my luggage and have a heart attack.

I almost carried my suitcase back to the car and drove off. I knew exactly what was expected of me as the mistress of the estate. If my romance with Doctor William Appleby had not recently ended with his engagement to a wealthy patient's daughter, I would not be standing by the door. Broken hearted, I needed the cocooning and love of these people as much as they needed me.

When I didn't hear the tread of Harold's shoes on the marble entry floor, I raised the brass knocker again and allowed myself the pleasure of three additional, precisely timed (as protocol defined) taps. I knew my aunts and uncles were waiting in the parlor immediately to the left of the foyer, but would not walk the twenty feet to open the door. That was the butler's duty.

After a second brief period of waiting, I gave up, opened the latch, and lifted my suitcase across the threshold.

For all my relatives' failings, good manners were not one of them. The gentlemen rose to their feet as if they were surprised by my sudden appearance and hadn't known me since I was born. They greeted me with extended arthritic hands. I ignored their impersonal gestures and hugged them instead. Rearranging their needlework on their laps, the women waited. When I finished hugging Uncle Norman and Uncle Stewart, I bent over each of my aunts and gave them a kiss on the cheek.

Evidence of my expected arrival was the clothes they wore. The women were attired in floral chiffon dresses (carefully tucked around their knees) and pearl necklaces (the only jewelry acceptable for daytime). The men wore bowties and jackets.

Their formality belied our relationship. Growing up, I spent weeks and months at Grant House either under the supervision of a nanny and the relatives while my parents were stationed in some remote village doing good deeds for the Peace Corp or with my parents while they were home between assignments.

I opened the drapes to brighten the parlor, an act worthy of a reprimand if I hadn't been deeded the house. I made a note to have Stella, the day help, wash the windows and send the drapes to the dry cleaners.

"Where's Harold?" I asked. In the past fifteen years I had not entered the house without the official inspection by the loyal caretaker.

Aunt Dorothy looked to the others for approval before she spoke. "It's his shopping day. We haven't seen him."

"If he was going to be late, he should have called." Aunt Mildred punctuated her comment with a disapproving 'tsk.'

I sat in an overstuffed chair, straightened the doilies, and placed my feet on the ottoman. It was only after I sat down that Uncle Norman and Uncle Stewart returned to their self assigned seats. Lying on the antique commode table between their seats were identically folded sections of the newspaper. The difference was the amount of the daily crossword filled in. I knew from experience that they bickered over the clues and judging by the number of words filled in on today's puzzle there had been quite a bit of heated discussion.

Uncle Stewart cleared his throat. With a great measure of formality that didn't match the years they had lived together and their family status, he said, "Harold received a telephone call last evening."

"I believe I also heard the phone ring," Aunt Dorothy added to the conversation. "Perhaps he arranged to have a meal with friends and was delayed."

Aunt Mildred interjected, "He still should have called. Connie won't know she needs to prepare the tea tray if he didn't call."

This bit of titillating conversation reminded me to check my cell phone for messages. I pulled the device out of my pocket and the eyes of my relatives followed the action. An alien spaceship landing on the lawn would have received the same amount of curiosity.

For the first time in my life, I observed Aunt Helen's face light up. Her needle stopped mid-jab into her sewing project. "Is that one of those phones without any wires and you can call from anywhere?"

"Now Helen, don't get yourself excited. It's not good for your blood pressure," Aunt Dorothy admonished.

I passed the phone to Aunt Helen. She turned it over in her hands and ran a tender finger over the metal cover. "Open it up," I encouraged. My phone wasn't the latest model, but to the relatives it was high tech. It had been a giant step for them to go from a rotary to a push button phone.

Aunt Helen managed to flip open the cell phone. The digital display flashed, "3 messages." Amazed at the technology, she snapped the phone closed and handed it back to me.

I noticed my uncles were leaning forward in their chairs, interested in the gadget, but too polite to ask to inspect it closer. I handed it first to Uncle Norman and after a brief examination of the small communication device, he passed it to Uncle Stewart, who studied the cell phone intently, opening and closing the cover and placing a finger on each button, determining its purpose.

Aunt Dorothy broke the silence. "We are working on new seat covers for the dining room chairs. We chose a peach color for the background with magnolias as the design. They will go well with your great grandmother's china. Would you like to see the ones we finished?"

"Why don't we wait until after tea to show Gi-Gi the covers for the chairs? She probably wants to go upstairs to freshen up," Aunt Mildred said.

I read between the lines of Aunt Mildred's comment. *Freshen up* was a euphemism for *use the bathroom and change from your jeans into a skirt*. I planned to make some changes to the way the household was run and bring it into the twenty first century, but I didn't want to shock them on the first day of my ownership. I nodded my approval of Aunt Mildred's suggestion and excused myself from the room.

As I put my foot on the first step, Aunt Mildred called out, "Stella aired the master bedroom and put fresh linens on the bed. It has the nice view of the driveway and it has a private bathroom. We thought you would be more comfortable sleeping there than in your old room."

"Thank you, I will take a look at the room. It has been years since anyone has slept there." I wasn't emotionally attached to my childhood bedroom and the items I was having delivered from my apartment wouldn't fit into the smaller room. If my memory was correct, in addition to the en suite bathroom, there was a sitting area off the master bedroom which would serve as an office and a place to escape when the aunts and uncles wore on my nerves.

I quickly unpacked the few things I had brought with me, set up my computer, and changed into a green skirt that matched the knit top I wore for travel. I brushed my short hair and reached for my ever present cell phone. I chuckled when I realized the gadget was still in the possession of Uncle Stewart and if I didn't ask for it back, he would squirrel it away in his room. Uncle Stewart was a hoarder. He never threw anything away.

CHAPTER 2

H E SHOULD BE fired." I heard Aunt Dorothy say as I stood with one foot suspended over the top step. I waited to hear the identity of the person who should be fired, although I suspected she was talking about Harold's infraction to their strict schedule.

From the shadowy appearance of the parlor I could tell someone had closed the drapes in my brief absence, guarding against the destructive nature of sunlight on the heirloom carpet and furnishings.

"Now, Dorothy, it isn't that bad. Tea is only fifteen minutes late," Uncle Stewart said, trying to calm his relative.

"This time it is only fifteen minutes, the last time was thirty minutes," she rebutted. "If Harold gets away with slovenly work habits who knows how long it will be next time."

"That was five years ago and he had a good excuse and said he was sorry. Serving the tea late twice in fifteen years is not a reason to dismiss the man. Besides, Gi-Gi hasn't come down from her room. We wouldn't be able to serve the tea until she joins us."

"Gi-Gi needs to be tough with the servants or they'll take

advantage of her sweet nature."

I descended the stairs, allowing my shoes to land on the squeaks and to slap against the wood. The less than subtle announcement of my arrival ended the discussion about the help.

"Oh, the tea isn't here yet? I'll go into the kitchen and see what is causing the delay." Without waiting for their permission, I scurried to the back of the house and pushed open the swinging door leading to the kitchen. The usual activity of whistling kettle, clanging silverware, and banging drawers was occurring.

The heavy shape of our long time cook was the only thing I saw. "Connie?"

She turned, squealed, arms open. "Gi-Gi, my child, it's been too long. Let me take a look at you."

It was a mystery how she could take a look at me when she was holding me so close, squeezing the breath out of me.

"Congratulations on being deeded the house." Connie released me long enough to allow me to draw in some oxygen. Then she grasped me in another bear hug. "You're just what the old folks need. They're too settled into the routines. You need to stir them up a little, get them moving again."

I pulled away. "We'll chat later, after they drink their tea. Right now they're about to mutiny because their tea isn't on time."

"Harold isn't back with the cake and cookies. If I had known he wouldn't be here, I would have baked something," Connie explained. She poured the boiling water into the china teapot.

I looked out the window to see if the car was coming down the driveway. "Connie, the estate car is in the stables." I bit my tongue. We hadn't had horses on the property for seventy years. Stable was our affectionate name for the building converted into garages. It was one of the things I would change.

"Then he forgot to bring in the cakes when he got back." Connie filled the cream pitcher and replaced the carton in the refrigerator.

"The aunts and uncles haven't seen him all day and he didn't answer the door when I arrived."

Connie stopped her tea tray activity. "That's not like him at all." Worry lines appeared between her eyes. "Now that I think about it, I haven't seen him either. I assumed, since it's his regular day for shopping, that he left early so he would be back when you arrived."

"Do you think he's sick?" I asked. Connie's concern was affecting me.

"I'll use the intercom to buzz his apartment downstairs."

I watched as Connie pushed the button on the antiquated system that conveyed the message to the butler's apartment that he was needed upstairs. "He didn't buzz back to let me know he got the message," Connie explained, gesturing with a ladle.

"You prepare the tea things. I'll run down and knock on his door." I didn't wait to hear if she had an alternate suggestion. I clamored down the first three steps, rounded the bend where the back entrance/Harold's private entrance was, and raced to the basement where a former butler had managed to construct his personal domain. I didn't wait to use a dainty tap on the door. Instead I pounded on it using my fist.

When I didn't get a response, I did what I did when I was a child. I peeked through the key hole. The perspective was limited, but it allowed me a clear view of the soles of a pair of upright shoes. It was enough to send me dashing up the stairs two at a time.

"Where's the key? I need the key."

"What key? What do you need it for? What's wrong?" Without waiting for answers to her questions, she fumbled through the junk drawer and held out the skeleton key that fit every door in the house.

As soon as it was in my hand I raced back to the basement apartment. I was turning the key in the lock when Connie caught up to me, breathing heavy from the exertion of the stairs, the ladle still in her hand. I wished she had smacked me over the head with the cooking utensil when I realized the door wasn't locked.

"Stand back," I commanded. I turned the knob and pushed open the door.

Just as I had surmised from my keyhole perspective, Harold was lying on the floor. It didn't take a nursing degree to determine he wasn't lying there voluntarily. With a vacant look in his eyes, a gray tinge to his complexion, and a bullet hole in his chest, there was no need for me to examine him. He was dead and there was no hope for resuscitation. Harold would not be serving tea.

"Connie, I'm depending on you. Go up to the kitchen and call 9-1-1. Tell the police not to use their sirens. Tell them to enter through the back door. Then fix the tea for the aunts and uncles and serve it in the front parlor. The drapes are closed. They won't know what happened until I break the news to them later."

"Why did he kill himself?" Connie's heavy bosoms heaved as she held back a sob. She reached down for the hem of her apron to wipe away a threatening tear.

A quick glance around the room didn't reveal a weapon. "He didn't kill himself. Someone shot him. Now please do what I asked you to do. Send the police down when they arrive. I'm going to wait here."

Connie's foot was on the bottom tread when she turned and asked, "What should I tell them? They have been waiting for you to join them for tea."

"Tell the aunts and uncles that I was suddenly overwhelmed by tiredness from the drive and went upstairs to rest." I waited at the door to Harold's apartment until Connie was at the top of the stairs, and then I stepped tentatively into the private domain of the butler.

As the only child in a household of older adults, I was welcome to enter everyone's personal space. I would drag my dolls or games with me and spend an afternoon playing on the floor. The assumed welcome into every part of the house was a courtesy I took for granted.

14

The exception was Harold's rooms in the basement. I was forbidden by the butler to enter. On the one occasion when I disobeyed his edict, I was marched out the door with the stern comment that it was unseemly for a young lady to be in a bachelor's abode. The door was firmly shut and locked. I was so humiliated that I never attempted to go back in.

Now with the butler dead, there was no one to block me from entering, although I still had the feeling I had to sneak into the room. I held my breath as if the residents upstairs would hear my movement and I would be reprimanded for being in his private space.

I reaffirmed my original opinion. Harold was dead and had been that way for some time. I had a nursing degree, but I didn't have the experience to determine the exact time of death. The blood was dry on the front of his shirt. From the size of the stain, the shot had been accurate and death immediate. A medical examiner would perform an autopsy and reveal further secrets of his demise.

Other than the fact Harold had served the family loyally for fifteen years, I didn't have any idea of the person he was. I vaguely recalled that his last name was Peters and he came from Philadelphia. I didn't know if he had family, brothers or sisters, nieces or nephews who needed to be notified of his death. I didn't know if he had hobbies, if he spent hours constructing miniature boats in bottles or if he collected stamps. I did know that in the years of his employment with the Grants, he had never returned to Philadelphia or took a vacation.

I used the time to study the contents of the room, hoping to find pieces to the puzzle of who the man had been before he became our butler. This would be my only opportunity. Once the police arrived, they would thoroughly search every square inch and every item, looking for clues to the killer's identity.

I made a quick assessment of the space.

Harold had lived a Spartan life if the contents of the sitting room were to be judged. The chair had once been in an upstairs parlor and discarded as being too worn and faded for that room (ditto the rug). There were no family photos hung on the walls or resting on the tables. The only indication that someone actually lived in the apartment was yesterday's newspaper haphazardly discarded, lying on the floor beside the chair. The solitary lamp still glowed.

Careful not to touch anything, I moved into the bedroom. Here was where Harold had spent his own money to provide creature comforts. The linens on the bed were smooth and invitingly turned down like in an expensive hotel. The blankets on the bed were definitely first quality and the same could be said for the sheets. The latest model television, a large flat screen with all the bells and whistles, was securely attached to the wall opposite the bed. The drawers to the dresser were firmly closed. I suppressed the urge to open them.

The closet door was ajar. With one finger on the edge of the wood, I opened it to examine the contents. On the right side of the closet, seven black suits hung on wooden hangers alternating with seven stiffly starched white shirts. The hangers were spaced a precise one inch apart. On the left side of the rod, several pair of casual pants and a vast array of sport shirts, hanging haphazardly on wire hangers, crammed the space. There were several boxes on the shelf above the rod, but I didn't have time to pull them out.

On the floor of the closet were two pairs of polished, black dress shoes, a pair of dockside shoes, a pair of sneakers, and a black metal box, pried open and left empty.

Voices on the stairs alerted me to the arrival of the police. I didn't have time to contemplate my discoveries. I did, however, take the necessary seconds to stick my head in the bathroom. Nothing had been disturbed unless the person who shot Harold was very neat, folding the towel and positioning the soap in the exact center of the dish.

I was standing next to the body when the first police officer entered the room. He huffed, mumbled his name, and asked, "Have you touched anything?"

"Only the door knob. It was unlocked when I entered."

The second fellow who entered the room went directly to the body, he muttered, "Dead." Unphased by the murder victim lying in the middle of the room, he turned toward me and with the most charming grin introduced himself, "I'm Tony O'Connor."

I have to admit the combination of the grin and the bluest eyes I had ever seen rendered me speechless. I stuttered my name, making it sound like there were half a dozen syllables instead of the two simple letters, Gi-Gi.

Tony was all business, as was the older, nameless officer with him. "What is the full name of the victim?" "What was his occupation in the household?" "When was the last time anyone saw Harold alive?" "Can you make a list of his friends?" "Where did he hang out on his days off?" The questions continued.

I could only answer the first two, deferring the other questions to Connie who had served tea to the residents and joined us in the butler's apartment. She didn't have any answers either.

Tony raised a questioning eyebrow. "I have heard of invisible servants, but I never knew it was true."

Connie opened her mouth to protest, thought better of it, and clamped her lips closed. We both knew it was Harold's desire to maintain his personal privacy and the formality of his position that created the barriers to total integration into the family. It wasn't the snobbery of the relatives.

Other professionals entered the small living space. It became so crowded with technicians, medical examiner assistants, and police officers that I began to feel claustrophobic. I tried to excuse myself from the room.

Tony sidled up to me at one point and asked, "Are there any other people living in the house?"

"Yes, five others, my aunts and uncles," I answered.

He jotted the information in a small notebook. "I thought the house was vacant except for the caretakers. I never see any lights on when I'm on patrol." Then he added, "I have to question them."

"Can it wait until tomorrow?"

"No, it's best to do it while we're investigating the murder scene. Most crimes are solved within the first twenty four hours. If I delay the questioning the perpetrator has time to cover his tracks, establish alibis, and witnesses tend to forget important details."

"But…." My voice trailed off.

"But what?"

"They don't know." I had the good sense to act embarrassed.

"They don't know what?"

I cleared my throat and let the words flow. "They don't know Harold is dead. They don't know Harold was murdered. And they don't know you are here."

"How could your aunts and uncles not know? There are at least six cars in the driveway and almost twice that number of people milling around the rooms down here." Tony shook his head in disbelief.

I tried to think of an explanation that would convey how naive and unworldly my relatives were. The best I could come up with was, "The house is large and built solid. Sound doesn't travel through the walls like it does in modern houses."

"Didn't they see the headlights?" He was in disbelief of what I was telling him.

"The drapes are drawn in the parlor," I countered.

"The fact remains, I have to question them. One of them may be able to provide information that will solve the murder."

"I don't want to upset them."

"Eventually, they'll find out. You can't hide the fact that the butler is no longer living here. They're going to ask questions."

"But, please, not tonight. I only moved back to the house this afternoon."

"I guess we're at a stalemate. I must question them tonight and you don't want me to question them tonight. I think the law wins." As an afterthought he added, "I'll be tactful."

I wanted to wipe the smug look off his face. There had to be a way to compromise. "I have an idea and I think you'll find the aunts and uncles are more candid with their responses if we approach them my way."

CHAPTER 3

AUNT DOROTHY, AUNT Helen, Aunt Mildred, Uncle Norman, Uncle Stewart. I would like you to meet a friend of mine, Tony O'Connor."

Immediately the gentlemen stood up and extended their hands. The ladies twittered and preened as if Tony was calling on them. Dorothy patted her hair and licked her lips. Helen adjusted the neckline of her blouse and straightened the hem of her skirt. And Mildred tilted her head to one side, studied Tony, and asked, "Are you single?" She patted the sofa cushion, gesturing he should sit beside her.

I almost laughed. Big strong Officer O'Connor, who faced unrepentant murderers every day, appeared to be terrified.

He shot a questioning look in my direction, shrugged his shoulders, and sat on the couch beside Aunt Mildred. When he agreed to pretend he came to visit me, he didn't know the microscopic scrutiny he would be subject to.

Dorothy addressed me, "Gi-Gi, ask Harold to bring some refreshments for our guest."

"I don't think Harold is available to do that at the moment. Why don't you get acquainted with Tony while I prepare the cart?" I didn't wait for a response to make my escape from the parlor.

In the kitchen, I grabbed a box of crackers and dumped them onto a plate. I added some cans of pop, a pitcher of juice, and glasses. I placed a bunch of grapes in a bowl and artfully placed a wedge of cheese next to the crackers. I took the ice bucket from the top of the cupboard and emptied the ice cube trays into it. I wheeled the cart toward the parlor in time to hear Uncle Stewart laughing. The sound caused me to stop, dishes rattling, almost spilling the juice.

What was Tony telling my relatives that was causing Uncle Stewart to laugh? Tony was supposed to be discreetly asking questions about Harold and his activities the day before. Nothing about the butler's current condition would be cause for so much as a grin.

I pushed the snack cart into the parlor.

Aunt Helen was wiping a tear from her cheek. I thought Tony had broken the news of Harold's death. "Are you okay Aunt Helen?"

"Oh, Gi-Gi, it was hilarious. Uncle Norman was telling us about the time he and Tony's grandfather climbed over a fence to get into the county fair without paying admission. Augie, that's Tony's grandfather's name, got his pants stuck on a wooden picket and the only way they could get him down was to remove his trousers. What a hoot! I've never heard that tale before."

I turned toward Uncle Norman, "You knew Tony's grandfather?"

"He was several years older than me, but yes, I knew him. He was an adventuresome chap."

Tony added, "My grandfather still works at the produce store in town. Why don't you stop by and visit with him? I'm sure he would enjoy swapping stories with you."

"I just might do that," Uncle Norman replied.

Did I detect a glint in Uncle Norman's eye that wasn't there before? I changed the subject before I could give it any thought. I wanted the police officer to finish his business. "Tony, wasn't there something you wanted to ask the family?"

I should have worded my question differently or I should have been more specific or I should have kept my mouth shut and let Tony question the aunts and uncles in his own style.

The question I asked led the relatives to an entirely mistaken conclusion. All of a sudden, the aunts and uncles were congratulating us, fluttering around, talking about champagne, and hugging Tony. I tried to back out of the parlor without anyone noticing, especially Tony. I had only met him and I had the relatives thinking we were getting married.

I heard a sharp whistle. "Harold is dead."

Silence. All movement stopped. So much for Tony's tact. Slowly everyone returned to their preannouncement seats and demeanor.

Dorothy was the first to speak. "Does this mean you aren't getting married?"

I stood in front of Aunt Dorothy and took her hand. "I only just met Tony. He's investigating Harold's death. He wants to ask you some questions about Harold."

I looked at the people in the room. Uncle Norman no longer had a glint in his eye and Aunt Helen, again, had tears (not from laughter) in hers.

I could have kissed Uncle Stewart when he leaned forward in his chair and asked Tony, "What do you want to know about Harold? We'll try to help."

The next two hours passed with questions, answers, and a few remembrances of kindnesses Harold performed for the relatives. From what I could discern, there wasn't any information that would lead to the apprehension of the killer. Harold had been the perfect butler, discreetly performing his tasks.

I watched the aunts and uncles. It was well past their normal suppertime and I hadn't heard one complaint. It was approaching their bedtime and again not one of them had mentioned the time. Instead, I saw five intelligent people addressing the topic of Harold's death in a cohesive manner.

Tony took notes, occasionally prodding their memories, but mostly he was listening to the aunts and uncles theorize about the death of the person who had been their faithful butler for fifteen years.

When the conversation wound down, Tony stood up, "You have been very helpful. If you think of anything else, I would be pleased if you called me." He reached into the breast pocket of his uniform and withdrew business cards, which he handed to each member of my family.

Aunt Helen sighed when Tony departed.

CHAPTER 4

I POURED COFFEE FROM the carafe on the buffet and took a deep gulp of the dark brew. Only after I felt the effects of the caffeine in my system did I face the five pairs of eyes staring at me expectantly.

"What?" I squinted against the sun shining through the dining room window.

"He seemed like such a nice young man," Aunt Dorothy said.

"Harold? He always performed his duties efficiently." I walked around the dining room table and closed the drapes.

"No, Tony O'Connor."

"He seemed like a very capable investigator. I'm sure he will do his best to capture the culprit who murdered Harold." I blew across the surface of the coffee before taking another sip.

"Did you notice the red highlights in his hair? That's his Irish heritage showing," Aunt Mildred mentioned.

I watched the group suspiciously. They were up to something

this morning. A subtle movement at the far end of the table alerted me to a gentle elbow jab administered by Aunt Dorothy to the rib cage of Aunt Helen, who in turn tapped Uncle Norman on the arm.

"You should register with the bank this morning. You won't receive your allowance from the trust fund until you do," Uncle Norman suggested.

I was familiar with the trust fund. Established by my great grandfather, prudently invested, and suitably tied up by legalese, it provided small incomes to the residents of Grant House and was sufficient to pay the help and maintain the house. "Thank you, but one day won't make any difference. I planned on staying around the house this morning. I'm expecting the rest of the boxes from my apartment to be delivered."

"We can take care of that for you while you're at the bank," Aunt Helen offered.

My suspicion gauge went up another notch. The day before, when I arrived, no one made the effort to walk twenty feet to open the front door. Accepting a package from a delivery person seemed beneath them. Accepting delivery of an apartment's amount of belongings was way out of their comfort zone. I doubted if any of them knew what was involved.

"Uncle Stewart, what's the balance in the trust fund?" I asked. I tried to sound nonchalant. I was positive that the aunts and uncles were plotting something.

"I don't recall. You can ask while you are at the bank." He didn't look me in the eye.

Now I knew something was fishy and it wasn't the smelts on the buffet. Uncle Stewart always knew to the penny how much money was in the trust fund. He watched over it like a farmer watches over his only seed and knew daily what the fund was worth.

I pulled a vacant chair away from the table and sat down. "What are you up to?" I asked the others gathered around the table.

"Nothing unusual. We're planning to spend our day the same way we always spend our days. Helen, Dorothy, and I are going to work on the needlepoint seat covers for the dining room chairs. Norman and Stewart are going to inspect the grounds this morning and do the crossword in the newspaper this afternoon," Mildred replied. "Isn't that right?"

Four heads bobbed in confirmation.

I bit into a sweet roll. A murder had occurred in the basement of the house and not one comment had been made about the butler's death.

If my instincts were correct, the aunts and uncles had something up their sleeves to promote a romance between Tony and myself. I needed to stop their efforts before they got started. I chose my words carefully. "While I was working at the hospital I dated one of the doctors. He broke up with me and immediately got engaged to another woman. I am still getting over the heartbreak he caused. I am not ready to enter into another relationship. Do you understand?"

This time all five heads nodded.

Satisfied they received the message, I picked a crumb from my blouse and put it in my mouth.

I almost choked when Aunt Dorothy asked, "Will Tony be coming to the house tonight to ask more questions?"

§§§ ≪≪

The confession regarding my heartbreak had gone over their heads. I had been in residence for less than twenty four hours and already I needed to get away. "I'm going to the bank."

§§§ ≪≪

Every curtain and every window in the house was open when I pulled into the driveway.

In addition to visiting the bank, I stopped at the grocery store to purchase items Connie needed. I carried the bags into the house through the back entrance and almost dropped them.

Dorothy was wearing an apron and standing in front of the stove, stirring a large pot.

Connie, in contrast, was sitting at the table, sipping from a tea cup. She shrugged her shoulders in response to my questioning look.

"Aunt Dorothy, that smells delicious. What are you making?"

"Vegetable soup," she replied, as if it was something she did everyday. Over her shoulder she added, "We had the delivery people put your boxes in the alcove of the master bedroom."

"Where is everyone else?"

"Your uncles are in the garage, trying to get the old Ford started." Dorothy didn't turn to face me. She continued stirring the soup, stopping only long enough to taste the broth.

"And?"

"Aunt Helen is going through Harold's clothes to see if there is anything that can be given to the church charity drive."

"And?"

"Aunt Mildred is in Uncle Stewart's study searching the files for the resume Harold provided when he applied for the job. She thought the background information would help the police find the killer."

I sat at the opposite end of the table and tried to make sense of the activity. I knew these people all my life and I never saw them do anything remotely similar to domestic tasks.

"Dorothy, I think I found something." I recognized Helen's voice as she ascended the stairs from the basement. Her face blanched when she turned the bend in the stairs and saw me. She hid what she had in her hand behind her back. "Gi-Gi, I'm surprised. You're home early. How did it go at the bank?"

I ignored her question, asking her, "What did you find?"

"Nothing. I was just trying to sort Harold's belongings. They should all be donated to the Salvation Army."

"Aunt Dorothy said you were going to donate his clothes to the church."

"She misunderstood. At breakfast we discussed giving them to the church, but we decided to donate them to the Salvation Army." Helen's cheeks reddened at getting caught in her lie.

I didn't get a chance to question her further. From the stables, I heard a loud crash and a swear word I didn't think either of the uncles knew. I rushed to the window and then out the door. Uncle Norman was lying on his back in the middle of the concrete garage floor.

By the time I crossed the driveway, he was sitting up and smiling. I ran a medically trained hand over his head to check for lumps. I checked his vision and his bones for fractures. The only ill effect he had from his fall was a grease smear across the front of his shirt. "What are you trying to do?" I asked as I helped him to his feet.

"I'm trying to get the old Ford started." Confirming his statement were tools scattered on the floor and a tool box with the drawers hanging open. From the rusty state of the wrenches and screw drivers, it had been a long time since they were last used.

"Why didn't you call the dealership and have a mechanic come out and start it?" I asked. It didn't seem like any of my questions were going to be answered that morning, but this time I provided my own distraction. "Is that a 1964 Ford Mustang convertible?"

"Yep, first year they were made."

I was in awe. I ran a finger through the thick dust.

"It was the fastest car around. The women loved it."

"Norman, come here. You need to see this," Stewart said.

The distractions of Norman's fall and then the Mustang caused me to forget about Stewart being in the garage. "What are you working on Uncle Stewart?"

"Nothing." He slammed the trunk on a newer model, fuel efficient, compact car I had not seen in the garage before.

"When did you get this car?" I asked.

"It's not mine." Stewart walked away from the car as if it

didn't exist.

I followed him. I couldn't remember ever seeing the family members drive. I was interested in finding out who had taken the initiative to learn to drive and purchase a personal vehicle. "If it's not your car, whose car is it?"

"Harold's."

"Harold? Why did he need a car? He had access to all the vehicles in the garage." I stared at the car. "What were you doing in the trunk?"

This time I didn't need an answer. It was beginning to make sense. They were trying to figure out who killed Harold. Mildred was searching the files for Harold's resume. Helen was searching Harold's apartment. Stewart was searching Harold's car. I just didn't know where the soup and the Mustang fit in the scheme.

With both hands on my hips and in a tone that made my patients obey my orders, I said, "Let's go into the kitchen. We need to talk."

The men dusted their hands and followed me into the house. I gathered Helen and Dorothy. I sent Connie to the third floor to request Mildred come down to the kitchen.

When all the residents of Grant House were assembled around the table, I started. "Who would like to tell me what you are doing?"

"Nothing," was the joint response.

"Nothing? I come home from the bank and find the five of you searching Harold's apartment, his car, our records, cooking, and doing mechanical work and you tell me *nothing*. I think something is going on here and I want to know what it is before I toss all of you out on the street." It was an empty threat, but they didn't know that. I waited for the relatives to answer my question.

There was an exchange of meaningful looks between the people gathered at the table. As if by some silent vote and he was elected, Stewart stood up, and said in voice that would have made a politician proud, "We are appalled that a murder took place under our roof and we have decided to solve the crime and exonerate the Grant name." He sat down again.

"Murder is serious business. It's a matter for the police. If you continue to interfere, evidence you find may not be allowed in court." I circled the table. "Further more, what if the killer decides that you are too close to his identity and harms you?"

Mildred stood up. "We don't care. We need to seek justice. Harold was our butler and he was shot in our house. We need to find his killer."

I was surprised by the determination in Aunt Mildred's voice. She had always been the most complacent of the Grants. The others nodded their heads in agreement with her statement.

"What about the danger?" I asked.

"There're five of us, six counting you. We should be able to outwit one person."

"What about the evidence? You could find yourselves thrown in jail for tampering with the evidence and interfering with justice."

Dorothy spoke up. "That's what the soup is for."

"How is soup going to prevent you from charges of tampering with the evidence?"

"We called Tony and he's coming for dinner. We'll give him any evidence we find and he can say he found it."

"Ah, now I know how the soup fits into your plan, but tell me, what does getting the Mustang running again have to do with solving Harold's murder?"

"We may need to chase the killer or make a quick getaway. There isn't another car as fast as the Mustang." Norman's chest puffed out as if he was the proud father.

"More likely, you'll need the car to escape the killer." I hated to burst their bubble of excitement, but they needed a dose of reality and someone to keep their aged bodies safe. "What you are doing is dangerous!"

"What have we done that is dangerous?" Helen challenged,

her arms folded across her chest. "Taking clothes off hangers isn't dangerous. Cooking soup isn't dangerous. Going through our personal papers isn't dangerous. Putting a battery in a car isn't dangerous."

I noticed she hadn't included searching Harold's car on the 'not dangerous' list, but I didn't call it to her attention. I had run out of arguments and the soup smelled delicious. I had to admit I was the teensiest bit excited at the thought of seeing Tony again.

I left the kitchen to sort through the boxes delivered that morning. I would leave the aunts and uncles to their tasks. By tea time they would tire of the activity and fall back into their usual routine.

※※ ※※

By mid afternoon, I heard the powerful engine of the Mustang roar to life. Uncle Norman surprised me with his mechanical skills. His driving left a little to be desired as I heard him grind the gears (several times). If the sounds coming from the garage were any indication, he was going to need a new transmission before he got to the end of the driveway. I tried to remember if my car was out of the way of a possible collision.

On the other hand, he was doing quite well for someone who hadn't driven in the past fifteen years. Harold had taken care of that daily task.

From the kitchen came the mouth watering aroma of freshly baked rolls. I was tempted to leave my task to taste one of the rolls, but I was waiting for the older members of the household to come to their senses, which they obviously hadn't done yet.

At four o'clock, most of the boxes were untouched. I carried the emptied cartons to the trash and ignoring my family members, returned to the master bedroom to take a shower, wash my hair, and change into something suitable for a Grant House dinner with a guest.

Ignoring the family members was a moot point, as they weren't visible. The aunts weren't in the kitchen and the uncles weren't in the garage. I assumed they were exhausted from their flurry of activity and retired to their respective rooms to rest before dinner as I had predicted.

The hair brush was in my hand for a final attempt at creating a sleek hairdo when I heard footsteps and conversation in the hall outside my room. Feeling childish, and for the second time in two days, I bent low and spied through a keyhole. When that didn't provide satisfactory information, I put my ear against the door and listened.

"I remember Norman being an excellent driver."

"But he hasn't been behind the wheel in decades."

"I think it's like riding a bicycle or swimming, once you learn how, you never forget. At least that's what Norman said."

"I don't know."

"Think of the adventure."

I took another peek through the keyhole and saw Aunt Dorothy and Aunt Helen walk past. At least I thought it was them. The voices sounded like their voices, but the persons in the hall were wearing slacks, something my aunts would never wear. Furthermore, the word *adventure* was not in their vocabulary.

I opened the door in time to see the tops of their heads as they descended the stairs. Maybe I was mistaken about their clothes.

Or maybe not. Minutes later I heard car doors slam and the roar of the Mustang's engine. I raced to the window in time to see the backs of five gray haired heads and the taillights as the convertible, driven by Norman, turned onto the main road.

I said a silent prayer for their safety and wondered what I would do in the big house if I had to live in it by myself.

*****

I paced back and forth from the foyer to the back door. It had been an hour and the aunts and uncles weren't home yet. I pictured all sorts of trouble. (The Mustang dangling over a cliff being the chief image.) I hesitated when the telephone in the hall rang. I wanted it to be my relatives calling to report they safely arrived at their destination. I feared that the caller was the local hospital reporting injuries to five senior citizens.

When I picked up the phone, all I heard was voices bickering in the background. "Hello? Hello?" I yelled into the phone.

"Gi-Gi? Is that you?"

"Uncle Stewart, are you alright?"

"Dry rot."

"Dry rot? What do you mean?" My mind whirled through my nursing school education as if it were a virtual Rolodex. I had never heard of a medical condition called dry rot.

"The tires on the Mustang were dry rotted. All four of them are flat." His statement was mixed with scratchy noises as he attempted to master the use of the cell phone.

"Where are you?"

"We're about a mile from the house."

"Why didn't you call sooner?"

I heard the embarrassment in his voice as he said, "It took that long to figure out how to use the doggone cell phone."

"I'll be right there." Knowing that the aunts and uncles were safe, I delayed my rescue mission long enough to call the local tow truck service and the Ford dealership. If the aunts and uncles were going to be crazy enough to ride around in the Mustang, the car needed to be inspected and a license plate needed to be issued.

As an afterthought, I looked up the number for a driver training school and made appointments for Uncle Norman and Uncle Stewart.

A quieter group of senior citizens rode back to the house.

A long-faced Norman was the last passenger to get out of the SUV. He apologized for the inconvenience of having me pick them up. "I should have thought of the tires before we went onto the highway."

Stewart, who was waiting by the car door, patted Norman on the back. "It was fun while it lasted," he said. He took the cell phone from his pocket and offered it to me.

"No, you hold on to it. I think you're going to need it."

My relatives walked toward the house like they were walking to the hangman's noose. I wondered if I had made the right decision to come back to the family home and care for these people.

In an effort to make them forget the glitch in their plan, I called out, trying to sound cheerful, "Don't forget, Tony will be here for dinner in twenty minutes."

Dorothy waved in acknowledgement, but the others kept walking with their heads hung low.

CHAPTER 5

TONY LOOKED AROUND the table making an almost imperceptible shake of his head. He thought he had been invited to dinner for conversation and some laughter like at his family gatherings. So far everyone had eaten in silence. The only sound in the room was the accidental tap of a spoon against the side of a soup bowl.

His feeble attempts to start a conversation were met with blank stares. Comments about baseball, politics, and the weather had been met with glares from his fellow diners. Resigned to eat his soup without the fellowship of the others, he tried one more time. "Have you thought of anything that will help us find the person who killed Harold?"

I didn't feel like talking. The actions of my relatives had caused me to rethink my life plan. I tried to help with the chatter, but my heart just wasn't in it. I felt sorry for the off-duty officer. He was looking especially handsome this evening and had even brought small bouquets of flowers for each of the aunts, but I still couldn't summon the positive energy to wipe out the depressive atmosphere.

In response, I handed the question off to Aunt Mildred. "You were upstairs today going through Uncle Stewart's files. Did you find anything?"

Dragging out the words, Aunt Mildred said, "At breakfast, we thought we kept a copy of Harold's resume from when he applied for the job of butler. I mean Stewart keeps everything. It's strange, I went through most of Stewart's files, but I didn't find it."

"That was a good idea. If you can find the resume I will be able to check the references, and hopefully find out something about Harold's past. The information could lead us to the killer."

Mildred lowered her head. "To tell the truth, we don't remember his last name. If I knew that, I may be able to locate the document."

Tony wiped his mouth with the linen napkin. "You don't remember his last name? Didn't you write out his paychecks?"

Finally, Uncle Norman had something to say. "The bank writes out the checks to pay the help from the trust fund."

I interrupted. "His last name was Peters."

Tony scratched his head and acted like he hadn't heard what I had said. "You have people do your check writing?" He didn't wait for an answer. He pulled his notebook from his back pocket. "The bank is a good lead. What's the name of the bank? It's likely Harold had his account at the same bank. We may be able to trace Harold's activities and find his friends based on the transactions he conducted."

Uncle Stewart didn't want to be outdone by the praise Tony offered Mildred and Uncle Norman. Stewart said, "I searched Harold's car."

"He had a car? I didn't know that." Tony looked out the window, toward the garage. "No one mentioned it last night."

"We didn't know he owned a car until this morning. And it's strange, because he was permitted unrestricted use of the cars in the stables," I interjected. "It's one of those hybrid cars that run on electricity."

Tony's eyes widened. "You have stables? First you tell me that you have someone to write out your checks and now you tell me that you have stables."

"They were converted to a garage long before I was born." Aunt Helen studied the contents of her soup bowl.

Norman became an active part of the conversation, steering the conversation back to the topic of Harold's car. "The car Harold purchased is a hybrid. In addition to fuel savings and cutting back on air pollution, it also eliminates noise pollution. Stewart and I have discussed the car and have a theory about why he purchased that particular model as his personal vehicle."

For Tony, the dinner had changed dramatically. My relatives were contributing positively, not only to the conversation, but to the effort to identify Harold's killer. "I would be interested in hearing your theory."

That was all the prompting Norman and Stewart needed. They vied with each other for the opportunity to speak. Finally, Norman leaned back and allowed Stewart to do the talking. "We think he snuck out at night. Harold purposely selected that model of car because of the low level of noise it created. Once we were in our rooms for the evening, with either the radio or television on, he could leave the house by way of the back door, get in that little car, and go anywhere he wanted, do anything he wanted with us being none the wiser."

"You didn't know about his car?"

"Harold kept the garage door shut and we had no reason to go out there."

"What about when you wanted to go out to eat or shop at the mall?" Tony asked.

The aunts and uncles answered in unison. "Harold drove the

estate wagon."

Norman tapped Stewart on the sleeve. "Tell Tony what you found in the back seat of the car."

"Books of matches from bars," Stewart whispered as if it was scandalous.

"Do you remember the names of the bars?" Tony asked.

"Better, I put them in a plastic bag. You can take them with you." Stewart twisted in his seat until he could reach into his pocket. He pulled out the bag and displayed it the way an angler displays a trophy fish.

Tony accepted the offering. "Anything else?" His eyes made the circle of people sitting at the table.

"I have to agree with my uncles," I said. "Harold went out after they retired for the night."

"Based on what?" Tony asked.

"Last night, while I was waiting for the police to arrive, I looked around Harold's apartment." Five pairs of eyes widened in shock as if I had committed a heinous breech of social etiquette. "In his closet were the suits he wore for the job, but the majority of the closet was filled with casual clothes. The type of clothes men wear when they are drinking in bars."

Helen joined the conversation. "I saw the clothes too and I have to agree with the Gi-Gi. Harold had a lot of casual clothes, but I never saw him wear anything but his suits."

"There, I knew you would come up with helpful information." Tony leaned back in his chair and studied his notes.

"But." Helen's single word hung in the air. We held our breath while she formulated the thoughts to complete her statement. "But I don't think the matches were Harold's. He didn't smoke. He never disappeared to have a cigarette. He never smelled of smoke when he was around us. His teeth weren't yellow. He didn't have any flecks of ash on his suits."

Dorothy nodded in agreement.

I got caught up in the speculation. "What if he had a girlfriend and she smoked. She caught him cheating on her and she shot him in a jealous rage."

Tony tapped the pen against the notebook. "She would have visited him in his apartment several times before last night. He hadn't tidied the sitting room before her arrival. He was comfortable with her visit."

Helen waved her napkin in front of her face, as if the slight breeze created enough extra oxygen to prevent her from fainting. "Harold was having a relationship? Here? In our house?"

"Knock it off. I went to the same college you attended. I knew your reputation. I also know how old you are and you aren't old enough for a case of the *vapors*," Stewart said chastising the drama queen. He added a leer to take some of the venom out of his comment.

In a huff Helen stood up, taking her soup bowl into the kitchen. The door swung shut behind her.

Her exit gave me the opportunity to ask a question, "What if it was the first time the woman visited, and the visit was unexpected?"

Tony jotted the question in the notebook.

I asked another question that had been weighing on my mind. "What conclusions did the investigators make about the empty metal box on the floor of the closet?"

"Excuse me," Tony said.

I thought he hadn't heard me, but he was reaching toward his belt before I repeated my question.

"That's a humdinger of a cell phone," Stewart said.

Tony's cell phone was top of the line. It had all the computer aspects built into the display: email, internet connection, GPS. If Norman and Stewart were impressed by my antiquated version, they were drooling over Tony's phone. While I admired the cell phone, Tony answered the call. I listened without shame. If he wanted to keep his call private, he should have left the room.

I was disappointed with Tony's side of the conversation,

which consisted of a series of Yeses and Noes. When he finished the call, I lowered my eyes as if I had been studying my soup bowl the entire time.

"That was the dispatcher. I'm needed. There's been a multi-car accident out on the highway." Tony stood up. "You've given me some strong leads and when I am able to, I'll work on them. In the meantime, if you think of anything else, you can call me at the station and leave a message."

There was a moment or two of polite thank yous and compliments regarding the dinner, then Tony was gone.

I started collecting the dirty dishes and utensils from the table.

Norman raised one finger into the air as if he had an idea and put it down. After several more seconds elapsed, the finger was raised into the air again. "There's no reason why we can't follow up on the leads," Norman said.

"What leads?" Stewart asked, leaning forward, his interest obviously piqued.

"The bars." Norman looked around the table to see if everyone understood his intention was to go to the bars to find Harold's friends.

Helen's head popped out of the kitchen. "The bars? I haven't been to a bar in thirty years."

"I wouldn't know what to do at a bar." Dorothy twittered with excitement.

"You walk in, sit down, order a drink, drink the drink, and leave," Norman responded.

"That's it." Dorothy sounded disappointed. "I thought all kinds of dirty secrets happened in bars."

"There's more to it than what Norman said. There's flirting and dancing. There's people watching and …," I offered. I didn't like the direction the conversation was headed. It would be up to me to discourage the relatives from doing something crazy that would jeopardize the official police investigation.

"Oooh, it sounds interesting. I want to go. What should

I wear?" Helen's hands fluttered and her feet danced with anticipation.

"Sit down Helen," Mildred commanded. "No self-respecting woman goes into a bar."

"But I don't want to be a self-respecting woman. It's boring. All you do is needlepoint seat covers for the dining room chairs."

"Helen has a point," Dorothy interjected. "She's still young. She should go out in the evening."

I choked, covering the noise with a series of fake sneezes. Helen was the youngest of the aunts, but she was still on the far side of sixty.

"And I think I should go with her to make sure no one bothers her in an unsuitable fashion." Dorothy added, "There is safety in numbers."

Norman looked at his watch. "The way I figure it, Harold escorted us to our individual rooms right after the evening news. He went down to the kitchen for our milk and was finished with his duties by eight o'clock. He needed another thirty minutes to take a shower and change his clothes. I would guess he left the house around nine o'clock and arrived at the bar a little after that. If we're going to question the people he knew we need to follow his pattern. We should also arrive at the bar no earlier than nine."

"We need to decide how we're going to find out what Harold did when he was at the bars."

"We need to find out who he met when he was in the bar."

"I remember a trick from one of those detective shows on television. This guy goes up to the bar and asks for Harold. When the bartender asks why he wants to see Harold. The detective says he owes Harold money."

"Whoa! Didn't we have a discussion about the possibility of a woman killing Harold?" I asked.

Norman straightened his imaginary necktie. In a smooth voice that would make a late night DJ proud, he said, "I think I can handle the ladies."

This was getting out of hand. I pounded on the table to get everyone's attention. "No one is going to any bars."

Five people glared at me.

I caved under the pressure. "Unless I go with you."

The frowns turned to smiles. The three women hurried up the stairs to start preparing for the evening. Helen looked over her shoulder and said to me, "We would be disappointed if you didn't go. We're only doing this for you."

I couldn't follow the logic of how this was about me, but I was in no position to argue. At this point I would have done anything to cheer my relatives.

Norman stared into space and said to no one in particular, "In the old days, I enjoyed a fine cigar now and then."

CHAPTER 6

I WAS INTERRUPTED FOUR times while I dressed for the highly anticipated (not by me, but by the others) bar excursion. Once by Helen, who wanted to borrow something low cut. I gave her a knit top with a scoop neckline. Once by Dorothy, who asked if her flower earrings were too fancy. I loaned her a pair of plain gold hoops. Twice by Mildred who borrowed a blue tank top and then decided it didn't show enough cleavage and came back wanting to borrow a push-'em-up bra, which I refused to loan to her.

When the women gathered in the foyer, they were met by Stewart, who, if I wasn't mistaken, had added a little shoe polish to his hair and Norman who was wearing his prescription sunglasses, to look cool daddy-o (his words, not mine).

Connie, who had stayed late to watch the aunts and uncles leave for their surveillance at the bars, just shook her head. I hoped it provided her with the entertainment she anticipated.

43

I loaded the passengers into my SUV and, I have to admit, they appeared disappointed. After riding in the Mustang, my vehicle seemed stodgy. At least I knew we would arrive at our destination safely. There was a moment of confusion regarding who would navigate. I settled the matter by plugging the GPS system into the outlet. "Which bar are we going to go to first?"

Stewart pulled a note card from his pocket. "I made a list of the establishments from the match books and organized a route. If we spend fifteen minutes at each of the saloons, we should have enough time to find Harold's friends, question them about his activities, and report our findings to Tony at a respectable hour."

I thought he was being over optimistic, but I kept my mouth shut and allowed him his delusion.

"I'm going to order a cosmopolitan. I read an article at the beauty parlor that it's the drink of choice for modern women," Aunt Helen said.

My tongue was going to be a very sore if I had to bite it every time the aunts and uncles said something stupid. I knew the contents of the drink was mostly alcohol and hoped to divert my aunt's attention to something non-alcoholic. I had a mental image of leading my staggering relatives out of a bar, into the car, and up to their rooms later.

Their attention was riveted to the GPS and I was able to drive without any further comments from the backseat crowd. It was only when I stopped at the first bar that they looked up.

Beeping the car locks, I watched the revelers enter the bar.

The aunts and uncles tried to appear like they were experienced bar people. Right up until the moment Norman stepped through the door. (He had forfeited the role of gentleman holding the door for the ladies in favor of being the first person in the establishment. His intention was to determine if the atmosphere was suitable for the delicate sensibilities of the women.) He took one step into the bar and stopped, gawking as if he had never been in a bar before. The others piled into the back of him like starving people at a buffet. Stewart, at the end of the parade, nudged the group forward.

By the time I joined the group they were waiting to be seated by a nonexistent maitre'd. I slipped around the chorus line of my relatives and led the way to a table with six chairs.

"What is on the floor?" Mildred asked. "My shoes are sticking to it."

"Don't look down," I replied. The condition of the floor did not bode well for the cleanliness of the bathrooms. I needed to get the aunts out of there before nature called.

The men were looking at the other patrons of the bar, especially a duo of big haired, big busted blonds sitting on bar stools in front of the old fashioned juke box. A waitress wearing short shorts and a thin fabric tank top strolled up to the table. The men ordered top shelf scotch and water. The waitress extended her arm into the air, then lowered it, indicating that the bar's top shelf did not go up as high as the liquor requested.

I took charge. "The gentlemen will have draft beer, the ladies will have a glass of your house white wine, and I will have a diet cola."

"How did you know to do that? Have you been in a bar before?" Aunt Mildred asked, adding a "tsk" to express her disapproval.

Aunt Helen hadn't said a word, her mouth hanging open since she had walked in the door, watching the activity of the other customers.

The drinks arrived and the waitress lingered, check in hand, waiting for someone to pay it. All of a sudden Norman and Stewart became paralyzed. Neither of them could reach their wallet. I paid for the drinks, and gave the waitress a generous tip. She charitably placed a hand on my shoulder in a gesture that led me to believe she thought I was a counselor for a group of *special* people.

The songs selected by the pair of blonds started to play and they moved from the stools to the dance floor.

My uncles regained full mobility. Norman jumped out of his chair so fast it almost fell over. He joined the women on the dance floor and started moving in a jerky motion reminiscent of a jitterbug. Stewart studied the women and entered the dance floor fray in the form of an arthritic twist. Dorothy pushed her chair back and joined the small group. Her dance style was a fast, one person waltz, involving twirls and dips.

For the moment, Helen and Mildred appeared to be content watching the eclectic dancing.

I slipped away from the table and went to the bar. The bartender stopped wiping the counter. He moved to stand in front of me, prepared to take my order.

"Do you know Harold?" I asked.

"I don't know a Harold."

I couldn't come out and say, "Harold was our butler and he was murdered. We're looking for his killer." Instead I did what anyone who lived with my aunts and uncles would do. "I owe him some money and I'm trying to find him so I can pay him back."

The bartender threw back his head and started laughing so hard, I thought he was going to fall over. "That's funny," he managed to say. He turned off the laughter and became serious like someone turning off the water flowing out of the faucet. He looked me in the eye and said, "I got some good news for you. You don't have to pay him back. He's dead."

I hadn't realized how fast the news of Harold's demise would travel in the small city. I drew upon my acting skills. I put a hand against my chest, a strickened expression on my face, and uttered, "Dead," in what I thought was a shocked voice.

The bartender winked at me. "You have a great sense of humor. What are you doing later?"

I ignored the pick up line and rejoined Helen and Mildred at the table. I noticed their first glasses were empty and a second glass of wine sat in front of both of them. The waitress came over to the table with the tab for the drinks in her outstretched hand and asked for more money. I paid her. She leaned over and said, "Next time, ask for Hal."

Hal? Who the heck was Hal? The bartender? The only way I would ask for Hal was if I woke up the next morning and discovered dinosaurs and the beginning of another ice age.

I watched the uncles dance while I finished my Diet Coke. After I slurped the last of the drink through the straw, I unhooked my purse from the back of my chair and rounded up the group. The others fell into line behind me with Stewart and Norman looking longingly over their shoulders at the young women on the dance floor.

What seemed to be the strangest part of the evening was the smiles and twittering fingers of the girls as they said good night to my uncles. "Bye Stewy. Goodnight Normy."

Stewy? Normy? It hit me like a thunder bolt. The bartender's name wasn't Hal. The waitress was trying to tell me Harold used the shortened version of his name when he patronized the local bars.

I whistled as I drove to the next bar on the list. The use of a nickname was a minor detail, but it gave me an excuse to call Tony. I had something to report. In spite of my protestations about my heartbreak, I will admit, I was looking forward to talking to him.

We entered the second bar like seasoned professionals. There wasn't any gawking. The women quickly found a table. They ordered their drinks. Norman and Stewart still had paralysis when the bill arrived.

The diet cola tasted a little odd, but not intolerable. I drank it and asked for a refill.

Norm and Stewy put some change in the juke box, argued over the selections, and waited for some women to start dancing. No one did.

While they were selecting the music, I strolled up to the bar and asked the bartender, "Has Hal had been in yet tonight?"

"I haven't seen him tonight. Why?"

I didn't have an answer. I wasn't good at thinking on my feet. I fell back on the line that had caused the other bartender to fall over laughing with one modification. "He owes me money and I want it back."

"I don't know when he'll be in or if he'll be here tonight. He comes and goes. Why don't you talk to his girlfriend? She'll know when to expect him." At least the bartender hadn't laughed.

I glanced over to the table the bartender indicated. The only thoughts I had about Harold's romantic interests pertained to him getting caught cheating on his girlfriend or breaking up with her. Either way there was a possibility I was facing his killer. The woman, the bartender pointed to, certainly didn't look like the type of woman Harold would date. In spite of the ruffles around the neckline of her blouse, the woman looked like she could pick up a piano and hold it over her head while she mopped under it.

I hesitated for a minute, took a deep breath, and walked over to the table. "Hi, my name is Gi-Gi. I wanted to ask you some questions about Hal."

"Who?" The voice had a gravelly, masculine quality to it.

"Hal."

I felt a tap on my shoulder. I turned. The bartender was standing beside me with a finger pointed toward the next table.

"Sorry, my mistake." I moved to the next table, where I introduced myself and started the conversation again.

This time, the woman seated at the table more closely resembled the type of woman I would have picked for Harold. She appeared to be his approximate age and was sensibly dressed. Her medium length brown hair was freshly washed and styled and her makeup was skillfully applied. She was drinking a beer. When I asked if she had seen Hal this evening, she replied, "Hal should be along shortly. He said to meet him here at ten o'clock."

I tried to judge the sincerity of her comment. I was hoping

she was lying. If she was waiting for Harold then she didn't know about his death. I didn't relish the thought of being the bearer of the news. Unless she was a talented actress, it also eliminated her from being the person who pulled the trigger.

"May I join you for a minute?"

Reluctantly she nodded her head. I sat across the table from her where I could watch her facial expressions. I wanted to be able to judge her reaction when I told her the news. "I didn't catch your name."

"Darby Jackson." She glanced toward the door in a manner that suggested she was anticipating Harold's imminent arrival or she was searching for an excuse to end the conversation.

"How long have you been seeing Hal?"

"Not very long. Maybe six weeks. What is this all about?" Darby's voice quivered a little bit as she spoke.

"I'll tell you in a minute, but I was hoping to get a little information from you first." Based on my recent break up, I didn't think the duration of the relationship had been long enough for Darby to establish emotional ties strong enough for her to murder Hal if he was cheating on her or breaking up with her. I could still get some information from her.

"Are you his wife? Is that what you're going to tell me? The lying, cheating bastard." Spittle flew out of her mouth when she said the word wife.

"To the best of my knowledge, Hal is not married," I said. Although the possibility that he was married and hiding from a wife had not crossed my mind before. The next time I talked to Tony, I would discuss it with him. If Harold had a secret life of bar hopping, what else had he hid? I decided not to worry about his marital status at the moment and concentrate on what Darby knew about Hal. "Do you know what he does for a living?"

"He has an unusual job. He's a butler for a bunch of old people."

At least Harold had been honest about his job. "A butler is

an interesting occupation. Not too many people have butlers any more. Did you ever go to where he worked and meet the people he worked for?"

"No, but we drove past the house once and the house was totally dark. It looked haunted. Harold told me he expected to come into a lot of money when the residents of the house died."

I ignored her negative comment about the house. It was something Tony had also said. I made a mental note to have timers installed on the parlor lights to dispel the haunted house reputation. "He told you he was going to inherit money from the people living in the house?"

Darby thought for a minute. "Hal never said it in so many words. He told me that he expects to come into some money. I assumed it was from the people he works for." Another moment of silence passed, followed by, "Are you from the IRS?"

I thought Darby had started to relax. I could tell from her question about the IRS that she was still trying to figure out why I was interested in Hal. I tried to think of a harmless, non-threatening question. "How old is Hal?"

"I think he is in his late thirties, but he acts a whole lot younger." Darby glanced at her watch. "He should be here any minute and you can ask him these questions."

"Do you know where he grew up?"

"Like I said, he should be here any minute. I don't feel comfortable talking about Hal. If he wants you to know his personal information he'll tell you." Darby took a sip from her glass, ending of the discussion.

I tried to decide if Darby's evasion of the question was from her lack of knowledge about Harold or if she was sincere in saying that Harold liked his privacy and would answer the question himself when he got to the bar.

It was on the tip of my tongue to tell Darby about Harold's death. I wanted to see her reaction and see if the new knowledge made her more willing to talk about our former butler. I didn't get a chance. Out of the corner of my eye, I saw something that disturbed me and made me want to become invisible. The nameless, older police officer, who had investigated Harold's death, entered the bar and was making a direct line for the bartender. In two minutes, if he asked the right question, he would be approaching Darby's table.

I hastily scribbled my name, address, and cell phone number on a napkin and got up, turning so that my back was toward the bar. I walked over to the table of relatives. "Come on. Let's go."

"But we just got here." Aunt Helen giggled. If I hadn't been so worried about the policeman questioning the bartender, I would have notice that her speech was slurred and she was a little bleary eyed. Her complexion was rosier than usual.

"Let me finish this beer." Uncle Stewart tipped his bottle and gulped the last of the contents.

I counted the glasses on the table. There had been a lot of drinking while I was chatting with Darby. I threw what I hoped was enough money on the table to cover the bill adding an extra twenty for a generous tip. "Come on."

I didn't wait for my little band of merry makers to follow. I wanted to disappear from the bar before the officer noticed us. I walked out the door and hoped for the best.

CHAPTER 7

I FELT LIKE I had had too much to drink the night before and then I remembered I had only ordered diet cola. What was the pounding and why was the sun so bright? I pulled a pillow over my head and rolled so my back was toward the window.

I heard tapping again and hoped it was part of my dream. When the tapping continued, I identified it as someone knocking lightly on the door.

"Gi-Gi, you have to get up," Connie said from the other side of the door.

"Go away. I don't want to go to school," I mumbled.

The door opened and the pillow was yanked from my head. "You have to get up. There's a woman in the parlor."

"Tell her to go away." I squeezed my eyes shut.

"I think it's important. You should talk to her."

I opened one eye. "Who is she?"

"I don't know, but it looks like she's been up all night, crying. I brought you a cup of coffee. You have to get up and get dressed. There's a man in the kitchen who wants to talk to you."

I was confused. Both eyes were open now. "A woman in the parlor?"

"Yes and a man in the kitchen. I thought it would be best if they didn't see each other until you had a chance to talk to them."

I pushed back the covers and reached out for the coffee. After gulping half the hot liquid, I felt my blood begin to circulate. "Where are my aunts and uncles?"

"In the dining room."

A woman in the parlor, a man in the kitchen, and the aunts and uncles in the dining room. It sounded like a game of Clue, but this wasn't a game. This was real life. I squinted toward the clock and tried to decide why two people were visiting at this early hour of the morning. I didn't think either one was selling Avon.

I trotted into the bathroom and took care of those needs, then picked up the clothes from the floor that I had worn the night before. It was a coin toss who I was going to talk to first.

I chose the parlor and the woman. Bad choice.

I instantly identified the woman. Her eyes were red rimmed and her hair looked like she hadn't combed it, but I recognized Harold's girlfriend, Darby Jackson. From her appearance, I guessed someone had told her the news, Harold was dead.

She was still wearing the clothes she wore the night before. I felt better about picking mine off the floor and wearing them.

I didn't say anything. I stood in the doorway. I didn't want her to feel welcome. I waited to hear what she wanted.

Darby skipped the pleasantries. "Why didn't you tell me?"

I read between the lines. Someone had told her that Harold was dead and she wanted to know why I hadn't mentioned it. "I figured it wasn't the time or the place to tell you Harold was murdered."

"Murdered?" She started to cry. "The cop didn't say he was

53

murdered; only that Hal was dead."

"Let me edit my comment. He died of suspicious causes."

"Suspicious causes? What does that mean?" Darby wiped the tears from her cheeks with the back of her hand.

"The police are investigating his death because they think he was murdered." I looked around the parlor for a box of tissues. There were none. Stella needed to add a box in every room until the facts regarding Harold's death were revealed to everyone.

"Who killed him?" There was an accusing quality to Darby's voice, like I was responsible either directly or indirectly for our butler's death.

"We don't know."

"Are you a police officer?"

"No."

"Then why were you at the bar asking me questions?"

"The incident occurred in this house. The man was part of our household for fifteen years. I have a right to know what happened." I moved into the room and sat in the chair across from her.

Darby sniffed. "I was in a relationship with the man. I think I also have a right to know what happened."

"You were in a relationship with the victim of a violent crime. You are probably the person who knew him better than anyone else. You're in the position of being able to tell the police information that will put his killer behind bars."

There was a long pause. Darby took a deep breath. "I lied."

"You lied? You lied about what?" I tried to keep my voice soothing, hoping to gain more information.

"Harold didn't tell me he would meet me at the bar at 10 o'clock. I went there hoping he would show up." With her head tilted downward, she looked at me through a waterfall of hair partially covering her features to see how I took the news.

Darby continued, "I met him six weeks ago. When he came into the bar, he would buy me a drink and sit down at the table and chat. I wanted the relationship to go further, but all my efforts just bounced off him as if they were bullets and he was made of steel. The night we drove past here was all my doing. I pretended a friend was supposed to give me ride home, but forgot to pick me up. I asked Hal to give me a lift which, being a gentleman, he did."

I thought her analogy of bullets and steel was inappropriate considering the manner of Harold's death, but I tried to stay focused on Darby's conversation. "What about the stuff he told you about coming into some money?" I asked, trying to make it sound less important than it was.

"That was true. He did indicate to me that he expected to come into a large amount of money soon."

"So he didn't come out and say it." I hoped if we could find out how he was going to get the money, it would provide the lead needed to find the killer.

"Not in so many words, but he was always talking about what he was going to do with the money, the type of car he was going to buy and trips he was going to take."

"Did he say how he was going to get the money?" I crossed my fingers and hoped he didn't expect to entice the relatives to put him their wills, then kill them off. I dismissed the notion. After working at Grant House for fifteen years, Harold had to know that all of the money was tied up in the trust fund and the relatives didn't have any personal wealth.

"I don't recall him saying anything about how he was going to get the money. I figured he was just talking moon dust."

"Moon dust?" I questioned. I had never heard the expression before.

"Yeah, dreaming about having money and what he'd do if he was rich, like people do when they play the lottery." Darby's complexion had returned to normal, although her eyes still showed evidence of a night of crying.

"So you don't think he was actually going to come into a large sum of money."

"Nah, although he always had money in his pocket to buy beer. He didn't expect me to pay for my own drinks like most of the other guys at the bar."

I thought about Harold's finances and said, "He wasn't making a fortune working here, but he didn't have any expenses either. He slept here and ate here for free. He only needed seven suits and a couple pairs of shoes."

"Well, I guess I'll be going." Abruptly Darby stood up as if to leave. "Let me know when the funeral is going to be."

"I don't think there will be a funeral. To our knowledge he didn't have any relatives and other than you we don't know any of his friends."

"There was someone in his life, his mother or a sister or someone, because no matter how intense our conversation was, he always stopped at exactly eleven o'clock and made a call from the pay phone at the bar."

"Every night?" At least the phone call indicated he had contact with someone on a regular basis. Who was important enough in Harold's life that he would call them? It went back to the conversation Darby and I had the previous evening when she asked if I was his wife. I needed to pass the information on to Tony.

"I can't speak for every night, but on the evenings he was with me, he made the calls. I never listened to the conversation. We rarely mentioned them. I usually made a trip to the ladies room while he made the call."

"And you don't have any idea who he called?"

"No, other than the fact that he excused himself from the table at the same time, I have no idea who he called."

"How long did the call last?"

"Strange, I never thought about it, but the calls were about same length each time, about three minutes long. He was usually sitting at the table when I returned from the restroom."

I played butler and opened the door for the departing Darby. I closed it before she was in her car. I still had a guest in the kitchen and I wanted to check on the aunts and uncles before I faced him.

The drapes were closed in the dining room, not for fear of sunlight fading the wall paper or the carpet, but from hangovers and headaches. I concurred with the decision to keep the lighting mellow, although my desire was more from lack of sleep and the need for more caffeine.

The men were seated at the ends of the table in the chairs with the arms. They were both dozing. Stewart had his shoes on, without socks. I noticed he had opted for a pair that didn't require tying. Norman's head was tilted so that his chin rested on his chest. Drool hung from the corner of his mouth. The women were awake in the general sense of the word, but the bottle of aspirin in the middle of the table indicated they felt a touch under the weather. No one bothered to say good morning and that suited me.

After determining my older relations were only a little worse for wear as a result of their bar experience, not permanently affected, I took care of the coffee issue by filling a cup on my way to the kitchen. A triangle of dry toast completed my breakfast.

I slowly pushed open the kitchen door in a secretive manner. The hinges didn't cooperate, squeaking loudly enough that Uncle Stewart opened one eye. He allowed it to close. I made a mental note to ask Joel, the gardener and handyman, to add a drop of oil to the hinges.

The sound also alerted the occupants of the kitchen of my arrival. I immediately recognized the older officer who had arrived in response to the 9-1-1 call regarding Harold's death and from the bar. I had a feeling he was here to chastise me for interfering in his investigation. My angst diminished only slightly when I saw the empty plate on the table. Connie had fed him a large breakfast.

Room for Murder

When she saw me, Connie gave me a *world peace rested on my shoulders* look of relief. She started to untie her apron, leading me to believe she was leaving, never to return.

"There's no need for you to disrupt your routine, the officer and I will go into the parlor for our chat." I added my own *look*, conveying the message for her to put her apron back on and don't dare leave me alone.

I waved a come with me gesture and the officer followed me through the other door, the one that bypassed the dining room and led into the hallway and along to the parlor. I quickly settled in the delicate rocker. I was afraid it would collapse under his weight or his girth would trap him between the arms and I would need a saw to hack his way to freedom.

I breathed easier when he sat in the overstuffed chair usually occupied by Uncle Norman. This was accomplished with only a minor groan, either from the chair or the man's knees, I couldn't tell. "You'll have to excuse me. There was so much distressing activity going on the other night. I don't recall your name."

"It's Everet Swanson." His speech had the slightly garbled quality of someone with a mouthful of food, but I was able to discern what he was said.

"Well, Everet, what news do you have regarding the death of our butler?"

"I was hoping you would provide the news. I thought you or one of the other residents remembered something. Any little bit of information would help us find his killer."

"We had this discussion with Officer O'Connor last evening. He was very thorough." I was operating under the assumption that Officer Swanson hadn't seen me at the bar the previous evening. Unless he said something to the contrary I was going to continue to assume we had made our escape unnoticed.

"And I hope you will repeat your findings to me."

"I was under the impression Tony would pass along the information to you." In fact I knew Tony had relayed the tidbits to Everet, especially about the books of matches, otherwise, the older officer would not have been in the bar, questioning the bartender. I clamped my lips shut so I didn't reveal anything.

"I did talk to Tony last evening. His report was very detailed. I talked to the bartenders at the establishments printed on the matches. I also talked to the car salesperson at the dealership where Harold purchased his car."

"That was a very good idea. What did the salesperson say?"

"Luckily the salesman remembered the transaction. Not too many of those hybrid cars are made and Harold had to wait three months to get one. But what made the transaction memorable was that Harold paid for the car with a cashier's check. He didn't need a loan to purchase it."

"Harold had to provide insurance information and his driver's license when he purchased the car. That should give you a paper trail to follow." I felt smug as I offered the suggestion.

"Odd thing. The dealership's copy of the transaction is not in the file."

"Trace the license plate."

"The license on Harold's car is a stolen plate."

"Stolen? This is too bizarre. Why would Harold drive around with a stolen license plate on his car?"

"Thieves thrive on that sort of thing. They go to the mall and exchange plates with an unsuspecting person. They get away with it because very few people memorize the numbers and even if they do, they don't check the numbers every time they get in the car. It may be weeks or months before they notice the switch, if they ever notice it."

"Do you suspect Harold was the thief or the victim of someone stealing his license plate?"

Officer Swanson thought about it for a minute and said, "I don't know, but it puzzles me."

I rocked in the chair for a moment while I absorbed the news Officer Swanson had conveyed. "Did you talk to the original owner of the license plate?"

He nodded. "It seems the person it was originally issued to, a nice, church going, family man, has sold his car and was issued a new plate."

The information Swanson revealed was intriguing. The entire auto transaction, license plate, and registration had disappeared, leaving no way to trace Harold's past through it. It was either a series of unfortunate events or someone (Harold?) had gone to great lengths to eliminate a paper trail linking him to it.

"This talk about the license plate brings me to the other reason I came here this morning. I would like to go through Harold's apartment and look for his wallet and other personal papers."

"I thought the investigators did that the night the body was discovered."

"I want to go through his room again. They may have missed something. We know more now and what didn't seem important may have significance."

"I'll have Stella show you his rooms. Feel free to open drawers and poke in the boxes."

"On my original visit I noticed an empty black metal box on the floor of his closet. Do you know what he stored in it?"

"No, I don't have any idea. The residents of the house are old fashioned in most things. It isn't proper for a young lady to be in a bachelor's apartment. I was only in his rooms one time before his death and that was when he first started working here, almost fifteen years ago."

"The box was heavy and pried open. It wasn't the type of thing you would use to store your socks. It had to be something valuable." Officer Swanson became pensive. He appeared to be looking off in the distance, but from where he was sitting there was no distance.

"Whatever was stored in that metal box is no longer in it." I stated the obvious.

"There might be something in Harold's room that will tell us what was stolen."

"You mean something like his paycheck stubs. He could have cashed every paycheck and kept the money in the metal box." I was stretching my imagination for what I would have stored in a locked box. I debated the wisdom of sharing with the officer the tidbit of information Darby Jackson had told me. Harold was expecting a large sum of money in the near future. Maybe the content of the box was going to help him achieve his goal.

"I should get started if I want to make it to the diner for the early bird supper." Everet heaved himself out of the over stuffed chair, pushing hard on the cushioned arms for leverage.

⁂

I continued to sit in the rocking chair, trying to think of Harold as someone who was a complete stranger. The man I knew was loyal and caring. He would not have hurt anyone. He had tended to my relatives in spite of their quirks. Not one of the residents had a bad word to say about him. He didn't deserve to be murdered.

Based on the family's experience with the man, I could logically conclude that Harold's death was a random act carried out by a crazy person. If that was true, the whole family could have been murdered by the intruder. I shook my head to clear the thought. I had to believe the murderer directed his or her action toward Harold for a reason. If we found the motive, we would find the killer.

The rhythmic hum of the hedge clippers outside the parlor windows reminded me that I hadn't spoken to Joel since I returned home. I planned to correct that omission as soon as I checked on the aunts and uncles. I wanted to ask him to oil the hinges on the kitchen door. This would provide the perfect excuse to question him about Harold. Not that I needed an excuse, Joel would give his perspective whether I wanted it or not.

Delaying my chat with the gardener, I detoured to check on

the relatives. The dining room was vacant. The dirty dishes had been removed from the table and the covered breakfast casseroles taken from the buffet. The aspirin bottle was still in the center of the table. I don't know what bothered me the most: finding a dead body in the basement or the absence of my relatives from the dining room. I tried to look on the bright side; at least they were mobile.

I refilled my coffee and went outside to see one of the guiding forces of my youth, Joel.

"Miz Gi-Gi, it is nice to see you home. It is a shame about our friend Harold, is it not?" So much for the pleasantries. Joel got to the root of what was on everyone's mind.

"It is a shame." I took a sip of my coffee. "Have the police talked to you?"

"Oh yez. Yesterday the young officer and this morning the older officer knocked on my door. They asked many questions."

I smiled. I knew Joel was born in this country and grew up on the other side of town, but his accent and patterns of speech made people think he was an immigrant.

I sat on the porch steps and waited. Joel had an opinion about everything and if I sat there long enough I would hear his thoughts about Harold, Harold's death, the police, the weather, the president….

Joel laid down the hedge clippers. He pulled a handkerchief from his pocket, pushed his hat up, and wiped his brow. "The television is always talking about global warming. They blame the heat on cow poop, plastic water bottles, car fumes, but no one blames the sun. Smart people work in the shade."

"Joel, what did you tell the police about Harold?"

"Ah, I told them Harold always did his duty. He took good care of the old ones. He minded his own business."

I smiled when Joel referred to the aunts and uncles as the old ones. He was the same age as Uncle Norman. "That's true, but why would anyone want to kill him?"

"I don't know." Joel sat on the porch step one below where I sat. I had to lean forward to see his face.

"Did you see or hear anything unusual the night Harold was killed?" I asked.

"No, nothing unusual."

We both stared in the direction of the gate.

"What does that mean *nothing unusual*?"

"He did what he always did."

"Tell me." I waited. I knew Joel could see or hear all the activity in the stables below his apartment. If the garage door went up or down he would know. If a car started, even the quiet one Harold owned, Joel would know. He also had a view of the back door from his sitting room window. "You may know something that the police could use to find Harold's killer."

Several times Joel's mouth opened as if he was about to say something. Just as many times he closed it without saying a word.

I assumed it was one of the rules in the man code, the phenomena where one man won't rat out another man. The fact Joel wouldn't talk about Harold's activities led me to believe there was more to Harold than the butler routine he performed for the family. He lived a secret life; one Joel knew or at least partially knew about.

"Let me tell you what I know and you can fill in some of the blanks." I was hoping if I told Joel what I knew, he would feel more comfortable filling in the gaps. "After Harold settled the aunts and uncles in their rooms for the evening, he would change his clothes and go to the local bars."

I looked at Joel to see if I had given him enough information to get him started talking about Harold's late evening life. All the gardener did was nod confirmation of what I said.

I continued. "This activity was so important to him that he purposely purchased a car quiet enough not to disturb the residents of the house."

Joel nodded again.

"But he still had to raise and lower the garage door and you heard the noise."

I still hadn't said enough to get Joel to talk more about Harold's activities.

"Harold met women at the bars and drank beer, but that wasn't the reason he went to the bars. He made a telephone call from the pay phone every evening at exactly the same time, but I don't know who he called or why."

Finally, Joel entered the conversation. "He never had visitors. Only twice in the whole time he worked here did anyone come to visit, the night he died and once many years ago."

"Was it the same person?"

"I don't know. I didn't bother getting up to see who was visiting the first time. The residents were younger and Harold had just started working here. I thought a car in the driveway was just what it was, a visitor. I didn't know how rare the event would be. This time I looked out the window. I was afraid it was an ambulance coming for one of the relatives and I might be needed."

"What did you see?"

Joel's expression changed, as if he was no longer looking at the road, but was looking into his memory for a picture of that night. "I saw a light colored car with four doors and a woman got out. At least I thought it was a woman. The person was medium height and had chin length hair. If it was a man, he needed a hair cut."

"Can you describe what the person was wearing?" I asked.

"Nah, but I can tell you this. The person drove up the driveway as if they had been here before. She drove through the port cochere as if it didn't exist, no hesitation about where the person was going. I mean she had a choice of the front door, the port cochere entrance, or the back door. The driver knew exactly where she was going."

"But you just said Harold only had one other visitor the entire time he worked here."

"Yez, that is strange."

"Unless Harold brought the person here in his car, then the person would know where to go."

Joel thought about my comment. Pulling his self up using the newel post for leverage, he said, "I have to finish trimming the hedge before it gets too hot. Global warming, hmpf."

I sat on the step and thought about what Joel had revealed. Why had Harold been secretive about his personal life? What had he been hiding? Did he think he would lose his job if the family found out about his outside activities? How was he going to get the money he had mentioned to Darby?

The caffeine kicked in. Where thirty minutes earlier I would have killed to return to bed, I was now full of energy. I wandered into the house looking for a project that would take my mind off the death of the butler. Unpacking and settling in rose to the top of my list.

CHAPTER 8

I TRIED TO FOCUS on which project I should tackle when the smell of something delicious diverted my attention to the kitchen. "Hey Connie, what's cooking?"

"There's a batch of cookies fresh out of the oven. Officer Swanson looks like he constantly needs fed in order for him to solve Harold's murder."

The single piece of toast I had eaten earlier suddenly seemed less than adequate as breakfast. My stomach growled in agreement, so I helped myself to a couple warm chocolate chip cookies from the cooling rack and stood by the window to eat them.

I solved one mystery. I located Uncle Norman by the garage watching the delivery of his convertible. He had the appearance of a new father tenderly stroking the fender of the sparkling clean car. As I watched, Joel came around the corner of the house and joined him in the admiration of the highly collectable vehicle.

Joel was still holding the hedge clippers. The shade he had

been working in must have disappeared as the sun rose over the house. I watched for a few more minutes as the two men started an animated discussion of the merits of the car.

"I'll be right back," Helen's voice carried up the stairwell. A giggle followed.

The activity of a second member of my family was revealed. I had suggested Stella, the day help, as the person to accompany Officer Swanson in his investigation of Harold's personal property. Helen had taken her place. This was a more efficient use of the cleaning person's time, because Helen would have been doing nothing.

"Aunt Helen, what is going on down there?" I wasn't interrogating my relative, merely asking a casual question.

"Oh there you are. We thought you couldn't keep up with us old fogies and went back to bed."

I studied the knit top she was wearing. I knew she had worn it to the bars the previous evening because she had borrowed it from me. I tried to recall if she had been wearing it at breakfast or if she had changed into it when she went to the basement to help Officer Swanson. Either way, I didn't think she was wearing it for the same reason I was wearing the clothes I had picked up from my bedroom floor.

"No, I've been busy. There are always things to do in this big house." I changed the subject to the issue burning in my mind, who killed Harold. "Has Officer Swanson found anything useful to the case?"

"Everet has been very efficient." This statement was followed by a childish giggle.

The nuance of Helen using the policeman's first name was not lost on me.

Helen continued, "He is very witty and has led a very adventuresome life as a member of law enforcement."

"Oh?" I was willing to bet that most of his law enforcement adventures took place in donut shops.

"He was telling me that, just the other day he stopped a lady for speeding and she wasn't wearing any shirt." This comment was followed by another series of teenage type giggles.

"Did he give her a ticket?"

"I asked him the same question and he said he couldn't because he was afraid the young lady's father would sue him for looking at her chest." Helen giggled again.

I hadn't heard so much giggling since I had been at the mall on a Friday evening and a group of young girls walked past me. I never heard Helen giggle.

"Has Officer Swanson found anything useful to the case?" Perhaps this time I would get an answer.

Helen turned off her school girl persona and became a serious reporter of the activity of Everet Swanson. "He didn't find anything useful in the sitting room. In fact he noted that it was uncommonly barren of any personal items belonging to the victim. When Everet entered the bedroom to continue his investigation, he started with the boxes on the shelf in the closet. The first box contained travel brochures, some of them were fifteen years old, but the majority of them were recent."

I made a mental note to visit the travel agents in town and in the surrounding area. Perhaps one of them would remember something useful.

"What else did Everet discover?"

"Harold collected baseball cards. According to Everet, some of them are rare and worth a fortune."

"And?" I prompted. So far nothing Helen had reported sounded like it would lead to the arrest of the person who had shot Harold.

"That's all. He was lifting down another box when I came up to get some of Connie's cookies." As if saying it reminded Helen of the task, she took a plate from the cupboard and loaded it with a dozen cookies. She started to pour a glass of milk, thought better of it, and added the carton to the tray instead. She was on the top step when we heard a crash from the upper level of the house.

"Oooh, I hope Everet isn't hurt." Still balancing the tray, she hurried to check the physical state of the officer. I didn't. The sound had definitely come from the upstairs.

I wondered which of my relatives I would find buried under an avalanche of family mementos. Helen was in the basement. Norman was out in the stables with Joel admiring the Mustang. (If I hadn't been so concerned about the crash noise, I would have enjoyed the irony of a car named after a horse being in the stables.).

I hurried up the back stairs to Stewart's private domain on the third floor.

*****

Aunt Dorothy was standing in the center of Stewart's library, hands on her hips and a scowl on her face. Opposite her, posed in a similar manner, was Uncle Stewart. The two of them didn't even notice I entered the turret shaped room.

"You will," Aunt Dorothy argued.

"No, I won't," Uncle Stewart retorted.

"Yes."

"No."

I figured the childish argument would continue all afternoon if I didn't interrupt. "What is going on?"

"Stewart knocked over his newspaper collection and now he won't pick them up." Dorothy's eyes never left Stewart's face.

My uncle caved under the pressure of Dorothy's stern look and turned toward me. He explained, "She purposely knocked the pile of clippings over. She said they're junk and they need to be thrown away. She wants to sweep them into a trash bag without contemplating their importance."

Dorothy turned toward me as if I was the arbiter of their disagreement. "The newspapers are a fire hazard. One spark and the whole house will erupt into a raging inferno."

"She promised we would not throw anything away. That was the condition I imposed when I allowed her to search in here for Harold's resume. And she agreed to it." I waited my entire life for Stewart pout in the manner of a six year old.

"But the newspapers are a fire hazard."

I knelt to straighten the papers. I didn't need either of them to trip and break a hip. "Why are you saving these newspapers? It doesn't appear like you save every newspaper, just certain ones."

Stewart spoke up, defending his hoarding practices. "My interests are eclectic. Sometimes I'm stumped by a crossword puzzle and I'll save it until I think of the answer. One time there was an interesting grammar mistake and I'm saving the newspaper until I research it."

"Here's a note on the front of this one, *Page 14*. Let's see what is on that page." I found the appropriate page. "You saved this newspaper because of an obituary. In the margin you wrote, *This guy deserved to die. Too stupid to live.*"

"Why would Stewart write that? It's a terrible thing to think," Dorothy commented.

I scanned the obituary. "Listen to this. Arthur ran himself over trying to change the tire while the car was parked on the hill in front of his house."

"See. I told you the newspapers are a fire hazard. It's not like he saved the newspaper from Kennedy's assassination or the one from the Challenger explosion,"

Dorothy said as she walked toward the stairs.

I ignored her comment and continued to place the newspapers in a neat stack, occasionally Stewart's notation would pique my interest and I would open the section to the appropriate page.

"Uncle Stewart, look at this picture. Does it look like someone we know?"

Without even glancing at the page, Stewart answered, "No." He was still upset that we were touching the sacred items in his collection.

"Come on, just take a look. At one time you thought it looked like someone we know. Read the note you wrote in the margin. *I know this guy.* Blond, military hair cut, mustache, pierced ear." I pleaded.

Humoring me, Stewart glanced at the newspaper. "All those artist renderings of crooks look the same."

"Something about the eyes seems familiar." I gave the illustration another hard look. The caption didn't help. The picture was a police artist's sketch of a bank robber, drawn from the descriptions witnesses gave. I didn't read the article. I didn't know the criminal element of society. I wouldn't know the robber. I had wasted enough time trying to identify the person and tossed the section into the pile to be discarded.

I rested for a moment while I listened to two pair of feet climb the stairs. I was surprised to see it was Helen and Norman. "Where's Dorothy?" I asked. "She's the person who started the project of going through Stewart's papers."

"She decided to help Connie with the cooking. So she recruited us to help sort Stewart's treasures." Helen giggled, an occurrence that was becoming a permanent condition. "Everet is joining us for dinner."

I was disappointed that it was Everet and not Tony joining us for the meal, but I didn't say anything.

Helen stood watching us sort the newspapers into piles. "Tell me what we are trying to accomplish."

Stewart took a step forward. "What we are trying to accomplish is to find Harold's resume. I don't know why or how my collection of newspapers got involved. I would never mix business papers with my personal items." He swooped down and gathered the discard pile into his arms and began shuffling them until the corners lined up. He set them on top of the others and stood in front of the waist high pile protectively, clearly peeved that his private domain had been intruded upon.

I asked, "Where would the resume be if you still have a copy?"

"Let me think. I may have filed it with the other applications for the position under *Butler*. I kept all of them in case Harold didn't work out and we had to start interviewing again." He pulled out a file drawer and ran a finger across the tabs. "There isn't a file for the butler position. It's missing."

I suggested he filed the resumes under domestic help or servants. Norman and Helen joined in the guessing game. Stewart followed each of ideas and one by one eliminated them.

"I am certain I filed them under the word *Butler*. At the time, we contracted the services of a domestic employment agency. We received six resumes from the service. They were mailed flat in a manila envelope. Harold's resume was folded, sent separate in a white, business envelope. He didn't use the service. Now how do you explain that I can remember how many applications we had for the job and the envelopes they were sent in and not be able to find them?" Perplexed, Stewart rubbed his head (The dye he had used the night before was irritating his scalp?).

"They're not here," I said, without emotion.

"What aren't here?" asked Helen.

What planet was Helen living on? I wondered for a moment if she was suffering from a case of dementia, but her fits of giggles whenever the name of a certain law enforcement officer was mentioned, made me decide she was only suffering a bad case of puppy love.

With my last ounce of patience, I explained, "The resumes have been removed from the file cabinet."

"Why would anyone do that?" she asked.

The question was one I was asking. I didn't have the answer.

"Helen, you need to tell Everet that the papers related to Harold's initial employment have disappeared." I was the only one present privy to the knowledge that the paperwork for the car had also disappeared. It seemed too much of a coincidence that the only documents which would contain background information about our butler were gone.

Stewart slumped onto the cushion of the window seat. He seemed relieved that the documents had disappeared as opposed to him forgetting where he put them. His brain had not become addled with age, at least not yet.

I left the room on the third floor where Stewart stored his personal collections and returned to the kitchen. Not that I particularly want to be in the kitchen, but there wasn't another room in the house I wanted to be in either.

Connie, without her apron tied around her waist, was sitting at the table reading today's newspaper, sipping a cup of tea. Dorothy was humming as she lifted the lid from a pot and added cherry juice to the brew. When I looked at Connie for an explanation, she merely shrugged. Having the resident prepare two meals in two days (in my lifetime) was novel for the cook. I wasn't going to begrudge her a little relaxation and I wasn't prepared to make her redundant based on Dorothy's current activity.

"Where's Mildred? I haven't seen her since breakfast."

"She called a cab and went shopping at the mall." Connie answered without looking up from her reading. "The trip to the bars last night made her realize how outdated her wardrobe had become. Her words, not mine."

A quiver of fear went down my spine. The aunts and uncles rarely left the house and then it was to see a doctor or get a haircut. They usually traveled as a group, with one of the household staff for supervision.

As we chatted, a taxi pulled in to the port cochere at the side of the mansion. At first I was mystified by the identity of the person getting out of the cab, but when she turned around I saw it was Mildred, a Mildred with a new hair color and style (gone was the gray, permed hair). The outfit she was wearing would have been more appropriate on someone half her age and with a firmer body. But I couldn't deny the happiness I saw on her face.

The driver opened the trunk and started to extract shopping bag after shopping bag. Mildred had more baggage than I had brought from my apartment and I was moving here permanently with the sum of my worldly possessions.

My aunt entered the kitchen and executed a pirouette. "What do you think?"

I gulped and lied. "You look fantastic!"

"You should see what I bought and it was all on sale. I saved almost fifty dollars."

I did a second gulp. Aunt Mildred may have saved fifty dollars, but judging the number of bags, she had spent at least ten times that amount. One bag in particular captured my interest, the one from the cell phone store. She confirmed my guess by pulling the newest model cell phone from her pocket to display it.

Dorothy turned down the heat under the pot she was stirring and set down the spoon. I waited for Dorothy to chastise Mildred for overspending, for the inappropriate clothing choices, for going off alone, for purchasing a cell phone, for….

Instead, Dorothy examined the outfit Mildred was wearing and asked, "Where did you get those clothes? They are gorgeous and you look great. What else did you purchase?"

The question led to the extraction of the purchases, one by one, with the appropriate oohs and aahs from Dorothy. Connie, who was also interested in what Mildred bought, joined the admiration chorus.

The item that held my attention was the cell phone, a top of the line model that would rival Tony's for features. Stewart had had trouble mastering the call feature on my phone. I had no idea how Mildred, with her lack of technology skills was going to use her purchase or who she would call.

"I've been thinking I need to do some shopping and update my wardrobe." Dorothy commented, removing her apron as she spoke. I knew she was headed to the mall. "Gi-Gi see if the taxi has left. If he's still in the driveway, tell him to wait. I'm going to need a ride to the mall."

I suddenly had a headache and remembered the bottle of aspirin on the dining room table.

CHAPTER 9

I WILL ADMIT THE cherry cobbler Dorothy prepared was the best I ever tasted. Judging by the way Everet greedily accepted a third helping, he would concur with my assessment of the desert.

"Oh, Evvie, tell everyone what you discovered in Harold's apartment." Helen had managed to ensconce herself in the chair beside Everet, filling his plate, and generally tending to his every need. She picked up the serving spoon and offered a fourth helping of the cherry cobbler.

I caught the nickname Helen used for the police officer. In one day, she had gone from calling him Officer Swanson, to Everet, and now she was calling him Evvie. I wondered if by bedtime there would be wedding bells.

Evvie didn't have the social grace to swallow before he started talking. "Hair color."

"I never expected that man to be vain enough to color his hair," Stewart, who had added shoe polish to his own hair the

75

night before, commented. "He maintained it well. Who would have suspected that he was prematurely gray?"

I was absorbed in the eating habits of the officer and couldn't engage my brain to interpret his remark. Thankfully Uncle Stewart read between the lines and I could understand that the officer was trying to tell us Harold dyed his hair.

"But it wasn't what I found that was important; it is what I didn't find that is interesting." Everet shoveled more cobbler into his mouth.

I rested my elbows on the table. If our guest could forgo social convention and talk with food in his mouth, I could disregard the preaching about elbows on the table. "What didn't you find?"

"I didn't find anything to indicate where he came from or social security records or education. People keep those kinds of records. They're important."

"What about a driver's license?" Uncle Norman asked.

"He had one." Helen reached over and wiped the corner of Evvie's mouth.

"That's a relief. We allowed him to drive our vehicles."

"While I was searching the apartment I had one of the guys at the station run his license through the system. It came up negative."

Mildred, dressed in a new pants suit and sporting her new hairdo, acted like the conversation was the most boring discussion she had ever heard. She commented, "You mean he didn't have any tickets or accidents on his record."

"No, I mean there wasn't anyone by the name of Harold Peters or anyone else registered to that license number." Everet followed his comment with a belly wrenching burp.

Helen gently fanned the air in front of her nose and slid her chair two inches further away from the officer.

No paper trail. Interesting. First the car dealership didn't have a record of Harold's transaction when he purchased the car. Then we couldn't find the resume he used when he applied for the position of butler. Now we were hearing that his driver's license was a fake. Three missing documents were two too many to be a coincidence.

I could easily dismiss the resume disappearance as being a case of Stewart purging his files some time in the last fifteen years. I could explain the car dealership losing the paperwork for Harold's car purchase as careless filing on the part of a secretary. But the state not having any record of his driver's license was noteworthy. The state didn't make that kind of mistake. For all three documents to vanish had to have been done deliberately. Harold was definitely paranoid of someone finding him. Who? Why?

I wasn't the only one at the table who reached that same conclusion.

Norman looked gleeful as he stated the obvious, "We definitely have a murder and a mystery on our hands."

"We took his fingerprints. We're hoping there is a file somewhere in the system that will link Harold to his earlier life." Everet adjusted his belt.

"Was his real name Harold Peters?"

"That's a question the department is trying to answer. We've even contacted the federal authorities."

"The FBI? The FBI is investigating the death of our butler!" Helen squealed. She immediately reeled in her excitement. Pandering to the ego of the man sitting next to her, she said, "I'm sure you can solve the murder without them." She patted Everet's arm.

"The murder of our butler," I amended Helen's comment.

Dorothy looked around the table, as if she was evaluating each person's potential as Harold's killer.

"Stop that." Norman said, "You're giving me the heebie geebies. No one in this room killed Harold. We liked the man."

"At least we know the butler didn't do it." Dorothy's flip comment caused the rest of us to look in her direction.

"We need to be more respectful to the memory of the departed," Mildred reminded the group, without looking at the faces of the people at the table. She was staring down at the cell phone on her lap.

"I wasn't being disrespectful, only honest."

Stewart commented, "We thought highly of the service he performed for the family, but we still need to keep a realistic view of the parts of his life that we didn't know about. Someone hated him enough to murder him."

Connie came in and collected the dishes from the table. I got up to help, but my real motive was to create an opportunity to call Tony. I had things I wanted to tell him about the case. Things I didn't want to confide to Officer Swanson.

I wouldn't admit even to myself that I longed for the company of the intelligent, well mannered, handsome man.

After living in a world of crazy older people (was it really only two days?), it was a breath of fresh air to talk with someone my own age. To further enhance the experience, I chose the gazebo in the garden as a place where we could have some privacy away from the prying eyes of my family and enjoy the beautiful evening. I asked Joel to sweep the dead leaves out of the lattice structure and to bring the wicker furniture and cushions out of storage for the occasion.

Unfortunately the family interpreted the spot as the perfect romantic venue for a young couple to whisper sweet nothings to each other.

I countered their opinions by telling Aunt Mildred the purpose of meeting Tony. To further convince them of the platonic nature of the visit, I repeated my woeful tale of the recent break up with the doctor from the hospital. I figured she would tell the rest of the relatives. I don't think they believed me. As soon as Tony got out of his car, in the earshot of everyone, I asked the leading question, "Have you found any clues about the person who shot Harold?"

It was important to get him alone. I didn't want the aunts and uncles intercepting Tony and making the meeting a public gathering. I had details I wanted to tell Tony without the others hearing them. Of course, I was stupid enough to ask the question while grabbing Tony's hand and steering him toward the gazebo.

Judging from the vase of flowers on the table and the fairy lights strung along the railing, Joel hadn't gotten the memo that this was a business meeting and not a romantic interlude.

Tony and I were still getting settled when Aunt Mildred brought out a pitcher of lemonade and two glasses filled with ice. She lingered long enough to ask Tony about the wreck that had caused his sudden departure the evening before. He politely answered her question.

Ten minutes after her departure, Aunt Dorothy arrived, wearing one of her new outfits. She brought an array of cookies. Tony politely took one of the sugar cookies and praised the person who baked it.

Uncle Norman's excuse for visiting the gazebo was to offer a bug repellant candle to discourage *those nasty mosquitoes*. A brief dialogue between the men ensued about fruit flies being attracted to the lemonade.

Aunt Helen just happened to pass the gazebo on her nightly (?) stroll through the garden. She offered to fetch a shawl for me to ward off the damp. She didn't leave until I assured her (repeatedly) that the temperature was still in the eighties and I wouldn't need one.

I watched for Uncle Stewart. It was like waiting for the proverbial other shoe to drop. You knew it was going to happen, you just didn't know when or, in this case, what excuse he would use. If I wasn't desperate to talk to Tony alone, I would have found the oldsters' actions amusing.

I couldn't concentrate on Harold's murder until Stewart made his pilgrimage to the gazebo. I watched the back door, waiting for my uncle to appear. My nerves were stretched expecting the visit to come like a gorilla attack from the garden behind the gazebo. At one point I looked up at the trees to see if there was a vantage point where he could drop from and execute his planned disruption.

As discreet as I tried to be looking for Uncle Stewart's arrival, Tony noticed. "Your Uncle Stewart is on the third floor of the house," Tony reported. "I can see his silhouette on the window blind."

I looked at the window in question to confirm Tony's observation. "I'm sorry. I was trying to be subtle. I didn't mean for them to interfere. They're protective and don't have many interests other than the murder and what I am doing at any given moment."

"I don't mind. It shows how much they care for you."

"I came here to take care of my relatives. I didn't expect the roles to be reversed."

"It may be a good thing. It gives them something to think about other than their own aches and pains."

"You're right." I shifted in my chair. The wicker was digging into the back of my legs. The white twig-like material may have a summery, romantic reputation, but it lacked comfort and strength. "I doubt Aunt Mildred has walked any further than the dining room all summer and today she was shopping at the mall. Aunt Dorothy has been cooking and Helen has taken an outside interest also."

Tony lifted an eyebrow.

I explained. "Everet Swanson was here today and was invited to stay for dinner."

"Ah." The single utterance indicating that he understood everything I implied in the statement. "I won't warn him. It may be a good thing. He also needs more to his life than work and eating his next meal."

"He spent the day in Harold's apartment, searching for clues to the motive for the murder and the identity of the killer."

"See what I mean. Today was his day off. He was supposed to be relaxing."

"I didn't take him for a workaholic," I said.

"He isn't. It's just that his wife died three years ago and he doesn't like being in his house alone. He uses work as an excuse to get away from the grief."

"If Aunt Helen has her way, there will be plenty of activity to make him forget his grief."

We sat in silence, watching the shadow of Stewart move back and forth in his upstairs sanctuary.

After several minutes, Tony asked, "Did he find anything?"

"Who?"

"Everet. Did he find anything?"

"He didn't find any clues, but that was significant. He didn't find a wallet or any papers leading to Harold's past. He did find a driver's license, but that turned out to be a forgery. It was like our butler didn't exist prior to him taking the job here."

"Nothing?" Tony took a sip of lemonade, tracing the pattern etched in the glass while he thought about my comment. "A normal person doesn't worry about unnecessarily divulging personal information, and they certainly don't go to any trouble to erase the paper trail of their lives."

"There's more. We searched Stewart's files today. We thought Harold's application would provide the names of his former employers and personal references. The folder containing the resumes sent by the employment agency and Harold's application is missing."

Tony sat a little straighter. "Stewart probably filed them in the wrong spot."

"No, I went through all the files. The resumes are not there."

"He filed them fifteen years ago. He tossed them out and doesn't remember doing it."

"No, you don't understand. Stewart is a hoarder. He isn't as bad as those people on television, but once something is stored in his room, he doesn't throw it away unless he is forced to," I explained. "That isn't the only thing. At the dealership where Harold purchased his car, the paperwork is gone."

I waited for Tony to react. He would make a great poker player. His face didn't betray his thoughts.

Hoping to stir up some insight from Tony, I asked, "Do you know about the license plate?"

"What about it?"

"It was a stolen plate. Everet didn't know if it was stolen so that Harold's car couldn't be traced or if a thief stole his and replaced it. Up until today, I would have said the plate was stolen from Harold's car, but knowing that the resume is gone and the car dealership papers have disappeared, it makes me wonder if Harold did these things himself to avoid being found." After my statement, I wondered if Tony thought we had intentionally harbored a paranoid person or worse, a criminal. I quickly added, "There was never any indication Harold was anything other than the model butler that he was."

Tony pulled out his notebook and a pen. "I wonder if Everet checked the VIN number on the car. That would give us a lead."

"VIN number?"

"Vehicle identification number. It is attached to the car in different places. A thief can remove the obvious one on the dashboard, but frequently forgets the ones affixed to the engine and door panel."

"How will that help?" I fought the urge to rush to the stables to examine the hybrid car Harold drove.

"I doubt it will help much. It seems Harold went to a lot of trouble to hide his personal information. A search of the records associated with the VIN number is only going to provide us with the current information we already know about him. Still it does seem a tad paranoid for him to go to so much trouble to destroy the paper trail of his identity."

"I met a woman who knew Harold," I offered.

I felt like I conquered the world. I had made a slight inroad into the case that no one else had accomplished, until Tony asked, "Did she know Harold during his tenure as a butler or did she know him from his life in Philadelphia?"

Sheepishly, I admitted that Darby Jackson knew Harold only as far back as six weeks. More boldly I added, "She said Harold made a call from the payphone every night at eleven o'clock."

"Now we're getting somewhere. Did she tell you what number he called or who he called?" Tony put the tip of the pen against the paper.

"I asked that question. She didn't know the information."

"Do you have a phone number for her?"

"Ah, no," I said, realizing why I was a nurse and not a detective. "Did you write down her address?"

"No, I gave her my information but I didn't get hers. How many Darby Jackson's are there in the world?"

"More than I want to call."

"Can't the police trace the calls? Get the call records for the pay phone."

"Only if I can get a judge to say that it is needed to solve the crime. I don't think

that's going to happen. Rarely does a judge agree to issue a warrant when it is the victim who is making the calls. With a public telephone the privacy issue with the other people using the telephone may be a deterrent to getting the warrant. They're innocent people conducting innocent activity. If a police officer was to seek a warrant, the judge would definitely weigh the value of the telephone numbers obtained versus the invasion of privacy."

"It may even be harder than you think."

"Why do you say that?" Tony replaced the notebook and pen into his pocket.

"I suspect Harold didn't use the same pay phone every night.

He went to different bars and made the calls from whichever bar he was in."

"That would make it more difficult to get a copy of the records for the pay phones."

"You could try." The bug repellant candle wasn't working. I swatted at a mosquito buzzing around my face.

"Of course I will try, but it doesn't mean it will happen."

The light went off in Stewart's room and I was distracted.

"We need to conduct this conversation away from your relatives. Someplace without the distractions. Maybe we should go to a restaurant tomorrow evening and we can finish our talk then." Tony stood up.

"It's still early. Stay a while longer." I pleaded, half excited he asked me to dinner the next night and half disappointed that he was leaving so early. I had some other points regarding Harold's murder I was curious about and I didn't think I could wait until the next evening to find out the answers.

"Before you leave, what is your theory regarding Harold's lack of a past?" I asked, hoping Tony would sit down and discuss his theory.

"I don't have one. I just learned about the dead ends to his life in Philadelphia. For all we know, he may have randomly selected Philadelphia as the place of his ficticious life because it is so big it would be hard to track an individual in that city, especially fifteen years after he left it. He could have been from anywhere."

I had to admit the thought had crossed my mind. Harold wanted to hide from his past and he may have created the few details we knew because he had to have a background. All of it could have been a lie.

"Guess. I think he left behind a loveless marriage, a wife and children. He faithfully calls his children every night at eleven o'clock to remind them that he loves them. Or maybe he left because the woman he loved got engaged to another man and Harold was devastated."

"You're too romantic." Tony smiled. "I think he left Philadelphia because he got laid off from his job and this was the only one he could find."

"Then why does he make a call every night at the same time?"

"He has a standing date with his bookie. He watches the games at the bars and then calls his bookie to see how his bets did and to bet on the sports for the next night."

I got excited. "Then it was his bookie who shot him. Harold was behind on his gambling debts. The metal box contained the gambling slips and the bookie stole them to hide the paper trail."

"There's no proof of that. That's the problem with theories. When you have a quasi-logical one everyone jumps on it. Instead of it being one of many theories, it becomes the truth and everyone forgets the other evidence." Tony was standing close and I had the feeling he was going to kiss me goodnight.

"What are the other clues?" There was a breathless quality to my voice that I couldn't control. I could feel the heat from his body.

"There aren't any, but that doesn't mean none exist. It means we haven't found any other clues yet. If we continue to theorize, we may overlook something that is important, but doesn't fit the theory." At this point, Tony's lips were saying one thing while his eyes were carrying on a conversation of their own. I liked the talking his eyes were doing.

Slam. The back door slammed shut. "Gi-Gi, how do you turn this thing off? It keeps ringing and every time I open it up, a William Appleby's name appears on the screen. What does that mean?"

"Uncle Stewart, that means the caller is William Appleby and you keep disconnecting the telephone call."

"He's on the line now. He wants to talk to you and he sounds angry." Stewart walked the short distance to the gazebo and handed me the cell phone. He muttered as he went back to the house. Unfortunately, the garbled words were clear enough and loud enough for Tony to hear. "Dames and their boyfriends."

Tony stepped back, the mood was broken "I'll let you take your call."

"Tomorrow night? Dinner?"

Tony waved a noncommittal response.

I watched as he strode across the grass and got in his car. I didn't know if he was angry. I didn't know, based on his gesture, if our arrangement to have dinner together was still on for the next night. At this point I thought about murdering Uncle Stewart for his poor timing.

"William, what do you want?" I said into the phone.

"I have an appointment tomorrow near your town and I thought I would stop to see you."

"No, I don't think you understand. You are engaged to Mary Ann Trumley. I don't think she would appreciate you stopping to visit me." Merely saying William's fiancée's name made my stomach queasy.

"She is on vacation with her family in the Bahamas."

"It doesn't change the fact that you are engaged to be married. Quit calling me. Don't visit me. I'm busy tomorrow."

I heard a chuckle from the other end of the line. "Doing what? Washing your hair?" Rinsing your delicates?"

"It is no longer any of your business what I do with my time. You are not welcome. Stay away."

"Come on, Gi-Gi. We can still be friends."

"No, we quit being friends when you started dating Mary Ann." I snapped the phone shut. Dr. William Appleby was the most egotistical human in the world. I hoped the gesture would convey the message that my words couldn't get across. I shook my head and wondered what I ever saw in the man.

I blew out the candle, unplugged the fairy lights, and carried the tray back into the house. By the time I put the lemonade in the refrigerator and covered the cookies with plastic wrap, I forgave Uncle Stewart.

Uncle Norman poked his head into the kitchen, "You have enough time to come with us. You can wear what you have on."

I looked at the clock. "Are you kidding me? It's late. Where are you going?"

"Bar hopping. Mildred has all those new clothes and wants to show them off." He added, as if it was the most normal thing in the world, "We may find someone who knew Harold and pick up some useful information."

I noticed his clothing. He was wearing a floral shirt, a souvenir from a trip to Hawaii he took twenty years before, and his white sans-a-belt pants. On his feet was a pair of white wing tip leather shoes without socks. "Are you going on a cruise?"

"I knew you would appreciate the duds." Uncle Norman chuckled and ran a hand over his scalp to smooth his thinning hair. "I do look sharp, if I have to say so myself."

"You're not going by yourself, are you?" My question didn't need a verbal answer. The swinging door opened at that moment and the rest of my relatives paraded in wearing their bar hopping attire.

I had moved home just in time. My relatives were insane.

I weighed my options. I could order them not to go out, but they would rebel. I could let them go by themselves, but I witnessed their lack of street smarts the night before. (I didn't want to go to the police station to bail them out of jail.) Or I could go with them and be the voice of sanity.

Reluctantly, I agreed to go to the bars with my aunts and uncles only on the condition we went in my car and I drove. I ran up the stairs to get my purse, checking to make certain my credit card was still there. I knew I would pay dearly for the evening, in more ways than one.

CHAPTER 10

I RAN MY FINGERS through my windblown hair. The back seat of the Mustang had been cramped with four women crowded into it. Norman drove with Stewart riding shotgun.

Dorothy's hair had not moved during the ride to the bar. I didn't know if she had found an aerodynamic position in the car that didn't get affected by the wind, or if the can of hair spray she used to maintain her bouffant cancelled out the negative impact of the convertible. Either way her hair looked like she had just stepped out of the beauty salon.

Helen treated us to a view of a wedgie as she emerged from the backseat, which she plucked out and then wiggled her hips to further her comfort. It was not a pretty sight.

Mildred rearranged the neckline of her tank top several times, alternately lowering the fabric to display more cleavage and hefting her bosoms to emphasize their fullness. One of her purchases was the push 'em up bra I refused to loan her the previous evening. She was determined to advertise the benefits of wearing the undergarment.

Norman was still standing by his beloved car, removing the road dust with his white cotton handkerchief. I had a feeling Stewart was eager to go inside, but was politely waiting with us in the parking lot so he didn't have to pay for the first round of drinks.

As I glanced around at the other vehicles in the lot, alarms started going off in my head. I didn't have good vibes about this bar. My first clue was the row of motorcycles in the parking lot. I don't like to stereotype. I had noticed a large number of over fifty year-olds riding Harley Davidsons, but television typecasts motorcycle riders as being gang members. My second clue to the clientele of the establishment was a young lady with several skull and cross bone tattoos, rainbow shades of color in her hair, and metal studs in her clothing, face, and body. It appeared like she picked up her accessories at the local hardware store rather than the jeweler on Main Street.

When I walked through the door, I realized my assessment in the parking lot was correct. I immediately wanted to beat a fast retreat. Compared to this place, the bars we had visited the previous evening looked like the country club, the women debutantes, and the men gadabouts. I was trying to think of a way to get my menagerie out the door without shouting, "Hey these people are not nice!" when a trio of more muscle-than-brains, bandana wearing, pierced eared men weighing three hundred pounds and standing seven feet tall stood up from the bar and walked toward us.

I cowered and tried to grab a handful of shirts from Norman and Stewart to pull them back out the door. They were frozen in place.

"Good evening, Pops. We think it would be prudent if you and the women chose another place to have a cocktail this evening. Things tend to get a little rough in here."

I blinked. Never in my life did I imagine the thug-looking men standing in front of me would speak so politely.

My uncles agreed to the suggestion with nervous bobs of their heads, did an about face, and marched double time out the door, lucky to escape. Mildred, Helen, and I followed. It was only when we were in the car did I notice Dorothy hadn't followed. I panicked.

I didn't need to worry.

The door opened again. Dorothy had the personal escort of two of the men, a hand tucked into the crook of their bent arms. She was smiling and giggling as she left the bar and the men were patiently chatting with her.

"Anytime, ma'am." If he had been wearing a Stetson instead of a sweaty bandana, he would have tipped it.

I stared in amazement. As soon as Dorothy was safely in our midst, in front of my eyes, the gentlemen returned to their Neanderthal personas, their arms positioned to tackle a dinosaur with their fists.

Dorothy's eyes sparkled when she exclaimed, "Wasn't that fun!" She was still grinning from the attention of the two men, completely oblivious to the danger of the bar. I didn't have the heart to tell her. Besides I didn't think she would believe me and the chances were slim that she would ever return to that particular bar.

Norman carefully backed the Mustang out of the space, steering clear of the row of motorcycles. (I had a vision of them falling one after another, crashing into the one next to it until there was nothing but a pile of rubble.) He knew how lucky he had been to escape that particular bar and he wanted to stay lucky.

I reminded my companions we were looking for clues to solve Harold's murder and vetoed the next bar as being too upscale for our butler to patronize.

I located a restaurant that served alcohol and directed Norman to pull into the parking lot. It looked safe, even if it wasn't the type of place I would find any information about Harold. I hoped it would provide sufficient distraction to entertain my group.

The hostess seated us at a corner booth. I made sure Dorothy was in the middle where she couldn't cause any trouble. I didn't think anyone her age pouted, but she did.

"This place is boring." Dorothy complained (more than once).

I had to agree. The next youngest person after me was a forty something man clinging to the arm of a woman twice his age. I couldn't decide if he was a paid escort, a young, sympathetic relative, or if the woman was a cougar trying to get her claws into a much younger man. Or if he was tolerating her company in the hopes of getting some of her money. Was that Harold's plan to obtain the money Darby mentioned?

"Is that Morris?" Stewart whispered. "I haven't seen him in ages." My uncle slid out of the booth and strolled over to a table where two white hair couples were dining. Two minutes later a fifth chair was pulled up to the table and Stewart joined his friends.

I ordered a vegetable platter for the rest of us to share and a round of drinks. Norman handed over the keys to the car in favor of having an alcoholic beverage. He didn't need much persuading.

I was people watching and munching on a carrot when the restaurant door opened. Out of a mix of boredom and curiosity I watched as a solitaire man entered. I was dazzled by his good looks and it took a moment before I recognized him. "William?" I must have said it too loud, because my former boyfriend, the scoundrel who broke my heart by getting engaged to a wealthy patient's daughter only weeks earlier, turned toward me and smiled.

I don't know how he ended up sitting beside me, in the place Stewart had vacated. The waitress appeared at his side immediately. He ordered a double scotch on the rocks and a round of drinks for the table.

I introduced William to my relatives. I knew my aunts and Uncle Norman were impressed, but anyone who bought them a drink was worthy of their attention. Dorothy wasn't pouting any more.

William finished his first drink in one gulp and ordered a second scotch along with a steak dinner. Ignoring the other people seated at the table, he said to me, "I found your house and no one was home. The gardener didn't understand me. I guess he doesn't speak English. I told him I was your boyfriend and I wanted to wait for you inside, but he wouldn't unlock the door." William took a deep sip of his drink. "You should hire help who speak English, it costs a little more, but at least when you tell them to do something they understand and do it."

I was about to say, "Joel has been employed by the family since I was a baby. He speaks perfect English. He grew up across town." I didn't say anything. It was none of William's business and after he finished his meal, I wouldn't have to worry about William's opinion.

"It is sitting on some prime real estate. You should sell that white elephant you call a house and buy a condominium on the beach. How many bedrooms do you have?"

"Ten." The calculator part of William's brain whirred, assessing the value of Grant House. It was almost laughable.

"Whew, it must cost a fortune to heat that place." William looked at me with a strange expression, his fork suspended midway between his plate and mouth. "You never told me your family was rich."

"It wouldn't have made a difference." I didn't try to correct his impression or tell him the money was tied up in an eroding trust fund.

William didn't get the hint. "Let's get out of here. The old fogies are making me nervous."

I looked at the people seated in the booth. "I can't leave them. I'm the designated driver."

William raised his hand into the air. The waitress didn't even come over to the table. She turned toward the bar and ordered another drink in response to the gesture.

Satisfied that his alcohol need was taken care of, William tucked his napkin beside his plate and with his other hand took my hand in his. "Come on, let's go."

I pulled my hand away from his. "I explained to you. I can't leave. I'm the designated driver. If I leave they won't have any way to get home."

"Let them call a taxi. The driver will take them to their homes." William's voice sounded slurred. I lost count of how many double scotches he had.

"They live with me."

"That's got to change." As William said the word "change" his eyes closed and his head fell forward into his half eaten food. He was out for the count.

Reaching into his back pocket, I pulled out his wallet, and paid the check. The logistics of getting the passed out William into his own car (in case his stomach revolted against the alcohol, which it did) and the two cars back to the house included paying two busboys to drive his car and help me get him upstairs. I used the last of William's cash to give them a big tip.

CHAPTER 11

W HAT ARE YOU doing?" I asked Connie. On the kitchen counter was a silver tray lined with a linen napkin.

"Your houseguest requested breakfast in bed." Water splashed from the vase as Connie plopped in on the tray. A petal dropped from the flower.

"My house guest?" It took a second for it to register that William was awake. "How do you know he wants breakfast in bed?"

"Stella was dusting on the second floor and she saw the closed door to your old room. She didn't know Dr. William was in the room, so she let herself in. He gave her the food order and she relayed the message." Connie slapped the plate onto the tray.

I examined the contents. "Is that poached eggs with hollandaise sauce?"

"Yes, and dry toast points with the crusts removed, fresh squeezed orange juice, a slice of melon, any kind that is in season

94

will do, and a carafe of hot coffee with cream."

"But that's not your job," I protested. "You cook for the family. You don't cater for individuals. And he's not a guest. He's an unwelcome intruder who we allowed the use of a bed." As I spoke my mood went from curiosity regarding Connie's activity to rage. I stormed out of the kitchen, shoving the door so hard it slammed against the plaster.

I rapped on the door of my childhood room and let myself in without waiting for William to grant permission. I caught him fluffing a pillow behind his back as he prepared to eat his breakfast in bed. "You're not my breakfast, but you look good enough to eat."

"Get up. Get packed. Get out of my house." Spit flew out of my mouth with the words.

Still unfazed, William patted the bed beside him. "I didn't order enough breakfast for two people but I'll share."

"I don't think you understand. You will not be getting your breakfast delivered to your bed. You will not be getting breakfast – period. You will be getting out of my house. You are only here because a hotel will not allow you to register if you are not conscious and smell of vomit."

"You're so cute when you are angry."

I slammed a second door within two minutes.

By the time I reached for my first cup of coffee and ate the breakfast William had ordered, I returned to my normal, sunny disposition and greeted my aunts and uncles in the dining room in a civil tone.

"We heard the shouting. It sounds like trouble in paradise." The sarcastic comment made by Uncle Stewart raised my hackles (I have no idea what hackles are, but mine were definitely raised).

Without commenting, for fear of taking the frustration out on an innocent member of my family, I took my coffee out to the gazebo. I had a house guest I needed to remove, a murder that needed solved, and five aunts and uncles who needed something to do other than mind my business.

Fifteen minutes later I heard a car start and caught a glimpse of the dark Mercedes as it was driven down the driveway. I felt as if one of my problems had gone away and it was safe for me to reenter my own home. My breathing returned to normal and my fists unclenched as I walked back to the house. William had broken my heart. He had become engaged to a woman based solely on her daddy's bank account. He was not going to disrupt my life.

Connie kept her back to me as I reentered the kitchen.

"Sorry Connie, but that man drives me crazy. Imagine the ego. He is engaged to another woman and still thinks he can walk into my home and give orders like he owns it. I'm glad he's gone."

She didn't say a word. I figured it was her way of avoiding being the target of my next outburst. Moving into the dining room to apologize to the family, I would have preferred for the door to swing back and hit me in the face than view the person sitting in Uncle Norman's chair. It explained why Connie had kept her back to me. She wasn't afraid of me yelling at her, she was hiding.

I marched into the dining room, stopping beside William's chair. "What does it take to get it through your thick skull that I want you out of my house?" I said, punctuating each word.

"Norman said it would take at least a day to get my car detailed at the dealership. You can understand I don't want to drive it while the odor lingers from last night." He inspected the cube of cantaloupe on his fork.

"And where is Uncle Stewart?" I asked my former boyfriend. Someone in the household should be aware of the situation between William and me and lend support to my campaign to evict my unwelcome guest.

"Stewart volunteered to take my Mercedes to the dealership. He said he was on his way to have breakfast with an old friend and it would not be inconvenient. He said he'd get a ride home from his buddy." Having deemed that the melon was the perfect ripeness, size, and color, William popped it into his mouth.

I temporarily forgot my need to evict William while I considered his remark. Stewart had a friend. That was news to me. For as long as I lived in the house, the aunts and uncles had lived with a limited social life. Now when I needed the safety of their numbers, they suddenly developed the urgent need to see other people.

"I'll call a hotel and you can stay there while the car is detailed."

William appeared to have developed a selective hearing disorder or else he was ignoring what I said. "I have an appointment at ten o'clock and I was wondering if you could give me a ride."

"Call a car rental agency."

"Why would I do that? You have cars out back and servants to do your chores. You can spare a couple hours for a friend."

Exhausted from the emotional rollercoaster I rode since William sat beside me in the restaurant, I didn't have the energy to argue with him. I collapsed into a seat at the table and took a biscuit from the basket. I ate it without any butter or jelly. "What time do you want to leave?"

He leaned back in the seat and looked me over. "There is time for you to fix your hair, put on some makeup, and change your clothes. Wear something that will impress but don't take too long. I don't want to be late."

⁂

"A jeweler? I drove all over Timbuktu so you can purchase a bauble for the woman you jilted me for?" I couldn't believe the audacity of the man.

"It's not for Mary Ann. This is the only jeweler around authorized to carry the model of Rolex watch I want."

"Another Rolex watch? You're wearing a Rolex. What happened to the guy I dated who insisted on going Dutch because he had medical school bills to pay?"

"You could afford to pay for your own dinners and I didn't

97

make you pay the entire bill, only half." He spoke as if that made it right. "I need the watch if I am going to be a better doctor."

"A new Rolex watch will not make you a better doctor."

"If I expect to attract upscale patients to my practice I need to look upscale," William argued.

"So you think if you wear a top brand watch, you'll get patients who will pay their bills on time and you can pay off your tuition loans faster."

"Something like that, although, the interest rates on my loans are so low my tax man told me to only pay the minimum, besides once I'm married…." William's voice trailed off. Even he wasn't stupid enough to finish the statement out loud, although I could probably do it for him. "My in-laws will pay the loan for me."

I hurried to change the subject. "So why did I need to dress up?"

"Jewelers expect their high end customers to look high end."

"I'm not buying a new watch. I'm not going in the store with you. I'm going to the library. You can come get me when you finish at the jewelers." I was disgusted. William's actions only confirmed what I thought of him earlier. He was selfish, manipulative, and egotistical. I was beginning to feel lucky he was going to marry someone else and when I dug deep into my emotional soul, I was beginning to feel sorry for his wife-to-be.

I must have been firm enough or else William was afraid I would do something to jeopardize his watch deal because he asked me to stop my SUV several store fronts away from the jewelers. He didn't want to be seen getting out of a mid-price car.

I waited and when he had his hand on the door handle of the retailer I pulled up to the curb directly in front of the store, beeped the horn, and blew William a kiss.

※ ※

The library was cool, dimly lit, and not one member of my family was there. I spent the first fifteen minutes browsing the stacks, running my fingers down the spines of books I would like to read. It felt like a luxury I hadn't had in years: first studying to become a nurse, establishing myself in the career, the hectic romance with William, the break up, and the move into the family home.

For the moment, the indulgence would have to wait. I needed to make progress dealing with at least one of my problems. The easiest one was to figure out a way to get rid of William. I wanted to read about Mary Ann Trumley, the woman who had stolen William away from me. There was something odd about him being in my hometown while his fiancée was away on vacation. It seemed strange he wasn't freeloading off her family. I wanted to see if there was trouble in paradise. Reading the society page may provide a clue.

Knowing William, if there had been a break up he would react and seek revenge rather than forgiveness. Was his motive for calling me to make his fiancée jealous or was he truly so self centered that he assumed he was welcome in spite of the manner we broke up?

I didn't know if the Trumley family was worthy of the gossip column or if the newspaper would include anything on the progress of their wedding plans, but it was worth a shot.

I waited while the newspaper's web site booted up. The headlines flashed in the negative before settling into the normal black print on white screen. An artist rendering of a court room scene appeared as the feature story, reminding me of the newspapers stacked in Stewart's room.

I began to read the story. The release of a prisoner from a federal penitentiary had set the journalist on a campaign to investigate the crime committed, but never fully resolved. In the case illustrated by the journalist, a bank was robbed several years ago, an arrest was made, but the stolen money was never recovered

Chastising myself for losing sight of my purpose, I flipped to the society section. Starting with the Philadelphia newspaper from the day before, I worked backwards in time. Nothing appeared about Dr. William Appleby and his fiancée, Mary Ann Trumley. I continued to scroll backwards. Either the Trumley family didn't rate a mention in the society column or there wasn't anything to report. That didn't mean there wasn't any trouble in the relationship; it just meant the newspaper hadn't documented it. I was going to have to resort to nagging and yelling until he left my house.

I was daydreaming of all the torturous things I could do to make William leave, like having Uncle Stewart show him the collection of serving bells he displayed in the étagère. Uncle Stewart could talk for hours about the delicate items used to call the servants in the days before intercoms. If that didn't drive William out of the house screaming, I had other plans.

Of course there was Aunt Mildred's needlepoint. She could ask William to hold the skeins of yarn so she could roll them into balls. That tedious task would drive any sane person crazy.

A disembodied hand appeared in front of my eyes, floating randomly between the computer screen and my face. I almost committed a library faux pas. I almost screamed before I realized the arm was attached to a living, breathing human. William was trying to break my trance.

"Where is your new watch?"

"I traded in my old watch. The new one has to be ordered and will take a couple weeks before it comes in," he said as he glanced at his bare wrist. "Let's go. I'm hungry."

"There's a new diner on the way," I suggested. I saw the building when we were on our way to the jewelers and it looked clean and moderately priced. "I want to try the food there."

"I just purchased a new watch. I need to budget my money carefully. Why don't we wait until we get back to the house and eat there? Your cook can prepare something for us."

"It will be past lunchtime when we get back. All the others will have eaten. I don't want to make her fix a special meal just for us."

"That's what you pay her to do."

I didn't even try to explain to William that Connie had to prepare dinner for the family and that her time was filled without the added work.

CHAPTER 12

WHEN WE RETURNED to Grant House, Connie was up to her elbows in dishwater with Dorothy creating more dirty dishes. Pots were steaming on the stove and the one section of the counter was covered with flour. Delicious smells were coming from the oven.

"Connie, do you mind if I fix two sandwiches? William and I didn't eat on our trip." I opened the refrigerator to see what ingredients were available.

"A sandwich?" William questioned. "I can't possibly eat salty, processed meat and white bread."

"A salad?" I suggested.

"That's better. I'll lie down for fifteen minutes while you fix them. I don't want any onions. They give me gas."

I shot him a look that should have killed him but unfortunately it didn't penetrate his ego. I debated whether to demand that he fix his own salad or to enjoy the reprieve from his company.

"You're better off without him," Connie said without looking up from her task.

"I realize that. He'll be leaving tomorrow, when his car is returned." I don't know if I said that to reassure Connie or me.

"Don't count on it."

"Why do you say that?" I reached into the refrigerator to take out the lettuce for the salad.

"I recognize his type." Connie continued to wash the dishes.

"What type is he?"

"He's the type who always finds a way to extend their visit an extra day or two and they expect the best while they're here."

I arranged some slices of hard boiled egg and julienne ham on top of the layer of lettuce. "He will be leaving tomorrow morning."

"He didn't offer to pay for gas, did he?" Connie had only known William for less than a day and she had him pegged for exactly the type of man he was. I had dated him for almost a year. Why hadn't I seen it?

"No, he's driven me places and hasn't asked for gas money. I didn't expect him to offer."

"You were dating at the time. Now he's freeloading and asking favors. He should have offered to pay for gas." Connie opened the oven door and peeked at the progress of a cake. She added, "He probably didn't want to stop at a restaurant on the way home because he would have to pay."

"He will be leaving in the morning." I was being positive, but I recognized the truth in Connie's statement.

"Hmpf." Connie's single syllable summarized the situation.

I moved the salad plates to the dining room and went back into the kitchen for rolls and butter. Dorothy hadn't said anything about William while Connie and I had talked, but now she chimed in with her two cents worth. "Tony is a much better man. Are you still going out to dinner with him?"

I wondered how she knew about the arrangements. "I'm

planning on it. How do you know we were planning to have dinner together?"

"He called and said he would pick you up at six o'clock. He made reservations at Hayden's for six thirty."

I checked my watch (a Sears special not a Rolex). If I ate fast I would still have time to take a quick nap, shower, and do my hair. I went to the foyer to call William for lunch. I was debating the tackiness of yelling up the stairs versus the good manners of walking up and tapping on his door when the brass knocker on the front door was lifted and tapped the requisite three times.

Our visitor had the good breeding of someone who knew how to use a knocker properly. I should have been thinking about who was on the other side of the door.

A man in his early twenties, holding a small suitcase was waiting on the porch. He looked like a traveling salesman. His complexion was dusty. I wondered what he was selling.

"Hello, how may I help you?"

"My name is Robert Peters. I'm here to visit my brother Harold. He told me I could stay with him for a few days."

My legs turned to rubber. Harold had relatives who needed to be told of his death. How was I going to break the news to this man that his brother was murdered in the basement of my house?

"Would you mind waiting on the porch for a moment?" I didn't wait for the man to respond. I closed the door and put my back against it. I had to think about what to do.

I did the first thing that came to mind. "Stewart! Norman! Helen! Dorothy! Mildred!" I yelled.

Unfortunately the walls of the old house were thick and no one came to my aid, except William. "What is all the screaming about? I was sleeping."

"I need your help."

"Is someone sick? Are you having chest pains?"

"No, worse. But if I did have any of those symptoms, you

would be the last person I called." I was thrown off track and I needed to deal with the brother of our deceased butler. "I need you to get Dorothy and Connie from the kitchen and see if you can find anyone else."

William gave me a strange look, like I had just asked him to shingle the roof, but he sulked off toward the kitchen to do as he was told.

I peeked out the little hole in the door and didn't see Robert Peters. He was probably sitting on the swing, waiting politely, wondering about the delay in seeing his brother.

I was still standing with one eye against the peep hole when my little troop returned from the kitchen. "What's wrong? What do you need?"

With one finger up to my lips, I indicated for them to be quiet. "Harold's brother is waiting on the porch. He doesn't know Harold is dead," I whispered frantically.

"Is that all?" William commented. He turned as if he was going to go into the dining room to eat his salad.

"Whoa, I can't do this alone. You're going to stand here and help me tell the brother what happened."

"I don't know what happened. Your butler was murdered. What's that got to do with me?"

I gave him a one word command like I would give a dog. "Stay."

William stood still, but I could tell he was going to be the weak link in our tactful attempt to break the news of the death of our butler to his brother.

"Invite him into the parlor," Aunt Dorothy said.

This sounded like a good plan. I could pump Harold's brother for information before I disclosed the state of his health or rather his lack of health.

I opened the door and waved Robert in. "Sorry for the delay. Please have a seat in the parlor. Connie, would you please bring a beverage for our guest?" I grabbed Dorothy's hand and pulled her into the front room with me. William, dragging his feet, followed.

"Robert, where are you from?" I asked, once we were seated. William started to examine his fingernails as if he was contemplating a manicure.

"Philadelphia," Robert answered.

"Philadelphia is a big city, exactly where did you live?"

"In the downtown section."

This wasn't the answer I was looking for. Most people would have said a street name or a neighborhood or a landmark as the area in which they lived. "That's a large area, could you be more specific?"

Unfortunately I didn't get an answer. Connie set a new record on how fast she could prepare a beverage tray. She chose that moment to return to the parlor laden with a cart filled with various soft drinks, glasses, and ice.

Harold's brother ignored the glasses and ice. He popped the tab from a can of soda and took a long sip. He muttered a thank you or at least something I interpreted as thank you. He didn't seem very talkative, so I tried another topic, "Do you have a large family?"

"No, just my brother and me."

"Do you talk with your brother often?" I bit my lip waiting to find out if Robert was the recipient of the eleven o'clock phone calls.

Robert's response was a vague, "Not as often as I would like."

"What do you do for a living?"

"I just lost my job. The economy, you know."

"Yes, the economy has hurt everyone. Where did you work before you lost your job?" I kept hoping William, Dorothy, or Connie would help carry the conversation, but every time I looked in their direction to encourage participation, they ignored me in favor of staring at Robert.

"You don't look like your brother," Dorothy finally commented. I thought it was rude to bring up the subject of appearance but it seemed to be one that Robert had been asked in the past.

"Yes, we had the same father, but I was a child of his second wife. That's why there is an age difference between us. Harold is almost fifteen years older than me."

"Where did Harold go to school?"

"That's a question you should ask him. He doesn't like people talking about him."

It was almost the same answer Darby had given me when I asked questions about Harold. "We have noticed that he is secretive about his personal life."

William decided the trite conversation was interrupting his routine. "Your brother is dead."

Robert blinked and then shook his head. "What did you just say?"

"I said, 'Your brother is dead.'" William enunciated the words clearer and louder than the first time.

I would have jumped in and reworded the statement to soften the blow, but I was in shock. How could William be so heartless? Where was his compassion? Where was his bedside manner? Why had I been blind to this man's selfish personality?

"Dead?" Robert's mouth froze, as if he was still saying the word. "I talked to him two days ago."

In a genuine act of concern, Dorothy got up and patted Robert on the back. "I know this is a shock. We are still grieving his death. Have a sip of your drink. Would you like something stronger?"

Without remorse, William shrugged his shoulders, "It had to be said and like ripping off a Band-Aid, it's better to do it quickly."

"But not like that. Why don't you go into the dining room and eat your lunch?"

There was a bounce in William's steps as he left the room to eat his meal. After all that had been his plan all along.

Connie was also appalled by William's less that tactful method of breaking the news to Robert. "Would you like to lie down?" she offered.

"How? When?" Robert managed to ask. I realized he was asking about his brother's death, not about lying down. "I talked to him the other day and he said nothing about being ill."

"Your brother was a victim of a violent crime." I waited for Robert to digest this information and then I continued, "He was shot, once in the chest. His death was immediate."

"Did the police catch the man who did it?"

The front door opened and the rest of my family entered, laughing and joking. One by one they sobered as they absorbed the atmosphere of the parlor.

"How do you do? My name is Stewart Griffin. I'm a cousin to Gi-Gi's mother."

Robert stood up. "I'm Robert Peters."

"Peters did you say? Our butler's name...." A sharp jab in the ribs delivered by Norman interrupted Stewart's sentence.

Dorothy slunk behind the others and made her escape. I let her go. She did her part in consoling the visitor. She trotted up the steps to the second floor. I felt a little jealousy and wondered if I could also leave.

Helen gave me a questioning look.

"Robert has been informed about his brother's death. We haven't discussed the details." I gestured to the small group to join us.

"We don't want to interrupt what is obviously a private moment," Norman said, speaking for the newcomers.

"Gi-Gi, why don't you call Officer Swanson? He'll be able to fill in the details of the case," Helen suggested.

I could have kissed her. Even though Helen was probably looking for an excuse to see the older officer again, it was a good idea. Officer Swanson would have experience in situations like this and it would give me a reason to politely escape the room.

The officer had to be more tactful than William had been.

I used the phone in the kitchen to make my call. I should have gone up to my room, locked the door, used my cell phone, and never left the room again.

"Connie, I need some strawberry jam," William yelled.

With one hand covering the lower half of the phone, I poked my head into the dining room. "Connie's busy. It's in the refrigerator."

"Can you get it for me?"

"Get it your self. I'm busy." I pulled my head back into the kitchen.

From the other room, I heard William say, "I hope you don't intend for me to share the bathroom with that man."

I didn't reply to William, he didn't deserve any measure of courtesy. His manner of delivering the news of Harold's death to his brother had upped his level of selfishness to the stratosphere. When I finished the call to the police officer, I intended to call the dealership and bribe the mechanic to finish William's car today.

Officer Swanson agreed to come over to the house right away and no one answered the phone at the car dealership. I wondered if William had bribed them not to finish the car today.

I snatched a cookie from the jar and thought about what I was going to say to Harold's brother. I took a second cookie. I hadn't had lunch and if I delayed in the kitchen long enough the officer would be here and he could explain everything to Robert. I wiped the crumbs from the counter and looked around for a reason to stay out of the parlor a little longer.

Not finding a good excuse to remain in the kitchen, I had to return to the parlor and relieve the others of their duty towards Robert. I got lucky. No one was there, which worried me more than if they were all waiting for me.

The knocker sounded random raps. Did Harold have more relatives coming to visit? Robert said he was the only immediate relative, but that didn't mean there weren't cousins. Perhaps this was the dealership returning William's car. I crossed my fingers that it was the latter rather than the former.

I held my breath as I opened the front door. "Oh, heck."

"Is that any way to greet your dinner date?" Tony was smiling. My remark hadn't changed his pleasant demeanor.

"I forgot."

"You forgot!" Tony didn't seem upset. He casually walked into the house as if he had been there before and felt comfortable. "Where is everyone?"

"I don't know. They were all here fifteen minutes ago, now they've disappeared." The image of Harold's brother flashed through my brain and I started to tell Tony about his arrival.

As if on cue, Uncle Norman called from the top of the stairs, "Is that Tony?" He didn't wait for an answer, with surprisingly spry taps on each tread, he joined us in the foyer.

"Gi-Gi is that what you're wearing to dinner?" Norman asked. "Why don't you change into one of your pretty dresses while I chat with Tony? I have some interesting insights into Harold's murder I want to share with him."

Dismissed like a young child, I raced up the stairs. Uncle Norman could entertain Tony while I changed my clothes. Instead of the anticipated leisurely routine, I hurried through my toilette and rushed to rescue Tony from Uncle Norman. I expected Tony to have glazed eyes from listening to Norman recount his college days or his brief career in the military. I found the duo had been joined by the rest of the family as well as William, who with his lower lip jutted out, appeared to be a little disgruntled not being the center of attention. Robert was absent from the gathering.

As soon as I entered the room, William grabbed my hand and pulled me back into the foyer. "Who is that guy?"

I pulled my hand out of his. "One of the officers investigating the murder," I explained. I don't know why I didn't tell William that Tony was my dinner date.

"He is acting like your relatives are friends instead of suspects."

"Do you think they are suspects?" I was stunned. In all the scenarios I had imagined regarding Harold's murder, never had I viewed one of my relatives as the culprit.

"They were in the house at the time of the murder. Of course they are suspects."

"If you think one of them could kill another human then you don't know me or my family. They are totally harmless. They would give you the shirt off their backs and they are as honest as a preacher."

William turned toward me and tried a different approach. "You look lovely. Are you hungry?"

"Starving. I'm looking forward to going out to eat."

"Out? No one told me. I just finished eating lunch, but I'll have an appetizer. I have to change my clothes."

"You're not invited. I'm going out on a date."

"With that cop? What about me? What am I supposed to do for a meal?" William asked, forgetting he just finished a salad and declared he wasn't hungry enough for dinner.

"You just finished your lunch and if you get hungry later, there is some leftover soup in the refrigerator. Warm it up," I said as I opened the door. I waved to Tony to indicate that I was ready to leave.

CHAPTER 13

G ETTING OUT OF the Tony's small car at the restaurant, I asked, "Did you get a chance to talk to Harold's brother, Robert?

"No, your Aunt Helen said he was lying down." Out of habit, Tony checked the cars parked in the lot. "Let's not talk about the murder until after we eat."

In spite of the name of the restaurant being simply 'Hayden's, the food was delicious and plentiful. I wiped my mouth and asked Tony, "Are you ready to talk about the murder?"

"If I have to, but first I want to know how his brother found out Harold was dead. Did you call him?"

"I didn't know Harold had a brother," I explained. "When Robert arrived, he expected to stay for a short visit with Harold. He didn't know Harold was dead until William told him."

"I may be losing my mind, but I thought your uncles' names were Norman and Stewart. Who is William?"

"Remember when Stewart came out to the gazebo last evening. He said there was a call on my cell phone from my ex-boyfriend." I emphasized the 'ex.' "That's William. He had an appointment nearby and wanted to stop for a visit. I told him in no uncertain terms that he wasn't welcome. I wasn't interested."

"If you told him you didn't want him to visit and you weren't interested, why is he at your house?"

"It's a long story."

"I have time."

I sighed. There was no way I could avoid an explanation of William's presence in my house if I wanted a deeper relationship with Tony. I recounted the events at the bar the previous evening, the car needing a thorough cleaning, and concluding with *the selfish bastard will be leaving in the morning*.

Tony appeared to be satisfied that I didn't have any romantic notions about William. "So why was he the one to break the news to Robert about his brother's death?"

"I wanted William to stay in the parlor while I tactfully told Robert the news. I was working my way to telling him, asking questions, and just generally creating a rapport between us that was conducive to the topic of Harold's demise when William blurted it out. The news hit Robert like a sledge hammer."

Tony raised an eyebrow. "Doesn't it seem strange that your butler lived in your house for fifteen years and never once mentioned a brother? Doesn't it seem strange that Harold never had one visitor to the house and suddenly the brother shows up on the front porch and tells you he was to stay with Harold? All this occurring within a couple days after Harold's death."

"No, yes, maybe, I don't know. I didn't think about it. Robert seemed genuinely shocked at the news."

"You said you went into the kitchen to call Everet and when you returned to the parlor he wasn't there. Where did he go?"

"I don't know. That's when you knocked on the door. I assume Connie or someone else took him upstairs to one of the vacant bedrooms so he could lie down."

"Did Everet replace the crime scene tape over the door to Harold's apartment?"

"I don't know. I didn't go down there today. Why?" It dawned on me that there were a lot of things going on that I didn't know about. I promised myself that I would be more in tune to what was happening in the house from then on.

"I don't want your house guests to enter Harold's apartment and interfere with the crime scene."

"They don't have any reason to go down to the basement."

"Harold's brother may feel a need to go into the apartment, to feel closer to his brother."

I read between the lines of Tony's comment and interpreted it to mean, look for clues to find the killer or valuables among Harold's things, but I said, "When I get home, I'll make a point of telling him to stay out of his brother's apartment. He will have complete access to Harold's possessions after the police investigation is over."

Tony nodded his approval of my plan. "Last night you indicated there was something else you wanted to tell me about Harold's murder."

"No, but I did want to ask you some...." I was interrupted by someone calling my name. I turned and saw eight people standing at the hostess station. Unfortunately, I knew them all. I couldn't ignore them.

When they saw Tony and me they bypassed the hostess and swarmed our table. They all started talking at once.

Aunt Dorothy said, "We would have gone to a different restaurant if we knew you would still be here. We thought you would be finished with your dinners by now."

Uncle Norman said, "We wanted to try to cheer up Robert by taking him out."

William said, "Your cook left for the day. There wasn't anyone to prepare a decent meal."

The rest of them had something to say as well. There were so many people talking at once I missed most of the comments. If Robert said anything I didn't hear it.

I looked at Tony and he seemed to be enjoying the confusion. "I'll ask the waitress to pull a couple tables over so they can join us. We'll have dessert while they eat," he said, as if having eight people descend on us was a natural occurrence.

When the furniture arrangements were complete, I noticed William tried to sit next to me, but Aunt Dorothy outmaneuvered him, sliding into the chair in an amazingly limber move, providing a buffer. My aunt picked up the menu immediately and intently started reading it as if it was a contract for a life-long commitment to her meal.

William pouted, which was becoming a permanent facial expression for him. He should have been smiling at the thought that he was going to be able to freeload another meal.

Helen sat next to Everet, a surprise in the guest list. She immediately picked up the menu and started analyzing the choices. While discussing the calorie and fat content of the options with the off-duty police officer, she softened her intent to shrink his waistline by using the endearing terms of honey and sweetheart.

Mildred and Norman sandwiched Robert. I could see they were trying to include him in a conversation, but our newest guest was resisting their attempts. He appeared uncomfortable among the large group. He also picked up his menu and started to read it. I couldn't see his face to determine how he was coping with the news of his brother's death. I wished Robert had sat next to me so I could continue the questions I started to ask him when he arrived at the house.

After a few failed attempts at making conversation with Robert, Mildred and Norman stared at their laps. If I wasn't mistaken, Norman had joined the cell phone generation.

"Do you think Robert looks anything like Harold?" I asked Tony.

"I haven't had a good look at the fellow." Tony leaned forward to look at him now, but his view was blocked by the others and the menu. "My opinion would be slightly skewed. The only time I saw his brother was when he was dead. It didn't give me a good perspective of his appearance."

"Well, I don't think there is any family resemblance. Robert explained that the two brothers had the same father but different mothers. I still think there should be something similar like the shape of their noses or chins. Look at my aunts and uncles and me. We're not directly related but we have the same shape ears." I held back my hair so Tony could compare my ears to the ears of the others.

When the waitress began to take the food orders, I declined anything. Tony leaned around me and ordered the chocolate cheesecake with two forks. "We'll share."

He reached below the table and took my hand in his.

Everything in the room faded from my mind as I enjoyed the warmth of his fingers against mine.

I re-entered the world when the food arrived and Tony released my hand.

Everet was served a baked chicken breast, a salad, and a baked potato with no butter. I detected a slight grimace and decided Helen had ordered his meal. Helen's selection matched Everet's.

For someone who had declared they weren't hungry an hour earlier, William's meal was the most expensive item on the menu. He probably didn't even know what he ordered, he had simply pointed at the item based on the price.

Robert's dinner was the largest quantity of food. He didn't wait for all the meals to be served. As soon as his plate was placed in front of him he started eating so fast sparks flew from his silverware. He reached for the bread without bothering to look up. The waitress had trouble serving his side dishes.

Tony commented, "He's young."

Dorothy extracted a small notebook from her purse and

made a notation, then slipped it back in her handbag. When she caught me watching her, she smiled one of those smiles that look forced and quickly disappeared. She explained, "I remembered something I need at the store."

Uncle Norman mentioned a news item that had been on the front page and the others discussed the issue. Tony joined in, adding a humorous perspective of the event and before the last crumb was consumed, the folks at the table were laughing and carrying on. The exceptions being Robert, who keeping his head down, reached for another slice of bread, and William, who acted like it was all beneath him.

I didn't expect Robert to join in the raucous. He didn't know anyone and he had received the news of his brother's death only hours before. William could have tried harder to participate.

The bill arrived and Tony signaled to the waitress to bring it to him as he reached for his wallet with the other hand.

"No, wait." I looked over the check. "William, you owe thirty five dollars."

"Why me? No one else is paying for their meal."

"Why should Tony pay for your dinner? You're a doctor. Show everyone your new Rolex watch."

"But…." William started to make an excuse. He saw my anger and reluctantly pulled out his wallet. "Let me split the bill with you. It's the least I can do after imposing on Gi-Gi's hospitality."

I was more satisfied by forcing William to pay half the bill than I had been by the meal until the waitress returned to the table. She stood over William's shoulder and whispered in his ear. His complexion reddened. He reached for his wallet again and thumbed through the credit cards, shaking his head each time. His credit cards were maxed out! I knew he didn't have any cash because I had used the last of it to tip the guys who had helped me bring him home the previous evening.

Tony watched the humiliation occur. He signaled to the waitress to put the entire bill on his credit card. The matter of the check taken care of, the group pushed back their chairs and headed for the door.

Out of William's earshot, I apologized to Tony for William's poor money management skills. "When we get back to the house, I'll reimburse you for the meals."

"That's not necessary. I enjoyed every minute of the meal." Tony halted for a minute. "Didn't you tell me William was having his car detailed today?"

"Yes, and he ordered new tires put on."

"If he can't afford to pay for dinner, then he won't be able to pay for the detailing or the tires."

"I don't care. He can push the car out of the dealership. He can live in a cardboard box. Tomorrow, he leaves!" I turned to face my ex-boyfriend. As I did so I saw Robert looking intently towards the kitchen. I followed his line of vision. There was a tall man in the kitchen, wearing an apron, looking back at Robert. Very subtle communication was occurring: a slight jerk of the head, a barely discernable nod, and a hand raised to waist level indicating halt.

I turned away, shocked. These two men knew each other. What were the odds that two men from Philadelphia would run into each other in a restaurant here in town? Why didn't Robert go over to the other man and say hello?

Tony took my elbow and said something. I didn't hear what he said. I meekly followed, thinking about the exchange I had witnessed between Robert and the man in the kitchen. I decided I would tell Tony about it when we got in the privacy of the car.

Eight people were crowding into the estate wagon. They looked like circus clowns trying to squeeze into a Volkswagen bug. Tony took pity and invited the aunts to ride with us. His action prevented me from mentioning Robert's friend in the kitchen of the restaurant. I didn't want to upset the aunts or worse, start them on a hunt to find more clues to the murder.

The closer we got to home the more I second guessed

myself. The signals I witnessed were figments of my overactive imagination. It didn't make sense. Robert didn't know anyone in town. Harold's murder, William's (unwelcome) prolonged stay, and the unexpected arrival of a now grieving Robert were too much for me to comprehend.

I shook my head trying to clear it. I was looking for things that weren't there in order to put sanity back in my world.

After the aunts were out of the car and safely back in the house, Tony suggested we visit the gazebo again. "After all, we really didn't a chance to talk about the murder investigation."

There wasn't much conversation when we got to the gazebo.

CHAPTER 14

S o I WASN'T crazy. The noise I heard wasn't part of the dream where hordes of little green men pounded on the door trying to get to a bed. It was only one person, Aunt Helen and she was whispering my name, "Gi-Gi? Gi-Gi?" Each time she repeated it, she increased the volume.

"Come in, Aunt Helen. What's wrong? Are you sick?" I flicked on the nightlight, prepared to handle a medical emergency.

"I'm not sick. Are you sleeping?" she asked, as if sleep was possible when someone was knocking on the door, calling your name.

"Not any more. What do you need?" I tried to remain calm, but I knew that her visit was prompted by something more important than the need to discuss the color choices for the dining room seat covers.

"I heard people talking." Aunt Helen was wearing a short, shocking pink robe over her long chartreuse floral nightgown, no makeup, and blue curlers in her hair. If the conversation didn't open my eyes, the outfit did.

"Go back to bed. It was probably someone watching television with the volume too loud."

"That's what I thought at first, but after listening carefully, the voices seemed to be coming from outside. So I got up and looked. The voices were louder when I opened my window but I didn't see anyone."

"Did you recognize the voices? Could you hear what they were saying?"

"No, they sounded garbled."

"I'll check." Sometimes dealing with a group of geriatrics was similar to dealing with young children. I felt the need to humor them the same way a parent looks under the bed for monsters.

"Shouldn't you call the police?" Aunt Helen held out a cell phone for me to use. I didn't get a chance to wonder if her comment was intended to bring Everet to the house or if she was truly scared. I didn't get a chance to answer her because her knocking on the door woke another person in the house, the man sleeping across the hall in my childhood bedroom.

"What's going on?" William, hair tussled, was standing in the doorway. At least he had the decency to put on pants and a t-shirt.

"Aunt Helen thought she heard voices outside."

"I didn't think I heard voices. I heard voices," she clarified.

"I didn't hear anything and I'm sleeping on the same side of the house. It was probably someone's television," William said, dismissing her observation as unimportant. "Go back to bed. Some of us need our rest."

I didn't like his attitude toward my aunt. It didn't matter that I said the same thing. I didn't like William doing it. If Aunt Helen claimed she heard voices then I would get up and see what was going on.

"Wait for me out in the hall while I put on some clothes and shoes. We'll go downstairs and look for evidence of someone trying to get in." As soon as they closed the door I dressed in the clothes I had worn to the restaurant. Uncle Stewart still had my cell phone. Lacking anything more substantial, I slipped the hair brush into my pocket for protection.

"Let's go." I led the way. Guided by the dim light from the lamp in the foyer, I tip-toed down the steps. I didn't know what the proper protocol for catching midnight invaders involved, but I wasn't going to alert them to my presence or the presence of the duo following me. I did know that investigating a noise in the middle of the night should not be done by amateurs, especially when there was a recent murder in the house.

"I still think we should call the police. What if it is the killer outside and he came back to finish off the rest of us?" Helen followed two steps behind me with William two steps behind her.

His willing participation was a surprise. He was demonstrating enough courage to accompany us, but after the credit card fiasco, he needed to show some manliness. I wasn't going to send either of them back upstairs.

I whispered, "Killers don't alert their victims by carrying on a conversation. And would-be victims don't talk while hoping to capture murderers."

I tried the front door handle, locked. My little troop went into the kitchen. That door was also locked, but the foray into the kitchen allowed me to get the emergency flashlight out of the drawer. Helen got the rolling pin. William just stood there. His eyes bugged out, searching for potential danger.

The only door remaining to be checked was the one leading in from the port cochere. With a shaking hand I tried the knob, locked. "You can relax. Everything is locked tight. No one got in." I felt my muscles relax.

"What about the windows?" William asked. For someone who, mere moments before, dismissed the voices as figments of Aunt Helen's imagination, William was being thorough in our investigation.

We quickly went into each room a second time. I flashed the light on the window sills and checked the latches. I breathed deep. "Whoever was out there didn't get in."

I headed toward the stairs.

"Gi-Gi?" said a small voice behind me.

"Yes Aunt Helen?"

"What if the person locked the door after they got in?"

I reversed and went back into the parlor. This time I searched behind the chairs and sofa.

We proceeded to the dining room and did a thorough search. I was pushing the swinging door leading into the kitchen when we heard the crash and a scream. I pointed toward the house phone and ordered William, "Call 9-1-1."

It was stupid. In cases like this, the rule is to run away from danger and wait for the police. But I reacted instinctively. I ran through the kitchen and out the backdoor, positive the noise had come from outside. I flashed the light around the garden. "Who's there?"

I heard a moan and then a voice I recognized said, "Over here, Gi-Gi."

"Joel? What are you doing out here?" I stepped in the direction of the voice, shining my flashlight around the entire area as I cautiously moved closer to Joel.

"I got up to use the bathroom and saw the flashlight moving around the first floor of the house. I called 9-1-1, but I didn't know what was happening in the house. I couldn't wait for the police to get here. I hurried to get dressed and came out to see who was searching the house. I tripped over the garden hose and fell into the wheelbarrow."

"Are you okay?" Helen asked.

I felt like an uncaring clod for not asking the question myself.

"I think I sprained my ankle." He added a moan to make certain we knew the extent of his injury.

"Let me check it." I examined his lower leg. There wasn't an obvious break, but there was swelling and discoloration. "You need to have this x-rayed."

I coerced William into driving my car to the hospital by telling him I needed to hold the icepack on Joel's ankle. I figured it would speed up the emergency room process if we had a doctor with us. Even if it didn't speed things up, being in the waiting room would give William insight from the patient point of view of medicine.

*****

The sun was coming up when Joel was discharged to leave the hospital. He was on crutches, diagnosed with a severe sprain, and not allowed to put any weight on his foot for forty eight hours.

I glanced in the car mirror to make sure my dream wasn't coming true. There weren't little green men pounding on the door, trying to get a bedroom, but as soon as I could get Joel up the stairs I would have another person bunking in my house. There was no sense in Joel going back to his apartment over the stables. Someone would have to take his meals to him, check on him, make sure he took his pain medicine, and supervise his trips to the bathroom. It would be much more convenient having him in the house. Besides, he was injured trying to protect us, he deserved some tender loving care.

William, with only a little prodding, helped me get the injured man up the stairs. I expected he would also help get Joel into bed, but William disappeared into my childhood bedroom and firmly shut the door before I could ask. I wanted to do the same thing.

I settled Joel into bed with a pitcher of water and a bell to ring if he needed anything. As I closed the door to a drowsy Joel, Dorothy was standing there. "Tony and Everet are in the dining room. They want to talk to you."

Tony and Everet, it must be important. "What about?" I asked, although I had a good idea they wanted to ask questions about the 9-1-1 calls Joel and William had placed during the night and discuss their findings.

"They wouldn't tell me. They only want to speak with you."

I rubbed my eyes. I only had an hour or two of sleep before Aunt Helen knocked on my door and declared there were voices outside, but I thought I could last another hour before I crawled back to bed.

As tired as I was, I still had to smile when I saw a doting Helen (without curlers and with makeup) sitting beside Everet. Everet didn't seem as enchanted with Helen this morning, but I thought his sour mood was the result of the scrambled egg whites and dry toast in front of him rather than the suffocating attention Helen was giving him.

Tony was indulging in a second helping of biscuits and gravy.

I reached for the coffee and decided against it in favor of going back to bed caffeine free when the conversation was over. "Good morning. What can I do for you this morning?"

"Someone was in Harold's apartment," Tony stated, his fork filled with real scrambled eggs. He stuffed the bite into his mouth.

I sat down. "Who?" I thought about the people in the house. The aunts and uncles may have entered the basement apartment out of curiosity. William may have gone to Harold's apartment due to his current financial state, looking for items of value. Robert had been alone for an hour or two, supposedly resting after hearing the news about his brother. He had the opportunity to visit the rooms belonging to the butler. Everyone had the opportunity and the motive for going into Harold's apartment.

"That's what we want to know."

"Was anything disturbed?"

"Not so that a casual observer would notice, but Everet is a trained professional. He knows exactly how he had left things. If he says someone crossed the crime scene tape then someone did."

"Will this affect the outcome of your investigation?"

"Fortunately, Everet went through everything and he's fairly certain nothing was removed and nothing was tampered with, but at this point in the investigation, we don't know what's important toward identifying the killer and getting the conviction."

"Did Helen tell you about the voices she heard outside her window? We called

9-1-1."

"Yeah, we heard about the calls when we were briefed this morning. The on-duty patrol unit responded to the call. Lance made a thorough search of the house and the grounds. He didn't find any evidence someone had been inside or outside the house, but he remained parked in the driveway until four in the morning, when he got another call."

Helen nodded confirmation of the patrol unit's presence during the night. "I definitely heard someone talking." I noticed she continued to be paranoid, evidenced by the rolling pin beside her elbow.

"We believe you," Everet said, adding a gentle pat on Helen's hand.

I heard multiple footsteps coming down the stairs. I still needed to tell Tony about the exchange between Robert and the man in the restaurant's kitchen. "Tony, I have something I want to discuss with you about the restaurant last night."

"Forget about it."

"But…." He was referring to William's lack of finances and the fact he was stuck with the entire bill for ten people's meals. I wasn't.

Connie came from the kitchen to replenish the dishes on the buffet at the same time the rest of the relatives entered from the hall. Suddenly the dining room seemed crowded and full of confusion as plates were filled and people found seats at the table.

"I'm going to bed," I announced to the group. "I don't want to be disturbed until noon. If anyone has a problem, they will have to handle it themselves or wait until then."

I made a grand exit.

CHAPTER 15

I ROLLED OVER, CHECKED the clock, and did the math. I had slept eight hours. By some miracle no one had an emergency requiring my attention. I stretched. I felt much better. That's when I noticed the silence. The house was too quiet. Where had everyone gone? Stella wasn't running the vacuum cleaner. Connie wasn't banging pots and pans in the kitchen. Joel hadn't rung his bedside bell. I hadn't heard any bickering between the relatives.

The silence was frightening. I hurried through my shower and pulled clean clothes from the boxes sitting on the floor. I needed to finish unpacking and mentally set aside some time after Joel was healed and the visitors were gone to do that task. Stella had aired the master bedroom and put fresh sheets on the bed before my arrival, but she hadn't emptied the closet or drawers of the contents. I had to do that before I could put away my things.

When I opened the door, I was greeted by a woman I didn't know. She put a finger to her lips to indicate I should be quiet and mouthed the words, "Joel is sleeping." She returned to reading a book and ignored me otherwise.

One problem resolved. I wouldn't have to worry about the invalid. I just hoped I didn't have to provide a bed for the woman. I glanced at the caretaker one more time and wondered who she was. She looked like a younger version of Joel. I decided she was one of his relatives. I shrugged my shoulders. I didn't care who she was as long as Joel was receiving appropriate care and I wasn't the one providing it. I continued down the hall.

William's door, my childhood bedroom door, was open. His bed was made and his suitcase gone. A second problem resolved. I assumed that while I was sleeping the dealership delivered the car and without a word of gratitude for allowing him to stay, he had departed. I wasn't concerned about his rudeness although a floral arrangement or a box of chocolates would have been appropriate. I was delighted to see that he was gone.

I almost whistled as I descended the stairs. I stopped mid-step. I had experienced the same euphoria the previous day. I reined in my hopeful emotion. How had William paid the dealership? I would ask Norman. I shrugged again. I really didn't care how William had paid for his car care, as long as he was gone. I would also confirm he had truly departed.

On the last stair I came face to face with my third problem – Robert. Without wishing me a good afternoon or at least saying hello, he said, "I can't find the keys to my brother's car."

"I believe Harold's car is under police investigation. They locked the car and took the keys. No one is permitted to touch it until the police have checked every aspect for clues to the identity of his killer."

"But Stewart said he drove it." I didn't know Robert's age, but he was whining, a tone that was becoming too familiar among my guests.

"Stewart drove the car before the police knew about it and deemed it part of the investigation."

"It was my brother's car. As his only relative, that means it is mine now and I need to get into town."

"Why don't you take my car or the station wagon?" I offered. I felt a selfish satisfaction. If Robert took me up on the use of one of the cars, I would have a legitimate reason to see his driver's license.

"They're gone. So is the Mustang."

"Stewart and Norman probably borrowed two of the cars and Stella or Connie took the estate wagon for supplies. Can you wait until one of the others return?"

"I need to go now."

"Why do you need to go into town?"

Robert paused. "Errands, important errands."

"If they are so important that you need to get to town this minute, you could call a taxi. Or if it can wait until later, you can take my car." I thought about any other possible solutions and something occurred to me. "How did you get here in the first place?"

"I walked."

"From where?"

"The bus station."

"That was a long walk. Why didn't you call Harold for a ride?"

"He was supposed to meet me. He didn't show up. I had to walk," Robert explained.

I tried to recall whether Robert had looked like he had walked three miles in the middle of a hot summer afternoon. All I remembered was the dusty, brown suitcase he had carried and my shock at discovering Robert's relationship to our butler.

"When do you think the police will let me have my car?"

"You'll have to file a petition in probate court, prove you are who you say you are, post a notice in the newspaper, and then you have to wait to see if anyone else claims it belongs to them. If no one claims the property and the court decides you are Harold's legitimate heir, you'll have to pay the taxes. Then you'll get the title to the car. I say it will be at least a year before you can drive it."

"A year? Pay the taxes? Post a notice in the newspaper? Prove I am his brother?" Robert sounded like he was overwhelmed by what had to be done. "What about the rest of his things?"

"Like…?" I wasn't a mind reader but I suspected Robert wanted access to his brother's money. I was correct.

"His money."

"You have to go through the same process. It will all be bundled together. If the courts decide you are the only legitimate heir to his estate, they'll give you everything at once. But don't spend any of it yet." My degree was in nursing, but I had been around enough people responsible for settling their parents' estates to have a general knowledge of the process.

"Why not?" Robert asked.

"The police haven't found any bank accounts and Harold didn't have any cash stashed under his mattress. You may have to use your own money to pay the taxes on your inheritance."

Robert's fists clenched. "I don't believe you. I think you're making up this legal stuff so that I don't get my brother's things."

"If it was up to me, I'd give you his things now just to get them out of the house. But if you don't think I'm telling you the truth ask someone else. Ask Tony. Ask William. Consult an attorney. They will tell you the same things I'm telling you."

Robert shook his head in disbelief. "What am I going to do for a year?"

"Rent an apartment. Get a job," I suggested. I didn't want Robert to think even for a minute that he could live at Grant House while he waited for Harold's estate to be settled in court. "You were only going to visit Harold for a couple days. Where were you going after your visit?"

"I think I'll walk into town." Robert neatly sidestepped my question, which didn't satisfy my curiosity.

"Call when you're done with your errands. Maybe there'll be a car available and someone can pick you up." I smiled and waved good bye. I didn't have the heart to tell Robert that the burial expenses would come out of Harold's money, if there was any.

I watched as Robert walked down the driveway and turned in the direction of town. He had skillfully maneuvered the conversation to get the answers he wanted and not provide the answers I wanted.

As long as he was gone, I had an errand of my own.

CHAPTER 16

I GRABBED AN APPLE from the bowl and started munching on it while I dug through the junk drawer. I found pencils, pens, gum bands, old receipts, flashlight, screws, screwdriver, and a ruler, but I didn't find the key.

The fact that the key wasn't there didn't sound any alarms. Everyone in the family knew where the key was and put it back when they were through using it. For the most part, skeleton keys, of the nature of the one from the drawer, were universal to Grant House and every other house built in the same era. If I needed it, I would get a key from one of the other doors.

In any case, the locks weren't complicated. As a child, I became very skilled at opening the simple locks with a paper clip. If I didn't get access to a key, I would use a simple metal wire to open the lock. I reached into the junk drawer and pocketed a paper clip as my backup plan.

I used the back stairs to get to the second floor. At the end of the hall there was a turn that if I was quiet enough, the woman sitting in front of Joel's room would not see or hear me.

My plan would have worked, but I didn't need it. The door wasn't locked, but the room wasn't empty as I anticipated.

"Uncle Stewart, what are you doing in Robert's room?"

Startled, my uncle jerked, but recovered nicely when he realized it was me. "There's something fishy about this guy and I thought I would go through his things and see if he is legit."

"You should respect a person's privacy."

"Not when there's been a murder in the house and this guy happens to show up on the doorstep right afterward. He could be anyone. He could be the killer come back to get what he wanted."

"Tut, tut." I shook my finger at my uncle like he was a bad boy. "What are you doing here?"

"I heard a noise." I said, but the words came out squeaky.

Uncle Stewart copied my gesture. He shook a single gnarled finger back in my direction, "Tut, tut. Don't lie. You were about to do what I am doing, searching for evidence that Robert is who he says he is."

"So? What have you found so far?" I asked.

"I haven't found anything, except my old tennis racket stored in the back of the closet."

"Robert only had a small brown suitcase when he arrived. He won't have much stuff to go through." I lifted the bed skirt and looked under the bed. (Stella was keeping up with the dust bunnies.)

"Well I didn't find anything useful. Maybe he is related to Harold and has his own phobia about privacy and no one finding out anything about him. No driver's license, no credit cards." Uncle Stewart looked inside the lamp shade, then turned the lamp upside down and examined the base.

"He was on his way to town. He probably took his wallet with him." Using the tip of my index finger, I opened the drawer of the nightstand. The contents were exactly as I remembered. I moved to the edge of the rug, lifting it carefully with the toe of my shoe. "If he isn't who he says he it, who is he?"

Uncle Stewart opened his mouth but didn't say anything.

"Quick, get in the closet," I whispered.

"Huh?"

"Someone's coming." I grabbed the sleeve of Uncle Stewart's shirt and shoved him into the closet. I squeezed in beside him. I pulled the door almost closed, leaving a thin crack so I could spy. The bedroom door opened slowly, a hand appeared around its edge. I tensed and held my breath.

I exhaled a sigh of relief. "Connie, what are you doing in here?"

"I think I am doing the same thing you're doing, protecting the family." She scanned the room as she spoke.

"Shh." This time the warning came from Stewart. He was already moving toward the closet. I followed, pulling Connie in with me. It was a tight fit. Our cook is not a petite person and the closets in old houses were not intended to hold three adults. The image of clowns fitting into a compact car occurred to me again.

This time when the bedroom door opened, it was Connie who spied through the gap. "Aha!" She punctuated her exclamation by pushing the closet door so hard that it banged against the wall.

"William?" My heart sank. He hadn't left. I had experienced a euphoric moment when I thought he had departed and he would not be interfering in my budding romance with Tony. "I thought you had your car back and you were returning to your medical practice."

"I have a problem. Can I talk to you privately?" William didn't raise an eyebrow at the discovery of three adults hiding in the closet.

"I'm busy at the moment." I anticipated the nature of his private chat and weighed the cost of him living with me another day or two versus the expense of paying for his car services. I would think about it later. In the meantime, I wanted him to stress over how he was going to get out of his financial crisis.

"I'll help you search Robert's room for evidence later, if you come with me now. I really need to talk with you." William looked like he was prepared to beg for something (money) and I was savoring the moment.

Connie and Uncle Stewart waved me out of the room and pushed the door closed so that they could continue to search Robert's belongings.

"What is your problem?" I asked with a bit of impatience. William was wearing on my last nerve.

"I have a guest."

I maintained my poise and asked, "Who is your guest?"

William took a step backwards, out of arm's reach. "Mary Ann."

"Mary Ann? Mary Ann Trumley? Your future wife? The woman you dumped me for? What is she doing here?" The mere mention of the woman's name brought murderous thoughts to my brain.

William took another step back and nodded.

My hands clenched into fists. "No! No! No! I will not have that woman in my house. I don't even want you in this house. I definitely will not have her in my house."

"That's part of the problem. She doesn't know it's your house. She thinks it's my house."

"And?" I fought for control. I knew there was going to be more and I wasn't going to like it.

"And Mary Ann is under the belief that the men and women living here are my aunts and uncles."

"How did she reach that conclusion?" I asked and quickly decided I knew the answer. She assumed that since William was living here that it was his house and naturally they would be his relatives. He hadn't bothered to correct her.

William shuffled his feet while he searched for words that would make him appear to be a victim rather that the perpetrator of the ruse.

I walked around in a circle. If I wasn't careful I would be sitting in a corner, sucking my thumb, rocking back and forth. "I thought Mary Ann was on vacation with her family at some exotic beach."

"I thought so too, but she claims she missed me so much she flew back early to see me. She decided it would be romantic to elope." He didn't look like he was partial to the idea of an immediate wedding.

"I'll help you pack your suitcase."

"I can't elope. You know I don't have enough money for the marriage license."

"I'll help you pack your suitcase and give you enough money for the marriage license. Consider it a wedding present." I had a vision of hope that the couple would get married and quickly leave on a permanent honeymoon.

"Elopement is out of the question."

"This is my final offer. I'll help you pack your suitcase, pay for the marriage license, and settle your bill at the car dealership."

"No, that isn't what I meant, although I wouldn't mind if you paid for the car. I'll pay you back." William didn't even blink at my offer. "Mary Ann has changed her mind. Now that she has seen the house, she wants to get married in the garden with the aunts and uncles in attendance."

"I'll pretend I'm a minister. I'll do anything to get you and that woman out of my house."

"Anything? Will you let me pretend this is my house until the day after tomorrow?"

"William, that isn't the way to start a marriage. You need to be totally honest before you exchange your vows. As much as I dislike Mary Ann and think you are a jerk, I can't let you start a marriage with Mary Ann thinking you have money to throw around."

"But...."

"No buts. If you don't tell her, I will," I threatened. I don't know why I cared about the success of their marriage, but I did.

"Please don't make me tell her tonight. Let me enjoy being the pot of gold at the end of Mary Ann's rainbow." William had puppy dog eyes and his hands were folded in a prayerful manner.

How could I force the issue of honesty when William looked so pitiful? "Okay, but you have only forty eight hours to tell her about the house and your financial situation. The clock is ticking."

A contrite William reluctantly agreed.

"What do we have to do to carry off this charade?" Now that I agreed to the masquerade I needed to know what role I had to play to carry it out.

"You're really going to help me."

"I'm a sucker for romance. What can I say?"

"We need to trade bedrooms. I told Mary Ann I own the house and allow the aunts and uncles to live here rent free. It would never do for me to have a pink child's bedroom when I am the master of the household." It appeared like William had given the farce more thought than his spontaneous appearance in Robert's room suggested.

"That won't be difficult. We'll flip flop the room arrangements. Most of my things are still in boxes. I'll just move them across the hall into the room you're currently using."

"I thought Mary Ann could use that room. It's directly across the hall and uh…."

"I understand. But where will I sleep?" Mentally I counted the bedrooms and the occupants. I came up one bedroom short. "The aunts and uncles have their own rooms. I can't ask them to share, not even for one night. That leaves five other bedrooms. If you use the master bedroom and Mary Ann is using my old bedroom, Robert is using one spare room and Joel is using the other spare room, the only one remaining is the nursery."

"See you answered your own question. You can use the nursery. At one point in your life you probably slept in there.

You'll feel right at home."

"There is only a crib in that room. That's not a real bed. I can't sleep in there."

William ignored my bed needs. "The other thing that needs to be addressed is at dinner tonight. I need to sit at the head of the table." He dusted the imaginary dirt from his hands like it was a done deal.

"I'll tell Norman to sit in a different chair." I was too emotionally tired to argue. If this was the way to get William and his fiancé out of my house I would suffer a little.

"There's no need to speak to Norman."

"Why not?"

"I already took the good man aside and asked him to sit somewhere else at the table tonight."

I sputtered, "You already told Norman to sit somewhere else? That means you assumed I would be willing to go along with this scheme of yours."

"Calm down, Gi-Gi. I was only trying to expedite the arrangements. I did it for you. I didn't want you to have to run around looking for everyone."

"Norman is back?"

"Yeah and he gave Robert a ride from town also."

"Robert is back? He just left the house."

"Do you need your hearing checked? I just said Robert is back. Repeating everything people say is not an attractive quality."

I didn't answer William. I rushed into Robert's room and hustled Connie and Stewart out of it and up the stairs to Stewart's private domain.

As we scampered to the upper level, I heard William's voice echo up the staircase, "Don't forget to dress for dinner."

CHAPTER 17

I ASKED STELLA TO stay an extra hour or two to help Connie serve dinner. Preparing and serving a four course meal for nine people and an invalid with a caretaker upstairs was beyond the scope of her normal work. I checked on the progress of the meal and found Connie sitting at the kitchen table reading a magazine.

"What is this, a mutiny?" I asked. I was beginning to think that the cook was overpaid for her services.

"No, preparation for the meal is finished. I'm taking a break before the guests sit down to eat."

I was curious about the meal. Even though I could smell something in the oven I didn't see any pots steaming on the stove. "What is the menu?"

"The first course is vichyssoise, a cold potato soup. It is in the refrigerator, already in the individual bowls properly garnished. All I have to do is set it on the table in front of each person." Connie flipped a page of her magazine.

"That was a good idea." I was impressed. The food she normally prepared for special occasions was good old American cuisine: roast beef and mashed potatoes with a roasted turkey served on holidays.

"The soup is delicious even if I have to say so myself."

"What is the second course?" I hoped it lived up to the standard of the first course.

Connie didn't look up from her magazine. "A summer fruit medley with a strawberry glaze."

My mouth was watering from the description of the fresh fruit. "It sounds refreshing. I think I smell the main course in the oven."

"Chicken cordon bleu with twice baked potato, asparagus in a balsamic vinegar marinade, very easy to serve and all the prep was done ahead of time. I only have to remove the pans from the oven when I serve the fruit medley." Connie thumped the magazine against the table.

"I hope the dessert lives up to the rest of the meal."

"Oh, it does. It's crème brulee. It's in the pantry. It gets served at room temperature. Stella is serving the beverages and removing the dirty dishes from the table."

"You outdid yourself with the menu and the planning."

"Oh, I didn't do it. Dorothy prepared the meal. All I have to do is serve it." Connie smoothed her apron, preparing to start serving the meal as soon as she got the signal.

"You mean Dorothy called a caterer." I shook my head, trying to make sense of what Connie was telling me.

"No, I mean Dorothy planned the menu, ordered the ingredients, and prepared it."

I entered the dining room in a state of shock. I had to look twice at Dorothy. She looked like the aunt I had known all my life, but never had I known her to fix her own breakfast, let alone a formal dinner for nine people. I took my seat next to hers and leaned over to tell her, "The menu sounds delicious."

She didn't respond, but her expression visibly brightened with the compliment.

There was a pause between when the rest of us were seated and the regal entrance of the engaged couple. William escorted Mary Ann into the room and held her chair. He sat at the opposite end of the table as if he always sat there. He nodded in my direction and I tapped my glass. This was the cue for Connie to begin serving.

The meal progressed as smoothly as Dorothy had planned. Each course was met with well deserved praise. Connie and Stella made an impressive display of serving the food and removing the used place settings.

If I looked hard enough for faults in the meal, it was the formality and stinted conversation. After the relaxed atmosphere the evening before at Hayden's restaurant with the laughter and kidding, this evening seemed stuffy and oppressive. I kept hoping Tony would show up and lighten the mood.

I studied Mary Ann. She accepted the role of mistress of the house as if she had been born here. As much as I wanted to hate her, I couldn't. She took a genuine interest in each of the people at the table. She made an effort to draw each of the aunts and uncles into the conversation. I wondered if she would act the same if she knew they were my relatives and not William's.

Even Robert made the effort to answer her questions.

"Bill, that was one of the best meals I have ever had. The staff needs to be complimented."

Surprised as I was by the informal form of her fiancé's name I still was aware enough to tap Dorothy on the thigh and whisper, "It was excellent."

William stood up. "Shall we go into the parlor for coffee?"

Stewart stood up and excused himself from coffee. "I need to make a telephone call."

Norman excused himself saying, "With Joel laid up, I need to close the stable doors and water the flowers."

Dorothy, still glowing from the success of her meal, excused herself saying she had to supervise the kitchen. I knew she didn't need to go into the kitchen, but she wanted to report the compliment to Connie and Stella personally.

Helen and Mildred also came up with valid reasons not to prolong their time with William and Mary Ann.

Unfortunately I wasn't quick enough (smart enough?) to think of a believable excuse for not joining the couple in the parlor. I trailed behind like the charity case I was portraying, promising myself I would leave as soon as possible.

It became more obvious I was the fifth wheel in the parlor when the two of them sat side by side on the sofa and held hands. There I was, the jilted ex-girlfriend, awkwardly ensconced in the parlor with the two lovebirds. I searched my mind for an excuse, any excuse to leave. I came up empty.

Fortunately, Stewart provided the perfect reason for me to leave. "Your cell phone is ringing," he said, holding up the small device.

I checked the caller I.D. feature, Darby Jackson. I didn't know any Darby Jackson. She was probably a telephone solicitor, trying to sell home improvements. I took the call anyway, grateful to have a reason to escape the parlor and away from the romantic atmosphere.

"Hello Darby."

"Is this the person who was at the bar the other night? Gi-Gi?"

I immediately recalled who Darby was. She was the woman who chatted with Harold while he waited for eleven o'clock to make his call. She was the woman who cried hysterically in the parlor the next morning. "Yes, how are you?"

"Fine. You asked me to call you if I thought of anything related to Harold," she said.

She had my attention. "Did you think of something?"

"This may not be important, but a few nights before he was murdered, Harold gave me a key. He made a joke of putting it on my key chain along with my car key."

"I think that's very important. The key may be the link to the murderer. Did Harold say what it opened?"

"No, as a matter of fact, he went into great detail about how he found it in the parking lot when he was grocery shopping. He made a joke about giving it to me for luck, but I think it may be important. The key looks new. It doesn't look like it had been laying on the pavement, run over by cars, and exposed to the weather. It still has those rough edges on it like when you get a key made at the hardware store."

"Darby, this may be the lead the police need to solve the murder."

"Do you think so?"

"Yes, and I think you should turn it over to the police."

"The police? I don't want to get involved. They already questioned me for hours and treated me like I killed Harold. I don't want to go through that again. Can't I give it to you and you can turn it over to the police?"

William called my name from the parlor. "We need more cream."

I didn't respond to William. I refused to act like his servant in order for him to impress the sweet Mary Ann. I said into the phone, "Where are you? When can I pick up the key?"

After the quick exchange of her address, I concluded the call. I went into the kitchen and told Dorothy where I was going.

"Let me get my handbag. I'll come with you."

There was safety in numbers and after the tremendous dinner she had assembled, Dorothy deserved a reward. I went out to the SUV to wait.

Of course, the gas tank was empty. Whoever had borrowed the car hadn't bothered to fill it. I wagered it was William, the cheapskate. Although with my relatives acting more like irresponsible teenagers than the adults they were, it could have been anyone.

I pulled my credit card from my purse in preparation for stopping at a gas station. When the back door of the house opened, all five of my relatives exited.

"Is this the girl you talked with at the bar?" Uncle Norman asked as he clicked his seat belt. "What's the address? I'll type it into the GPS."

I was surprised that after one lesson on the device, Norman was confident enough to program it, but what Uncle Stewart said shocked me. "Is this the young lady with the tight jeans, brown hair, and double D's?"

"Stewart, calm down. You're getting to be a pervert," Aunt Helen chimed in from the back seat. I could see in the mirror that her expression was playful as opposed to prudish.

"I have the perfect plan for checking out this woman. I'll use her bathroom. I'll snoop in her medicine cabinet and under the sink while you guys keep her talking. I think she may know more than she is telling us," Aunt Dorothy suggested.

"Aunt Dorothy, you stay out of her bathroom. In fact, I think Darby will be more willing to divulge information if I am the only one who goes in." I saw disappointment on her face, but I had to be firm.

"But I'm an old lady. Old ladies always need to use the restroom." Aunt Dorothy added a crackle to her voice to emphasize her age.

Helen and Mildred nodded their heads in agreement.

"No, and that's my final answer." I had to hold my position on the matter. If I gave an inch, the relatives would never respect my decisions.

At the gas station I got out of the car to fill the tank, satisfied that they understood.

⚜ ⚜

Darby opened the door and tried to hide her surprise when she saw the motley crew of senior citizens standing behind me. Shrugging my shoulders, I said, "Aunt Dorothy needed to use the bathroom and the others trailed behind."

I felt a slight breeze from heads bobbing behind me, confirming what I said.

Darby didn't have a choice. How could she deny an old woman the use of her bathroom, but she wasn't pleased with the mob of older adults invading her apartment.

"Sit there and don't touch anything. Aunt Dorothy, the bathroom is at the end of the hall," I ordered, indicating the solitary piece of furniture in the room, a long, well worn couch. "Darby, why don't we go into the kitchen and you can tell me again how you got the key."

I positioned myself where I could keep an eye on the relatives. They were behaving as if they were angels; spines stiff, eyes focused straight ahead, feet flat on the floor, hands folded in their laps. In fact their exemplary behavior worried me more than if they were chatting and jostling each other. They were up to something. I could tell.

I was so suspicious of their good behavior; I could barely concentrate on what Darby was saying.

I heard a flush and Aunt Dorothy exited the bathroom, giving a nod in my direction as she squeezed onto the couch and became a statue in the same formation as the others.

Darby took the pertinent key off her ring and handed it to me.

As if on cue, Stewart started coughing. There hadn't been any lead up to it. There hadn't been a small "ahem." When Uncle Stewart started to cough, it was belly retching, deep from his toes. There appeared to be no stop to his respiratory distress.

"It's one of his spells!" Dorothy cried out. She jumped up from the couch and positioned herself with her back to me. She appeared to be administering some type of first aid.

"Helen, do you have his medicine?" Norman asked, shifting his weight from foot to foot, wringing his hands.

Spells? No one told me Uncle Stewart had spells and what did Dorothy mean exactly by *spell*? My mind raced as I searched for the medical equivalent.

"I thought I had the pills with me. The pills were in my pocket when I left the house. Did they fall out?" Helen stood up and started patting her pockets. When it appeared the pills weren't in her pockets, she started lifting the cushions on the sofa.

"I'll get a glass of water," Norman said. He raced into the kitchen before I had a chance to react, and started randomly opening and closing the cupboards. When he didn't find a glass fast enough, Mildred joined him, opening first the refrigerator, shuffling ketchup packets and pickle jars, and then she opened the freezer door.

What was she doing? A simple glass of water didn't require a search of the refrigerator or the freezer.

"The pills may have rolled in here." Helen opened the coat closet door, shifting the garments back and forth, checking the pockets. She moved boxes on the shelf and then ran her hand along the floor.

Was Helen insane? A bottle of pills wouldn't jump out of her pocket and land on the shelf of a closed closet or into the pockets of jackets hanging from the rod.

Dorothy continued to hover over Stewart, blocking my view. Helen stood up and made little bouncy movements and small screeches.

Darby stood in the middle of the kitchen, in shock, a deer caught in the headlights look on her face.

Uncle Norman quickly perused the oven, then retreated from the kitchen. He launched a full scale search of the bedroom at the back of the apartment.

My confusion over Stewart's condition and the actions of my relatives delayed my nursing instincts from kicking in. By the time I examined my uncle, he looked normal, the color in his cheeks was normal, his pulse was normal, his breathing was normal, his eyes twinkled.

I gave a questioning look to Dorothy. She explained, "It was a mild spell. Luckily it passed without the medicine."

"I need to get these people home," I explained to Darby and hustled them out the door.

They walked to the car as if the next step would be their last and they continued their old people's act until the car was at the next intersection.

"What were you thinking?" I yelled.

Giggles erupted from my passengers, then snippets of conversation as they conveyed their findings to one another.

"She's clean."

"Yep, I agree."

"So do I."

"Excellent acting, Stewart."

"You did a pretty good job yourself."

"She doesn't have much stuff."

"Her medicine cabinet was almost empty."

"She doesn't have very many clothes."

"Not much furniture either."

"Healthy diet."

"Not many kitchen doodads."

"Stewart wasn't having a spell? You were acting?" I stopped the car at the curb.

"I was faking it the whole time." Stewart made a muscle. "I'm as healthy as a horse."

Norman seemed exceptionally proud of their act. "We planned it while you were pumping gas."

"You didn't have to do all that." I tried to sound disapproving of their actions in the apartment, but I didn't manage to sound convincing. I also had doubts about Darby wanting to hand the key over to me rather than the police. The motives were complicated by the exaggerations she had told at the bar. I tried to figure out how the relatives had reached their conclusions about Darby so quickly.

Aunt Dorothy explained, "What if it had been a trap? What

if she was in cahoots with Harold's killer? What if there was someone lurking in a closet or hiding under the bed?"

"And just what were you going to do if there was someone lurking in the closet or in the bedroom?"

"I would have shot him," Mildred said. She opened her purse and pulled out her cell phone that was the size of a small computer.

Was this the relative who wouldn't use an electric can opener because it was too technical? More importantly I asked, "How was a cell phone going to help if there had been someone in the closet?"

"I have an app for that," she said, quoting the commercials.

"Do you even know what an *app* is?" I challenged.

Mildred meekly slid the phone back into her purse without answering my question, which answered my question. She had no clue how to use the phone and she watched too much television.

I turned the conversation back to the actions of my aunts and uncles inside Darby's apartment. "Why did you think she was hiding something? She called me about the key. She was open about how she got the key. She could have kept it. She's trying to cooperate."

Norman defended their actions. "She didn't turn the key over to the police. When you've been around as long as we have, you get an instinct about people."

"Plenty of people like to stay out of the way of the police. Maybe Darby has a strong feeling that they have too much power or they misuse their power." I put the car in gear and pulled into traffic. "Norman, what do your instincts say about Robert? You had a chance to talk to him earlier today when you gave him a ride home."

"He's a one eyed snake in the grass."

I had no idea what Norman meant, but he said it with such negative emotion that I figured he didn't have a very good opinion of my young house guest. I wouldn't say it in front of the relatives but I also thought he was a one eyed snake in the grass.

"I agree," Uncle Stewart said. "I wouldn't trust him if he was holding the Bible in one hand and a cross in the other."

"That's exactly how I feel about him too." Suddenly I was telling the gang about the scene I had witnessed the evening before at Hayden's Restaurant when I saw Robert and the guy from the kitchen exchange a very discreet message. I concluded by saying, "I may have imagined it."

There was silence in the car as they processed the information.

I forgot about the key and the behavior of my relatives as they started discussing, one by one the significance of what I had witnessed at the restaurant. I forgot why I hadn't told them about the incident in the first place.

CHAPTER 18

I HAD A ROUGH night. I had pulled the crib mattress onto the floor and borrowed a pillow from Aunt Mildred's room. I don't know which was worse, the smell of the musty mattress or the strong aroma of lilac perfume emanating from the pillow. I do know I woke up several times during the night sneezing and cramped from being scrunched on the undersized mattress. The eyes of forgotten dolls stared at me in the dark.

I yearned for the departure of William and his future wife, when I could reclaim possession of the large bed in the master bedroom with its faded cabbage rose wall paper instead of the postage stamp size mattress and the building blocks with ABCs wallpaper.

I didn't like sharing the bathroom with Robert and Joel and his mysterious female caretaker. Joel only had another twenty four hours before he was allowed to put weight on his ankle and he could return to his apartment.

I sneezed again, a remnant of the dust in the mattress, not a summer cold. I squeezed my eyes shut to stop another sneeze.

Connie was in the kitchen, taking biscuits out of the oven when I stumbled, half asleep, down the back steps. I pushed the door to the dining room open and let it swing closed without entering. The only occupants of that room were William and Mary Ann. I didn't want to be in that situation again, where I was the third person, interrupting their romantic sweet talk.

"Do you have any coffee?" I asked Connie.

"There's a fresh carafe of coffee in the dining room." She was torturing me. She was aware that the engaged couple was in the other room and she knew I didn't want to spend time with them.

After the night I had, sleeping on the crib mattress, I didn't understand why she even suggested it but I played along. "I think that pot is empty."

She chuckled and poured some of the brew into a mug and set it on the table. "I don't blame you for not going in there." She didn't need to say anything more and neither did I.

I took a sip of coffee and waited for the caffeine to kick in. "Where is everyone?"

"They were up bright and early. They had things to do."

"Together? All of them?" I asked.

"Dorothy and Stewart didn't mention where they were going. I can only say they were dressed as if they were going to a funeral, but whoever heard of a funeral at this hour of the morning. Norman said he needed something for the Mustang. Mildred and Helen went grocery shopping and Norman was picking them up after he finished at the auto parts store."

"I didn't realize how active they were."

Connie returned the pot to the coffeemaker. "They aren't usually. I can't remember the last time they went to town without Harold driving. Mostly they sat in the parlor and politely bickered amongst themselves."

"I wonder if I can think of somewhere I have to go that would keep me out of the house for the entire day." As an afterthought, I asked, "What about Robert? Where's he?"

"I haven't seen him yet. He's probably still sleeping."

I felt a twinge of jealousy that he had a bed that was comfortable enough to sleep late.

"How long are you going to allow him stay?" Connie asked.

"Who? Robert?"

"Of course, I mean Robert. Who else did you think I meant?" Connie thought about her question for a second and then said, "I guess you have the right to ask 'who.' There are enough freeloaders here to start a flop house."

A bell tinkled from the dining room, which Connie ignored. She offered me a refill which I gratefully accepted, poured a mug of coffee for her self, and sat down across the table from me. "I don't like him. He's sneaky."

"I agree and so does Stewart, Norman, and the rest of the family, but why do you think he's sneaky?"

"Who's sneaky?" William pushed the door open, holding the cream pitcher. He was indignant, like we were talking about him (which we weren't) or purposely pretending we hadn't heard the bell indicating the people in the dining room needed something (which we were).

"People who listen to other people's conversations only hear bad things about themselves," I quipped, although the humor of the statement was lost on William. I quickly corrected myself. "We were talking about Robert."

"I agree. He is sneaky."

"Why do you say that?"

"I found him going through my toiletries."

"He was going through your toiletries? Maybe he forgot his toothpaste. Remember he was Harold's guest and he traveled light. He probably expected his brother to have shaving cream, toothpaste, and other grooming supplies he could borrow and not have to carry them in his suitcase. You can do that with family." I don't know why I was defending Robert; we were in the middle of having a discussion about how we thought he was less than forthright.

"I don't know why you continue to allow him to stay. He's nothing but a freeloader. He's broke and doesn't contribute to the household." I wanted to hold a mirror up to William's face, but I allowed him to continue. "He could at least help with the yard work since Joel is laid up with a sprained ankle. And can you imagine, he doesn't know the difference between a medical doctor and a lawyer. He was asking me about Harold's estate last night. Asking me how long it would take for the courts to award him his inheritance."

Connie pointed a finger toward me. "Yeah, he asked me the same questions. He wanted to know when he would get Harold's car and money."

Since we weren't feeding his ego, William ignored her comment. "Connie, we need more cream."

The cook jabbed her thumb in the direction of the refrigerator and mouthed the words, "Get it yourself."

My former boyfriend stood there for a few more seconds, debating whether Connie was going to change her mind and get up to refill the cream pitcher, then realized it was going to be a cold day before she did it. William approached the refrigerator like a reluctant gladiator approached a lion.

I took the opportunity to ask William, "Have you discussed finances with your girlfriend?"

"She's not my girlfriend, she's my fiancée," he corrected, with his head in the refrigerator looking for the cream. "I'll tell her. I haven't found the right moment to bring up the topic."

"Try right now and the direct method." Connie didn't hide the fact that she didn't like William.

"Time is running out," I told him as I rubbed my sore calf muscle, a reminder of the miserable night I spent trying to sleep on a crib mattress. I didn't just want a better bed, I needed one. I asked Connie, "Is Stella here yet?"

"She arrived about five minutes before you came down stairs. She said something about throwing a load of towels in the washer. What do you need her to do?"

William filled the small pitcher and left the kitchen. I had a feeling he knew the direction the conversation was headed and decided to make a quick exit.

"If she has time today, I was hoping she would air out the nursery."

The cook's eyebrows shot up. "Don't tell me we're expecting another guest and this one has a baby."

I shook my head and explained the bed situation to Connie.

"That's too much. The nerve of the man asking you to leave your own bedroom so he can hide the truth from his woman. The marriage will never last. Do you want me to kick him and his girlfriend, excuse me, fiancée out now?"

"Shh, she'll hear you. In a moment of weakness I gave him until tomorrow morning to tell her about his financial problems and the ownership of the house. If he doesn't do it by then, I am going to have the pleasure of tossing them out on the street, but first I'm going to tell her what a fraud he is."

I was taking the last sip from of my coffee when three things happened simultaneously. There was a knock on the back door. I heard thumping on the back stairs. The door leading from the dining room swung open.

Of the three, I figured the dining room would provide the most entertainment and focused my attention in that direction. Connie called, "Come in," to the visitor at the rear door and hustled her stout form over to the stairs to assist Joel and his companion.

"Gi-Gi, would you be so kind as to come into the dining room. I have something I need to talk to you about." Mary Ann's voice was so sweet, I knew something terrible was going to happen.

I obliged her highness, but first I relished making her wait. I rinsed my mug and turned it upside down on the drain board. I dried my hands in an exaggerated manner.

Taking a position at the side of the mahogany table that had been in my family for four generations, I waited for Mary Ann to start her spiel.

"As you know, I am aware of the relationship you and William enjoyed in the past. However, having you live in this house is beyond what you should expect of that friendship and to tell you the truth it is awkward for William and me. I think you are taking advantage of Williams' generosity. I am asking you to pack your things and move out immediately."

William sat there like a brick. His face was emotionless, staring at the china in front of him.

My jaw dropped to the floor. Only seconds before I was preparing to launch their fannies out the door and now Mary Ann was sitting in my dining room kicking me to the curb. Of course, William's silence spoke volumes about his spine.

"Are you nuts?" Tony said, from behind me.

I spun around and clamped a hand over Tony's mouth and pushed him back through the kitchen door. Out of the corner of my eye, I could see William come alive, frantically shaking his head and waving his hands back and forth, in an effort to keep the young police officer from saying anything more.

I didn't take my hand from Tony's lips until we were in the gazebo, out of view of the dining room windows.

"What is going on?" he asked when I finally allowed him to speak.

"It's a long story." It seemed like filling in the background of my actions was all I was going to get accomplished.

"I have time."

When I finished telling Tony about William's finances and his lie about the house being his, the police officer pounded the railing. "That rat! I can't believe he is trying to marry that woman without telling her the truth. He wasn't even man enough to tell her the truth when she was evicting you from your own home."

"I know I shouldn't care, but I do."

Tony's eyebrows shot up. He asked, "You still care about William?"

"Not about him. I'm lucky to have escaped that relationship and have no intention of going back to him even if he was available." I sniffed, and then explained, "I have this notion that marriages are supposed to be built on love, honesty, and commitment. I feel bad for Mary Ann. She isn't getting any of those things." Tears started running down my cheeks.

Tony stepped closer and wrapped his arms around me. "I feel the same way. My parents' marriage was built on those principles and it's lasted forty years so far." His lips brushed the top of my head.

Being in Tony's arms felt right. I felt protected. All my problems magically became insignificant.

Through my new found euphoria I heard the back door open and Everet call Tony. The moment disappeared.

"I'm busy here," Tony called back.

"We're needed. There was a break-in during the night at the barbershop. The murder investigation has to be postponed."

Tony slid his hands slowly down my arms. Looking me in the eyes, he said, "I'll be back and we'll finish our discussion. If it gets to the point where you have to move out, you can stay at my parent's house until that dunderhead doctor comes to his senses."

I tried to smile. "I have a feeling Mary Ann is the one who will come to her senses first."

"Only if someone tells her the truth." With that comment hanging in the air, Tony departed. Tony implied that I should be the *someone* to tell Mary Ann about her future husband's finances, but if the news came from me it would only sound like I was still upset over losing William. The message would be lost because of the identity of the messenger.

I had sixty seconds of peace and quiet to restore my

equilibrium.

The Mustang stopped under the port cochere. Helen and Mildred emerged from the back seat as Norman fiddled with the dashboard. The three of them were carrying plastic bags of groceries into the house. I hurried across the grass to assist with the task.

"Who is going to eat all this food?" I asked when I saw the cargo space of the vehicle. Every square inch was loaded with bags.

"We're planning a wedding for William and Mary Ann." Mildred's excited voice was an octave higher than usual.

"I thought it was going to be a quiet wedding with only the family attending."

Helen explained, "Mary Ann called her parents this morning and they are flying in to witness the marriage ceremony of their only daughter and I think they are bringing a couple of guests with them."

"This amount of food can easily feed us for a week or more." I stared into the trunk of the classic car.

"I don't have time to talk. I have telephone calls to make. We need to rent a tent and some tables and chairs. I have to line up a florist and a photographer. Thank heaven Joel installed the fairy lights around the gazebo before he sprained his ankle." Helen disappeared into the house, leaving the task of lugging the rest of the bags to me.

I thought of the wasted food and the excess expenditure. When Mary Ann heard about William's money situation and the truth about the house, there wouldn't be a wedding. For the moment, Helen and Mildred seemed so happy; I didn't have the heart to break the news to them. They would find out soon enough and maybe we could freeze some of the food.

I remembered making an offer to perform the ceremony and hoped William hadn't taken me seriously. I wasn't an ordained minister or a justice of the peace. I needed to tell Helen to add an officiate to her list. Just in case there really was a wedding.

I carried a load of bags into the kitchen.

Connie was sorting the groceries and giving commands with the authority of a drill sergeant. Helen and Mildred were doing her bidding, researching recipes, and dashing in and out of the pantry cupboard, fetching ingredients as Connie read them a list. The mixer was on the counter. Baking pans were being greased and floured. I felt the heat from the oven.

Norman, a tea towel tucked into the waist of his trousers, was standing in front of a cutting board with a paring knife in his hand, waiting for instructions.

Even Joel, with one leg propped on a chair and an ice pack resting on his ankle, had a bag of potatoes in front of him and was awkwardly starting to peel one. Judging from the way he held the peeler and the potato, he would be at the task for the remainder of the day.

I carried in the last of the grocery bags. A wave of weariness hit me and I looked at the clock. Mid-morning and I was not only physically tired, but emotionally drained as well. My night spent on a crib mattress caught up with me and I wondered where I could lay down and take a nap. I set the loaded bags on the pantry shelf, ignoring the contents, and crept up the stairs unnoticed.

As I walked toward the nursery and my miniscule bed, I noticed Robert's door was still closed. I purposely coughed and clomped my feet as I went past his room, hoping to disturb his rest. Inspired by the conversation earlier in the day, I stopped at the bathroom to look through my young house guest's toiletries. I was disappointed, none of his personal items were in there.

CHAPTER 19

I DON'T KNOW WHY I thought a nap would revitalize me. I was trying to sleep on the same mattress, legs and arms dangling over the edge, with the same musty smell, as I had the previous night. There was the added annoyance of car doors slamming and the occasional burst of laughter and snippets of conversation from the kitchen. Stella had taken the time to vacuum. Someone was hammering in the garden below the nursery window, preparing the area for the wedding ceremony.

After an hour of tossing and turning, I got up from my nap feeling, if it was possible, more tired and irritable than when I laid down.

The toilet seat was up. That was my first clue that Robert was awake. I checked the door to his bedroom. It was open, the bed was made, but the room was vacant. I did a quick perusal. Everything was still there. He hadn't stolen the lamp or the books from the shelf.

159

I glanced in the other rooms to determine his whereabouts (I didn't see him) and made my way to the kitchen where I could identify most of the residents' voices. From the bottom step I did a quick count and asked the question, "Has anyone seen Robert?"

Knives stopped mid slice, mixers quit mixing.

"I recall he asked to borrow a car to go into town," Uncle Norman replied. Heads bobbed in agreement.

"Which car did he take?"

The appliances started. The peeling resumed. Suddenly everyone was too busy to answer me. Not one person looked in my direction. "Did you let him take my car? Did anyone think to check his driver's license before he drove it?" I didn't get an answer.

"Guess what?" Dorothy entered the back door, prancing with excitement. She held up a square of white fabric as if it was an Academy Award. She unfurled the cloth and waved it above her head, an apron. She didn't wait for anyone to respond. "I got a job."

From behind her, Stewart held a similar packet. "So did I."

I stepped down to the kitchen level. Was I still dreaming? I wanted to pinch myself. "Jobs? Where? Why?"

"I'm going to be a cook at Hayden's Restaurant."

"And I am going to be their dishwasher for the brunch and lunch shifts on the weekends."

I sat on the vacant seat at the table, careful of Joel's injured ankle resting on the other chair. "But you never had a job before."

"I didn't think I would get this one, but when Tony said his grandfather was still working, I thought I would give it a shot." Stewart's grin was ear to ear.

Norman stepped forward and shook Stewart's hand. "Congratulations. That will certainly be a change-a-roo from what you usually do. Maybe I'll apply for a job somewhere." He scratched his chin as he contemplated the idea.

I opened my mouth to say something sarcastic. Fortunately

Connie stepped between Norman and me, cutting off the caustic remark I was about to make. She said, "Congratulations. When is your first day of work?"

I didn't hear the answer. I think my blood pressure was interfering with my ears and I could only think of the irony of Stewart washing the dishes for hundreds of strangers when he never washed a single dish in this household.

In the back of my mind, something clicked, "Aunt Dorothy, did you say you were going to be a cook at Hayden's?"

"Yes, isn't it great. Of course I won't be preparing any dishes by myself. I'll only be helping the chef by chopping and measuring ingredients."

I pulled her into the dining room. "You're not taking the job because of what I told you last night, are you?"

Dorothy squinted her eyes and puckered her lips like she didn't remember me telling the group about the silent message sent between Robert and the man from the kitchen at Hayden's. "I don't know what you're talking about. I applied for the job for the same reason Stewart applied for a job. We've been inspired by Tony's grandfather. We've been sitting here too long without using our talents. Instead of relying on the trust fund for our needs, we should be productive members of society."

She pasted an innocent smile on her face and spun around, pushing open the kitchen door. I heard her ask Connie, "What food do you want me to prepare for the wedding?"

Maybe I only dreamed I had told the relatives about the signals exchanged by the two men. I tried to clear my head. Last night I had slept on a crib sized mattress, I hadn't slept so I could not have dreamed it.

Mary Ann entered the dining room from the parlor and caught me standing there thinking about the jobs my relatives had acquired. "Gi-Gi, I see that you haven't started to pack. While that is my preference, if you are going to continue living here, you could at least be a contributing member of the household. The upstairs bathrooms need to be cleaned before my parents arrive. Maybe you could help Stella by doing that task." She smiled a fake smile. She was taking great pleasure in assigning the most despicable job in the house to me.

I had felt sorry for her, marrying a man who was less than honest with her. At that moment, I regretted giving her a moment of empathy. Mary Ann wasn't a benevolent mistress of the estate. I was at a loss for a smart retort. "I'll do that right away."

I left the room muttering all the things I should have said.

CHAPTER 20

STILL HOLDING THE bucket with the cleaning supplies, I stood back and admired my work. The en suite bathroom for the master bedroom sparkled.

"What are you doing in here? If Mary Ann finds you in my bedroom she'll call off the wedding." I thought William was going to have a heart attack and save Mary Ann from having to murder him.

"I'm earning my keep." I waved the toilet brush.

"What?" He took a step back. I don't know if he thought I was going to attack him with the cleaning tool or if he was afraid he would be contaminated by the exposure to real work.

"Your lovely fiancée decided, since I haven't moved out yet, I should become a productive member of the household. She assigned me the task of cleaning the bathrooms." I expected William to apologize or at least offer to clean the main bathroom in the hall, instead he flopped down on the wide bed.

"Close the door on your way out." William was beginning to believe the lies he told Mary Ann.

I set the bucket of cleaning products on the floor. I didn't know who had murdered Harold, but I was willing to hire the person to kill William.

"When are you going to tell her?" I asked, knowing that he understood the implied threat.

"Tell me what?" Mary Ann asked, from the doorway.

Right there, right then, I was tempted to tell Mary Ann the truth regarding the ownership of the house, but I had promised William I would hold off for forty eight hours and let him break the news to his fiancée. I scrambled past her.

This was the perfect opportunity for William to inform his bride-to-be of his financial position and as much as I wanted to see the expression on her face when he told her, I didn't want to see what was sure to be an emotional outburst.

As I hurried to get out of the line of fire, I heard William, butter would melt in his mouth, say, "Where we are going for our honeymoon."

After I scrubbed the bathroom in the hall until the chrome threatened to come off the fixtures, I turned my attention to the nursery. I was not going to spend another night in my own home sleeping on the musty crib mattress.

The boxes containing the things I brought from my apartment were scattered haphazardly against one wall, clothes from the day before were strewn over the rails of the crib, my purse was sitting on the rocker. I reminded myself that I only had another twenty four hours and the farce would be over. William would tell Mary Ann. He promised.

I opened the window, hoping the fresh air would improve the smell in the mattress. I straightened the boxes into neat stacks. As soon as the betrothed couple moved out, the boxes would be returned to the master suite and unpacked. The only thing to do was fold the clothes and put my purse in the closet.

Footsteps scampering up the backstairs and boyish giggling interrupted my task. "In here." The nursery room door opened.

"Uncle Norman, what are you doing?"

"We're escaping the cooking in the kitchen. We didn't know this room was occupied."

"This is where I'm staying until William and Mary Ann are married."

Stewart looked around the room. He wrinkled his nose in distaste. "Isn't this the nursery? Why are you in here? What's that smell?"

"It's a long story." I sat on the rocker in an unladylike position, too achy to care, and told them the abridged edition of why I had slept in the nursery.

"It isn't right. He should be truthful to that woman, even if she doesn't deserve it." Stewart expressed, with far less venom, my own opinion about William and Mary Ann's relationship.

Norman continued to look around the room. "Did you sleep on that mattress?"

"Yes."

"No wonder you were cranky this morning," he commented.

"The list of reasons for my emotional state goes beyond the mattress. Suffice it to say I was deservedly out of sorts."

"Well, it's the one we can fix. Let's go up to the attic and see what's there. I seem to remember an old army cot. It has to be better than the crib mattress."

"Does it smell better than this one?" I asked.

CHAPTER 21

ROBERT'S MYSTERIOUS disappearance was cleared up. He was sitting on the window bench as we passed through Stewart's turret room. Silhouetted by sunshine, he looked like he had an angel's halo, but I suspected he had a devil's heart hidden in his chest. After the wedding, I would tell him politely but firmly that he had to find somewhere else to live.

"What are you doing up here?" I asked him.

"Thinking."

I was getting accustomed to his one word answers.

The contents of the room didn't seem to be disturbed, but who could tell with the amount of stuff Stewart had accumulated over the years, including the piles of boxes he was currently moving. Robert could have gone through every file cabinet, every desk drawer, every box, and no one, including Uncle Stewart, would know the difference.

"Through here." Stewart stooped over and entered a doorway

that had been concealed by the boxes. The door was only as tall as my shoulders. I felt like Alice travelling through the looking glass.

"How did they get all this stuff through that small door?" I was surrounded by enough old furniture and knick-knacks to start my own antiques shop.

Stewart chuckled. "There's a larger door through the turret room at the other end of the house, but you have to move things to get in that way."

"This is a fire trap and everything should be pitched out," Norman stated.

"No, this stuff is valuable," Stewart argued.

"Don't start bickering. Let's find something for me to sleep on and get out of here. It's giving me the creeps." I ran my hands through my hair to check for cobwebs or spiders.

"Gi-Gi, look at that armoire," Uncle Stewart said. Still trying to convey his point, he indicated a large, upright chest set against the interior wall. "It's perfect. All it needs is a good polishing. People pay top dollar for that kind of thing. Open it up. You don't see craftsmanship like that anymore."

I didn't want to touch the grimy piece of furniture but I obeyed. The door opened with a creaking noise. Like the dough popping out of a can of biscuits, a white muslin balloon filled the door opening. I yelped in surprise. When I had recovered, I asked, "What is it?"

Stewart chuckled. "I forgot it was in there. It's your mother's wedding gown. Imported from Belgium, it was more beautiful than a queen would wear. It filled the aisle of the church. Your grandfather had to stand in its folds to walk her to the altar."

Norman had his own memory of the dress. "The hem, no, what do you call it? The train was ten feet long."

I had lived in the house all my life and I couldn't recall ever seeing the wedding gown. I wanted to remove the muslin dust cover from the dress and see it for myself, but I had a mission to accomplish. I needed to find some relic to sleep on that was more comfortable than a crib mattress.

Stewart started unsuccessfully shoving fabric back inside the armoire. When he got one side pushed in the other side popped out. Finally he shut both doors at the same time allowing only a thin strip of white muslin to show along the center. "I'll dig out the pictures of the dress later. We have to find something for you to sleep on tonight."

The uncles started poking behind chests and discarded chairs. I wandered around looking at the bric-a-brac, imagining what the objects would look like without the layers of dust.

"Here." Stewart's one word commanded my attention and I went to see what they had discovered.

It was a fold up bed. Metal frame, with a mattress that was stored in a 'U' shape, I didn't know if it would be much better than the crib mattress in terms of smell, but I would definitely be able to have all my limbs on the mattress at the same time.

The uncles began rearranging the furniture pieces stored in front of the cot. While they were busy I continued to browse the so-called family heirlooms to see if there was anything that could be used in the rooms below. Great grandmother had taken advantage of her husband's prosperity to select the highest quality furnishings. When my guests departed and the murder resolved, I would sort through the attic and do some redecorating in the rooms below.

The gable windows were filthy. I rubbed a circle of grime from the glass to allow sunlight in. No wonder the townspeople thought the house was haunted. I made a mental note to have Stella clean the windows.

I looked down at the driveway and cringed. Getting out of a small tan car was Darby Jackson. I watched as she opened the rear hatch and pulled out a small tote. This couldn't be good.

I called to the uncles. "Don't try to get that contraption down the stairs by yourselves. Robert is in Stewart's study. He can help." I hurried toward the miniature door, brushing dust (real and imagined) from my clothes and skin. I didn't need Darby to encounter Mary Ann and spill the beans about the ownership of the house.

⚜

Fortunately it was Everet who was acting as butler and greeted Darby Jackson. I wasn't surprised to see the older detective open the door. I was beyond that emotion. In only three days he had become a regular fixture in the household.

Out of the corner of my eye, I could see Mary Ann sitting in the parlor. A needlepoint seat cover was resting on her lap. Was she actually working on the needlepoint covers for the dining room chairs or was she trying to portray the image of the lady of the manor? I didn't have time to worry about what she was doing.

Darby leaned around Everet and said, "Gi-Gi, I need to talk to you."

"Darby, let's sit out on the front porch. There's a pleasant breeze." I pulled the door closed behind me. It was actually sweltering hot without even a wisp of wind to relieve the heat, but I didn't want Mary Ann to hear what we were saying. I had a second reason to keep my guest on the porch; the bag Darby brought with her was ominous and I didn't want her in the house with her luggage.

I was going to be firm. I did a mental counting of bedrooms and beds. No matter what she said, I was not going to invite her to stay in the house. If the uncles managed to get the cot down the steps to the nursery without damaging the bed or breaking any bones, I would have a real bed to sleep on tonight.

Darby didn't start with pleasantries. She went directly to the purpose of her visit. "I think someone is after me."

"What do you mean?"

"First, I had the feeling someone was following me while I was doing errands this morning and then when I got home there were little scratches and chips in the paint around the lock on my front door."

"Did they get in?"

"I don't think so. Nothing appeared to be disturbed."

I pictured her apartment with its scant furnishings. A burglar could thoroughly search everything Darby owned and not leave any indication that they were there. "Why would anyone try to break in to your apartment? Did anyone else in your building report a robbery?"

"I don't think so, but I didn't talk to any of the neighbors. I threw some things in a bag and got out of there."

"Did you report it to the police?"

"And tell them I have some paint chips around my door? They have more important things to do."

"There were several businesses broken into this week."

"Gi-Gi, I am so scared. I think whoever broke into my apartment did it because of my relationship with Hal."

"But you told me that you didn't have a relationship with Harold."

"We sat together at the bar. Someone watching wouldn't know we weren't friendlier than that. They would assume we meant more to each other."

I was scared as well, but for a different reason. I recounted the number of bedrooms in the old house. I could feel myself weakening. "Would you feel safer staying here for a couple days?"

"Oh Gi-Gi, thank you. I don't think I could sleep alone in the apartment. My nerves will be much calmer with other people around."

I didn't know how much calmer her nerves would be sleeping in a house where a murder had taken place and where the entire household was turned upside down preparing for a wedding that wasn't going to happen.

"Before you accept, you have to realize, the house is fairly full right now. A friend (I used the term loosely.) is getting married in the back yard tomorrow. He and his fiancée are staying with me. Harold's brother is occupying a room while he makes other arrangements. And my gardener had a slight mishap and can't go back to his apartment until tomorrow morning. The only bed available is an old fold out cot my uncles are bringing down from the attic and setting up in the nursery. I don't know what condition it's in."

"I'm sure the bed will be fine. I'm only going to stay a couple nights." Darby made a quick recovery for someone with a bad case of nerves.

In inverse proportion to the calming effect of not having to stay alone in her apartment was the tension I was feeling. I had to think of somewhere for me to spend the night. There was no chance I would sleep on the crib mattress again. I suddenly felt so weary, I didn't think I would be able to move from the porch rocker.

Darby got up from the chair and picked up her tote. "Do you want to show me where I am going to sleep? I'll put my things in the room and get them out of everyone's way."

It was with considerable effort that I managed to climb the stairs to the upper floor and show Darby the nursery and the bathroom she would share with the others.

The uncles or more likely Stella had replaced the crib mattress into the frame and set up the cot. The addition of fresh sheets and a comforter made it appear attractive and welcoming. The air quality was vastly improved. "Please make yourself at home." I tried to sound like I meant it.

"Gi-Gi?" Darby said as I turned toward the back staircase.

"Yes?"

"How are your aunts and uncles?" Politeness dripped from my guest's voice, but the underlying meaning was significant considering the theatrics they had performed in Darby's home the night before.

For devilment and maybe to keep Darby's visit as brief as possible I replied, "I made sure they took their medications this morning. They're fine."

"Did you find out what the key fit?"

I had forgotten the key. With all the drama going on in my life the key had lost its importance. Now the mention of the item gave me the idea to go down to the basement and see what progress the police had made solving the murder. If the crime scene tape was removed, I would be able to use Harold's apartment as my personal domain until the sham of a wedding was over. His bed had looked comfortable. Even with the stigma of being a murder victim's bed it would be a significant improvement over the crib mattress laid out in one of the sitting rooms scattered around the house. "We're still looking for what the key unlocks."

My trip to the basement was detoured in the kitchen where I reported to Connie the addition of one more person to feed. I also admired the progress on the cake and molded salads prepared for the wedding festivities. When the cook offered a ham sandwich, I couldn't refuse.

"I hope you don't expect Connie to wait on you. She has the meal to prepare for tomorrow." Mary Ann's voice sent a wave of nausea through me. I didn't know if I would be able to eat the sandwich Connie was preparing.

"It isn't for me," I lied, with only a quick glance at the knife being used to slice the ham. I didn't know if I would use it on bridezilla first or to cut the smirk from William's face.

The opportune arrival of Tony, handsome in his uniform, saved their lives. My murderous thoughts were replaced by desires of an entirely different nature.

Mary Ann bestowed the officer a royal nod and swept past him to her awaiting chariot, with William walking three paces behind her.

Tony surprised me with a kiss on the cheek and sat on the chair opposite me. "You should be counting your blessings."

I nodded agreement. "I had a narrow escape. I don't know how I was so blind to his pettiness."

"They're going to a counseling session with the minister. It should be an exorcism." Connie placed a ham sandwich on the table in front of each of us. Tony didn't hesitate to take a bite out of his.

"I'm glad I caught you. I wanted to update you on the pay phones at the bar. I managed to convince the judge to issue a warrant for the phone records. I should know the results tomorrow."

"That's good news." Progress at last. The phone records would reveal who Harold talked to each evening. That person should know something about Harold and perhaps a clue to the killer's identity. Then I could have my house back. "What about the butler's apartment? Is it being released?"

"Don't tell me you are still having bed issues."

I felt my cheeks heating up at the double entendre of his comment. "I have another house guest. One you may be interested in talking with."

Tony gave me a questioning look and I felt my cheeks heat up for a different reason. I felt a quiver of jealousy at the mere possibility of Tony showing a romantic interest in anyone but me.

I explained, "Darby Jackson claims someone tried to break into her apartment. There were scratches and paint chips around the lock area of the door. She thinks it is connected to her relationship with Harold."

"There wasn't any report filed about an attempted break in. I'll go talk to Darby, but I don't think it's related to the murder." Tony took a step toward the kitchen door. "Where is she?"

"She was unpacking her things in the nursery. Go up these stairs and turn left. It's the first door on the left." I took a step toward the stairs leading to the basement.

"Where are you going?"

"I'm going to check the progress in Harold's apartment. I need a place to sleep tonight."

"I wouldn't do that if I were you."

"Why not? I don't have any qualms about sleeping in Harold's bed."

Tony cleared his throat. "Everet finished his investigation yesterday."

"Great, then I can use the butler's apartment tonight." I moved another ten inches toward the basement stairs.

"Everet's car is in the driveway."

It was getting better and better. "I can get his official permission to use the apartment."

"Helen isn't with your Aunt Dorothy or Aunt Mildred."

How did Tony know that? I was getting a vibe and it wasn't a good one. He was trying to tell me something. I just couldn't figure out what the message was, so I asked.

"Think about it. Everet is down in the apartment. Helen is in the apartment. The investigation is finished."

I was speechless. The mental picture wasn't pretty.

"The offer of a room at my parent's house still stands."

"I can't leave. If I went somewhere else, Mary Ann would take over the house completely and I would never get back in." If I left the house now it would be to join the Foreign Legion or to lie on a deserted beach on a tropical island.

Tony disappeared up the stairs to interview Darby.

I needed something to do to get my mind off the activity in the basement.

CHAPTER 22

I ESCAPED TO THE attic (as far away from the basement as possible and still remain in the house). The solitude it offered was almost as nice as a warm, sandy beach. When Mary Ann returned, she wouldn't find me and assign another obnoxious chore. The added lure of long forgotten family heirlooms cemented my decision.

As I passed through the study, Robert was still sitting on the window seat, staring out the window. I casually waved a hand in his direction. He didn't acknowledge my greeting, which was alright with me. I didn't want to force a conversation with him. I suspected he was doing some investigating of his own and had assumed his current position when he heard me climb the steps. If he was conducting a search, he was being very neat.

I started my exploration of the attic with the sole intent of finding a sleeping accommodation. I didn't care what it was as long as it wasn't crib size or it didn't stink. One or the other I could deal with, not both.

Room for Murder

Uncle Stewart came by his hoarding instinct genetically. The attic was filled with every discarded piece of furniture and accessory the generations had ever purchased to decorate the lower levels of the house.

I smiled when I saw an oversized urn with elves and frogs hidden among the foliage painted in the glaze. After the dust and grime was washed off, it would be the perfect wedding gift for William and Mary Ann (if by some miracle the wedding took place). It was so ugly that it was probably worth a fortune. I heaved the elaborate vase onto a box by the small door and continued my search.

My next discovery was a fainting couch; the kind of thing women in old movies draped themselves on to look seductive. It was lying on its side surrounded by other pieces of furniture and shrouded by the inevitable sheet. I sneezed more than once as I unburied the treasure.

Of course, I had to try it out. I tried several poses of seduction and finally closed my eyes with the intent of testing its comfort for the night ahead.

A series of slamming car doors woke me. I went to the window and rubbed away enough dirt to see Connie leaving for the day, the aunts and uncles piling into the Mustang, and William helping Mary Ann into the passenger side of her car.

The lengthening shadows were my clue to their destination, dinner. Since I wasn't with them, I wondered who was going to pay and chuckled. I would have loved to be a fly on the restaurant wall to watch their antics to avoid the bill. While the thought amused me for a moment or two, it was replaced with the melancholic notion that not one of them had given a thought that I might like to join them. I watched the cars disappear in the direction of town, feeling like Cinderella left at home while her stepsisters went to the ball.

I gave myself a stern lecture. Those people didn't have to include me in everything they did. In addition, there were still two people staying in the house who needed dinner. As the mistress of the household, (when Mary Ann wasn't playing the role), I needed to tend to their meal.

I ran my fingers through my hair and straightened my clothes. Perhaps after dinner I could convince my remaining guests to help me move the chaise to a more suitable location in the house before bedtime.

I heard the sound of car tires crunching along the driveway. Aha, the aunts and uncles had missed me and were returning. I gave the car a quick glance and then did a double take. It wasn't the Mustang and it wasn't the high end sedan Mary Ann and William left in. And it wasn't the compact Darby had arrived in. I watched, waiting for the new arrival to get out of the car.

Robert exited the house. There was a bounce to his step that belied his mournful mood of the day. He waved a greeting to the driver and without a backwards glance got into the vehicle.

For someone who arrived from Philadelphia two days before and didn't know anyone in the area, Robert had made a friend quickly. I wondered about the inconsistency between Robert's awkward social skills and the new friend. Perhaps the person was a talker and only needed someone to politely utter encouragement to the conversation. The thought of a more active participation by Robert made me smile.

I still had one guest who required my hostess skills. Darby was downstairs, probably nervous about being in the big house by herself after the attempted break in of her apartment. I maneuvered around the forgotten furnishings in the attic and made my way to the child size door, chuckling at the ugly urn I had selected for the wedding gift.

I turned the knob and pushed on the door. It wouldn't budge. I tried again. Nothing. Someone had locked the door while I was asleep. It was puzzling. It was inconvenient. It was annoying, but it wasn't worrisome. I had the skills to pick the lock if I needed to do so.

The attic provided a haven for my nap. Now it became confining. I wanted out. Recalling Stewart's comment about a second door on the other end of the attic space, I picked my way to the opposite turret room. At one point I had to climb over a chest of drawers. I had to move several smaller pieces of furniture and once I created an avalanche of things, including a frame which I determined was a mirror, judging by the sound of glass breaking. Just what I needed, seven years of bad luck. If what I was currently experiencing was good luck, I dreaded what the future held.

The second door was of human proportions and unlocked. My incarceration was almost over. While I hadn't felt any danger or fear, I wanted out of the space. So, with a sigh of relief, I pulled open the door and came face to face with another obstacle, the back of the largest piece of furniture I ever saw. I didn't know what it was, but judging from the back, it was either a china cabinet or an ornate head board for a bed.

I was hoping it was a head board with the optimistic thought I would have a real bed to sleep in that night. I placed a shoulder against the wood and heaved against the structure. All I got in return was a moaning noise. I had to think about it for a second to realize it hadn't come as a result of my exertions. "Hello?"

No response.

"Hello?" I said with more confidence.

Still no response.

I put my weight behind my next push and was rewarded by a more melodic moan. I didn't know what demented, more muscle than brains, furniture mover had managed to bring the old organ from the parlor to the third floor and place it directly in front of the door to the attic. There was no way I was going to be able to move it by myself.

I wasn't fat, but I wasn't slender enough to slip through the narrow gap the mover had left between the organ and the wall.

Frustrated I slammed the door and sat on the first flat surface sturdy enough to hold my weight.

Plan B. I retraced my path back to the midget size door leading to Uncle Stewart's den, gathering the wire from the back of the broken mirror as I went.

The light was fading and I hadn't used my lock picking skills in a long time, but I managed to bend the wire into the reasonable shape of an 'L' and patiently tried to release the lock mechanism. After several attempts, I was successful and breathed a sigh of relief. I opened the door and faced a bright light shining directly into my eyes, immediately followed by an ear piercing scream.

CHAPTER 23

D ARBY, WHAT ARE you doing in Stewart's study?"
"I heard moaning and a door slam. I thought there were
ghosts." Her eyes were open so wide that they reminded me of
the victim's eyes in a horror movie. The beam of light from her
flashlight jiggled in her shaking hands confirming her statement.

I explained the sources of the noises she had heard.

"I thought you went to dinner with everyone else," Darby
stated.

"Why didn't you turn on the overhead light?" I shook my
head. "Why didn't you go to dinner with them?"

"I didn't sleep well last night. I needed rest more than I needed
food."

"Are you hungry now? We can go down to the kitchen and
raid the refrigerator. I think there is some leftover soup and
ham." I didn't wait for my house guest to answer. I turned in the
direction of the stairs. My stomach growled in anticipation of

Aunt Dorothy's flavorful soup.

It didn't take long for Darby and me to start laughing about the situation in the attic. If I staged a haunted house for a Halloween party, the door slamming, the organ moaning, and the broken mirror were classic elements.

I sobered when I thought about the one aspect still puzzling me. "Who locked the attic door?"

"Who knew you were in there?"

"Robert saw me going in." I pulled the tabs from the top of two cans of soda and placed them on the table.

Darby took a long sip from her can. "Is Robert one of your uncles?"

"No, Robert is Harold's younger brother. He showed up on the porch the same day you visited. He expected Harold to pick him up at the bus station and ended up walking here. When he heard the news, he was so upset, I didn't have the heart to send him away."

"I think you have your answer, but why would he lock you in?"

"He probably did it for spite. He thinks I'm personally keeping him from getting his brother's money and car. I tried to explain how probate works and that the procedure may take a year before he gets Harold's things. I don't think he believed me because he also asked William the same questions about when he would get his brother's assets."

Darby lifted the top of her sandwich and examined the content as if she couldn't identify the meat. "I have to agree with you. Why would you hand over a bunch of money to a stranger?"

I didn't answer her question. "I am not sure Robert is Harold's brother. I haven't seen his identification, no driver's license or birth certificate. There wasn't any paperwork or family pictures in Harold's apartment. There isn't anything to connect the two men." I blew on a spoonful of soup before I put it in my mouth. "Besides who gets Harold's things is a matter for the court to decide."

The back door opened and the aunts and uncles entered the house like a litter of puppies, jostling with each other to be first, laughing.

"See I told you she could still pick a lock," Uncle Stewart said to the group.

"You locked me in the attic?" My voice became shrill.

"Yep." He was standing there with his chest puffed out like he was proud of what he had done.

I sputtered, "Why? What if the house had caught fire and I had been trapped up there?"

Uncle Stewart's chest deflated. "We wanted you to rest a while longer. We figured that when you couldn't get out of the attic easily you would go back to sleep. We knew we wouldn't be gone very long."

Aunt Mildred held out a white bag. "Look what we brought for dinner, Chinese food, to-go."

"I can't remember the last time I ate Chinese food it was so long ago." Aunt Dorothy said, displaying an identical bag.

"Connie was so busy preparing for the wedding she didn't have time to fix our dinner. We told her to go home and put her feet up. We would fend for ourselves," Aunt Helen announced.

"And they gave us cute little chopsticks and fortune cookies for free," added Uncle Norman.

"I wish you had told me where you were going. Darby and I just ate soup and ham sandwiches."

Stewart, recovered from his reprimand, said, "There is always room for Chinese food."

Darby sat at the kitchen table staring at my relatives. She acted like she had never seen five old people excited over to-go food before.

As quickly as they had entered the back door, the aunts and uncles passed through the kitchen and went into the dining room. I could hear the rustle of bags and the chairs scraping back as they set out the cartons containing the food.

"Gi-Gi, come join us."

I looked at Darby, silently asking her if she would like some Chinese food. She shook her head. "I think I'll go upstairs and lie down."

I thought longingly of the army cot installed in the nursery. Darby was finding it comfortable or else she wouldn't be in a hurry to return to it.

When I entered the dining room, the aunts and uncles were already seated. The empty chairs reminded me, "Where are William and Mary Ann?"

"They wanted to go to some fancy restaurant. I can't wait to find out how he gets her to pay for their meals."

I was surprised to hear this coming from Norman. I thought he and the others were oblivious to the financial state of the future groom. I also thought it was ironic that Norman was interested in how William was going to avoid the dinner bill when he had twice ducked out of paying for drinks and meals.

In spite of the meal I shared with Darby, my mouth watered when I saw the assortment of Chinese food on the table. Before long we were laughing as we tried to transfer the food from our plates to our mouths using the chopsticks. Our interpretations of the fortunes inside the cookies provided further amusement, especially when Aunt Dorothy's read, "Careful mixing spices, makes tasty dish."

Stewart raised his glass, "I would like to propose a toast to the new cook at Hayden's Restaurant."

"Oh my gosh, I almost forgot. I have to be there at six o'clock in the morning." Dorothy exclaimed. Turning toward me, she asked, "Gi-Gi, will you give me a ride to work?"

"Aunt Dorothy, are you sure you want to take this job?" I asked. There were a number of reasons I thought she would back out of actually showing up. Her age, the fact that she didn't need to work for financial reasons and the physical demands of the job including getting up at an early hour were the obvious ones.

"If I had been born a little later, matured after women's liberation, I would have loved to have been a chef in a famous New York City restaurant. I'm too old for that dream now, but I am going to enjoy cooking for so many people."

I didn't know. I looked hard at the Mildred and Helen trying to discover what dreams they had that went unfulfilled as a result of women being suppressed prior to women's lib.

Aunt Mildred put her two cents in, spoiling Dorothy's excitement and answering my question. "A woman shouldn't have to work."

Uncle Stewart changed the subject. "Gi-Gi, I almost forgot one of interesting aspects of the evening. A woman in line at the Chinese restaurant handed us a coupon for two dollars off our order."

"That was nice of her." I gave up on using the chopsticks in the prescribed manner and resorted to stabbing the chicken teriyaki.

"She said there were coupons for all the restaurants and for food in the grocery store as well. We could save a lot of money if we use them when we shop."

"I think that's a great idea. Why don't you take charge of that project? We can use the savings for something special."

"I would like to take a cruise," Uncle Norman mentioned. "I hear that a lot of single women take cruises."

I envisioned using the savings toward a monthly dinner at a restaurant similar to Hayden's or taking the aunts and uncles to a movie. I did a quick calculation of how many cents off coupons it would take to send five people on a cruise.

"I bet there is a coupon for money off the price of a cruise," Aunt Helen said.

"I see coupons in the magazines at the hairdressers," Aunt Dorothy said with increased enthusiasm.

Uncle Norman was not to be outdone. "I believe I've seen

coupons in the Sunday newspapers."

"Haven't you seen them in the mail?" I asked.

"Harold always sorted the mail," Uncle Stewart said.

There was silence in the room. I don't know if it was the reminder of the butler's death or the realization that having a butler had taken away the small pleasures of day to day life that stopped the conversation.

"I need to go to bed if I'm going to be rested for work tomorrow," Aunt Dorothy declared.

One by one the others drifted out of the room until it was just Uncle Stewart and me. I got up to start removing the dirty dishes and empty containers. He joined me. "I better get accustomed to cleaning up after people. I start my job Saturday."

He turned on the water and started washing the dishes like a professional.

"Uncle Stewart, you act like you've done this before."

He thought about it for a moment. "I did. I let the others believe I never held a job before, but when I was in college I got into some minor trouble and needed to pay for the damages without my parents knowing about it. I got a job in the school cafeteria washing dishes." He started humming.

I brought the last of the dishes in from the dining room.

"Did you see the cot set up in the nursery? It'll provide a better night's rest than that old crib mattress."

"Ah…."

"Ah, what?" Uncle Stewart asked.

"Darby is using the nursery tonight."

"Gi-Gi, my girl, you need to be more selfish if you're going to survive in this world. There is no reason why you're letting William get away with pretending this house is his. You should be sleeping in the master bedroom."

"I guess I am so glad I escaped from the relationship with him that I feel guilty."

"I have to agree that was a stroke of luck. You should be

celebrating being out of that relationship." Uncle Stewart rinsed the soap from a plate and set it on the drying rack. "I wonder why Darby came here instead of going to one of her other girl friend's houses. She barely knows you."

"Good question and the night I met her at the bar she was by herself." I crossed my arms and pondered Darby's choice of a safe harbor.

"From what I've seen of her, she seems normal. Normal people have friends they can drop in on and spend the night."

I didn't know what normal was anymore. I picked up a towel, started drying the dishes and putting them in the cupboards.

"So where are you going to sleep tonight?" I noticed that he didn't offer his bed or one of the other relative's.

"I was going to sleep in Harold's bed or I found a fainting couch in the attic that is comfortable."

"That was your grandmother's chaise. She kept it in her bedroom. I don't think she ever laid on it. She mostly used it for her clothes. When she was getting dressed to go out, she would try on one outfit after another until she found the perfect thing to wear. Sometimes the clothes were stacked so high the maid refused to hang them up."

One story about my grandmother led to another. I was surprised at how fast the dishes got washed and put away.

Uncle Stewart folded the dishcloth. "Let's go down to Harold's apartment and see if it's suitable for you to sleep there."

His comment reminded me that I hadn't been down to the basement since I discovered Harold's body. I had intended to visit the apartment and conduct my own search for the motive behind his death.

❧ ❧

Uncle Stewart led the way, turning on all the lights to dispel any gloomy thoughts associated with Harold's death.

Once we were inside the apartment, Uncle Stewart sat on the bed and bounced. "The springs are good." He pulled back the

186

comforter. "The sheets are clean." He reached for the remote control, examined it, and pushed the power button. "Nice picture."

He inspected the bathroom and made a circle through the sitting room. "You'll be comfortable here tonight."

While he was doing those things, I made an inspection of my own. I checked for cobwebs hanging from the ceiling and places on the floor where rodents could enter the space. I decided that I would be comfortable in the apartment for different reasons.

When the door closed, I wasn't so sure Uncle Stewart was right. Creepy thoughts kept going through my mind. I only removed my shoes (I debated stripping down to my skivvies and bra.), laid on the bed, and pulled the comforter up to my chin.

Sleep eluded me. I did all the things I usually did when I wanted to fall asleep. I tried counting backwards from a hundred (like they do in the operating room, except I made it all the way to one). I tried to regulate my breathing until it was dreamlike, and I tried to relax my body starting at my toes and working up. Nothing worked. I didn't know if my sleeplessness was caused by my satisfying nap in the attic, the food I ate, or if it was a result of being in the apartment where a violent crime had occurred.

After a half hour I gave up. I wasn't going to sleep. I quit torturing myself, turned on the lamp and the television. None of the programs held my attention.

I was pushing the channel selection button one more time when a flicker of movement in the sitting room caught my eye. I immediately went into panic mode. I searched the bedroom for a weapon to defend myself. Nothing. I searched for a space in which to hide. Nowhere. I was vulnerable. I was a target for the assassin. I would have to use my wits. I held the remote as if it were a gun, pointing it toward the doorway.

"Everet, put away your weapon. It's Gi-Gi." Tony filled the entrance to the bedroom.

Everet glanced over Tony's shoulder to confirm the

pronouncement then turned away.

"I'll go out to the car and cancel the backups. Take your time. I have some cold cases to read." Everet left with a smirk on his face.

"What are you doing here?" I asked, quickly adding, "Not that I don't appreciate the visit."

"We got a call saying there were lights on and voices coming from the basement. We decided to investigate."

I didn't try to identify the person who was prompting the romance between Tony and me. It could have been anyone in the family. If I was honest with myself, it could have been me. I asked, "Who let you in?"

"The back door was unlocked."

"I guess it would be. William and Mary Ann are still at a restaurant and Robert went out with a friend. They're not back yet."

Tony positioned himself on the bed so that his back was leaning against the headboard. I scooted over next to him, a very cozy position.

"What are you watching?" he asked.

"Nothing held my attention." I yawned. I handed the remote to Tony. I don't know if his presence dispelled the gloom in the apartment or if tiredness finally caught up with me, but I immediately fell asleep. The next thing I remember is someone knocking on the door to the butler's apartment.

Tap, tap, tap. "Gi-Gi, are you in there?" Tap, tap, tap, "Gi-Gi, it's time for me to go to work."

Without opening my eyes, I responded, "In a minute." I worked my hand across the width of the bed, empty. Sometime during the night Tony left without waking me.

Aunt Dorothy chatted nonstop during the drive to the restaurant, but if I was quizzed about what she talked about I wouldn't be able to recall. I was busy with my own thoughts, thoughts about Tony.

CHAPTER 24

CONNIE WAS REMOVING the egg carton from the refrigerator to start breakfast when I returned from taking Dorothy to her job. I checked the time; it was only a few minutes after six o'clock. "Is everyone up?"

"There's been a bit of a snag in the wedding plans." Connie didn't sound like she had her first cup of coffee.

"What happened? Did William tell his beloved about his financial state and she called off the ceremony?"

"No, just the opposite. I think you're going to want to sit down for this news."

"I can take it."

"The wedding ceremony has been delayed two days. The bride's parents can't get back from the Bahamas until then and they have strictly forbidden their only child from getting married until they're here."

"That snake! William found a way to keep from telling her

about his finances. He's going to mooch off me for another two days!" I kicked the wastebasket, jamming my toe, and tipping the contents onto the linoleum. "How did you find out?"

Connie pointed toward a slip of paper lying on the counter. "Mary Ann left a note, asking me to put what I could save in the freezer and to serve the salads that will spoil to the aunts and uncles for lunch and dinner."

I sat down at the table and took off my shoe to examine my toe. "If you're serving the dishes you already made for our meals today, what are you cooking?"

"Oh, that's in the note too. I'm to make William eggs benedict and to deliver them to his room promptly at seven."

"I'll deliver them for you." I said with the sweetest voice, but evil intentions. I had a vision of me spilling the tray on his head.

"No, I'll deliver the breakfast." Connie turned to face me with the note in her hand. "You allowed him to start this charade. You should have said no at the beginning. Now you have to carry it out to its conclusion."

I regretted my weak moment. Before I had a chance to tell Connie how much I regretted it, Uncle Norman pushed open the kitchen door.

"Hey Connie, is the newspaper here yet?"

"I laid it on the dining room table like I do every morning."

"I'll look again."

I watched Uncle Norman leave. There was pep in his step I didn't remember seeing before.

I poured a cup of coffee and went into the dining room. I opened the drapes. I tried to appear casual, like I was simply waiting for a section of the newspaper to begin my day.

"What's up?" Uncle Norman asked as soon as he saw me.

So much for my casual look, I needed to work on my acting skills. "I was wondering if you made any phone calls last night after I went to bed."

"Phone calls? I don't know what you mean."

Either he was a better actor than I was or he was innocent.

"Someone, and I think it was either you or Uncle Stewart, called the police last night and reported voices and lights in the basement apartment. Tony and Everet showed up about an hour after the dishes were done."

"Tony's a nice guy, much nicer than that doctor friend of yours." Uncle Norman neatly sidestepped the inquiry regarding the call to the police.

"I think so too, but I need time to get over William. I don't want to enter another relationship until I am emotionally ready."

"William is a jerk. You should count it a lucky day when he decided to marry Mary Ann."

"I realize that, but I still want my friendship with Tony to take a natural course. I don't want people pushing us together."

Uncle Norman nodded his understanding, but I wondered if I really wanted them to stop pushing us together.

"Half the newspaper is missing. Do you want the comic section?"

※ ※

I was on my third cup of coffee and rereading the comic strips when I heard voices from the foyer, Mary Ann and William. I slid my chair away from the table. My first instinct was to run and hide before I was given another obnoxious task to perform by her highness. Against my better judgment, I moved closer to the doorway to eavesdrop. (I wondered what had happened to the plan to have eggs benedict served in bed.)

I overheard Mary Ann say, "William, you need to tell everyone that they need to find different places to live. Every time I turn around, there is someone else living here. I can't keep track of our guests and I can't continue sharing the bathroom with the gardener until we get married."

My former boyfriend mumbled something I couldn't decipher.

"I guess that would be better. I'll move my things into the master suite when we get back."

191

I covered my mouth to keep from laughing. From Mary Ann's comment I determined the solution was for William to give up the coveted master bedroom with the en suite bathroom and allow Mary Ann the luxury of the room.

I hoped she didn't figure out that all the bedrooms occupied by the relatives had en suite bathrooms. Anticipating the arrival of her parents, she would have the aunts and uncles relegated to sharing Joel's apartment or sleeping in the gazebo.

During the discussion between the future bride and groom, I saw a pair of women's shoes on the landing at the top of the steps. The person wearing the shoes turned and went in a different direction. They must have seen William and Mary Ann and executed a speedy retreat before they were exposed to Mary Ann's demeaning attitude.

The couple left the house via the front door without breakfast.

Uncle Norman looked up from his newspaper. "Why did you agree to him living here?"

I was getting tired of the question. I picked up my mug and beat my own hasty retreat towards the kitchen. My wrist was almost broken when I tried to push open the swinging door at the same moment someone on the other side pushed.

I stood back and allowed Aunt Mildred to enter the dining room. It was probably her shoes I saw on the landing and she had chosen to use the back staircase to avoid the loving couple.

Without any preface, Aunt Mildred started, "That woman entered my bedroom without even knocking. Fortunately I was dressed."

"What woman and why was she in your room?" I asked.

"Mary Ann." Aunt Mildred enunciated the name as if it left a bad taste in her mouth. "She said she was there to check on me like I was an invalid, but as soon as she entered, she went around the room picking up my things and looking at the bottoms. I think she was trying to appraise the value of the contents of William's house. I could almost hear her thinking, 'This is mine.

This is mine. This is mine.'"

Norman started to laugh, sputtering into his coffee.

I glared at him.

"Sorry, I choked," he said, as he wiped his mouth with the napkin.

I exited before Aunt Mildred asked me why I had allowed the charade to begin in the first place. The kitchen felt hostile. The bedrooms were occupied. I descended to Harold's basement apartment before the residents of the house declared mutiny.

The serenity, I was looking for, proved to be elusive. Aunt Helen was already in the apartment, crying.

Without saying a word, I wrapped my arms around her and gave her a hug. Being in the same room where the murder occurred was an emotional experience.

Helen sobbed out, "Hard worker."

"There, there, He was a hard worker."

"I thought he loved me."

I went along with her statement. I didn't know there was any relationship between Harold and Helen. "In his own way, he did."

Helen sobbed harder. "He told me how pretty I was."

"Harold liked to give compliments."

"Harold?" Aunt Helen pulled away from me and used her sleeve to wipe the tears from her cheeks. "What's Harold got to do with this?"

"I thought that's why you're crying. I thought you're crying because of Harold's murder."

"No worse." Aunt Helen started crying again.

"Worse?" I was confused.

"Evvie didn't call last night. I tried to get him to come over here by calling the police department and reporting voices and lights in the basement, but he didn't show up."

That cleared up who placed the call to the station and the reason why Tony showed up. I was still puzzled. If Helen wasn't crying about Harold, why was she in his apartment crying? So I asked.

"I have to repack all of Harold's clothes, but when I got down here it reminded me of Everet."

"So you were really packing Harold's clothes for charity?"

"Well…."

"I'll help you do it now. It will get your mind off Everet."

We proceeded to fold three of Harold's suits and put them in a garbage bag, when we heard footsteps on the stairs. "Gi-Gi, are you still down there?"

"Not still, but I am here now. What do you need Uncle Stewart?"

He held up three small squares of newspaper. "I found coupons."

The disappearance of the morning newspaper was resolved. "What are they for?" I asked politely, trying to take an interest in Uncle Stewart's new hobby.

"Fifty cents off maple syrup, two dollars off a meal at Hayden' Restaurant, and a twenty percent off coupon for the department store at the mall. I'm going to search for more." My relative turned to leave.

"Wait," Helen said. "I can use the coupon for the department store. Is Norman still in the dining room? I need him to take me to the mall. I need a sexy new outfit to capture Everet's interest." She snatched the coupon out of Stewart's hand.

Stewart confirmed that Norman was indeed in the dining room. The anticipated use of the coupon seemed to please him.

Holding the coupon to her chest, as if it was the solution to all of her problems in the romance department, Aunt Helen asked me, "Can you finish packing Harold's clothes by yourself?"

Before I answered her, Aunt Helen was hurrying towards the stairs.

"She just bought new clothes the other day." Stewart shook his head as if it were a crime for a woman to shop more than once in a week.

I checked the time. I thought it was too early for the stores in the mall to be open, but I didn't stop her. Preparing for her shopping trip and the anticipation of new clothes would take Aunt Helen's mind off Everet for the moment.

I folded the fourth suit and was reaching for the next one when I heard car doors close and the engine start. Maybe I should purchase a chauffeur's cap for Uncle Norman.

I finished folding the suits and stood back, debating the strategy for the second half of the closet. Do I strip the casual clothes from the hangers, toss all the clothes onto the bed, and then fold them, or do I start at one end of the rod and work my way across?

I was filled with the do-good spirit of donating clothes to the needy. I pictured a homeless waif standing on a doorstep, hat in hand, asking for a crust of bread or a pair of shoes. The homeless waif was replaced with the image of Robert standing on my porch with his small brown suitcase. Could Robert use Harold's clothes? I didn't think hand-me-down clothes fell under the terms of probate and if Robert really was Harold's brother (I still hadn't seen any positive identification.), he should be the person sorting the clothes.

Even though Robert didn't seem like the type of guy to be up and about at this hour of the morning, I was about to go upstairs to see if he was awake. That was when I heard movement outside the open apartment door. The subject of my thoughts was standing there, his back toward me. I watched for a second. He seemed to be listening.

"Robert?"

My one word startled him.

"I wasn't expecting anyone to be in the Harold's apartment. I thought it was still off limits."

If it's off limits, why are you here? I was surprised by the length of his statement. Maybe he was getting comfortable enough to talk to me. I still needed answers from him. I started with a seemingly casual question. "What are you doing up so early?"

"I couldn't sleep and I wanted to make sure nothing has been moved out."

"I'm glad you're up. I was coming to get you. I thought maybe you would want to go through Harold's clothes to see if there is anything you can use."

"Huh, sure." He agreed to go through the clothes, but he just stood there staring at the closet as if he had no idea what to do.

"Harold was taller and broader in the shoulders than you, but we'll start with the suits. Do you need a suit?"

Robert shook his head.

"What about the clothes on the hangers? Do you need any casual clothes?"

He shook his head again.

"I haven't looked in the dresser. Why don't you start taking the clothes out of the drawers and going through them? After you check the pockets for money or papers, put the ones you want to keep on the bed. The rest of the clothes go in the black plastic bags to be donated to charity."

Robert walked over to the dresser and slowly opened the top drawer. At the rate he was moving, the clothes would be out of style by the time we were finished. Even homeless people wouldn't want them.

I folded a shirt from the closet and watched Robert staring at the contents of the drawer. "Is it too soon? I can do it myself."

Robert touched the first pile of clothes. "I don't want his old underwear," he said and pushed the drawer shut.

"I'll dispose of them. Try the next drawer."

"I didn't know anyone was down here." The voice surprised Robert and me. We both reacted like kids caught with their fingers in the cookie jar.

I turned toward Robert to make the introduction to Darby. Instead of staring blankly at the drawer filled with socks, Robert intently studied the contents. He examined the toes and heels for wear and holes. He folded and refolded the socks, rearranging the pairs in the drawer.

Darby took a step toward Robert, squinted her eyes, and asked, "Do I know you?"

Robert didn't answer. He didn't raise his head.

I was beginning to think Robert's tough man act was a ruse to cover his shyness. I took pity on him. "Have you met Robert? He is staying with us. He looks familiar because he's Harold's brother."

"I think I know you from somewhere."

I didn't see the resemblance and there was still the issue of identification, but there was no reason why Darby would know him. Robert was from Philadelphia.

Hoping to distract Darby, I changed the subject, "What brings you to the basement?"

Darby's hand twitched. "Exploring the house. Later I plan to sit in the gazebo and read."

"Are you going back to your apartment today?" I sounded as anxious to have her return to her own home as I felt. The army cot had looked comfortable and given the circumstances, I would like to try it.

"No, I thought I would avoid it for one more day."

"Darby, do you think your apartment was targeted because of the key?"

She jerked like she received an electric shock and then she relaxed. "I didn't even connect the two events. No one other than you and your relatives know I possessed the key. By the time of the break in, you had it and your relatives knew that as well. If someone else knew about the key it was because Harold told them about it. But I don't think he would have said anything."

To hide my rudeness, (I mean, the woman had a right to be afraid), I changed the topic and asked, "Don't you work? Isn't your employer expecting you?"

"Not at the moment. I'm between jobs." Darby had the

decency to blush from embarrassment. "I filled out a ton of applications, but no one has called me."

"What are you trained to do?" I don't know why I was concerned about her lack of employment, I was also between jobs, but I needed access to my computer to start my job search. My computer was in the alcove of the master bedroom and I would have to wait until William or Mary Ann vacated the room before I started my job search.

"I have experience in a laundry and in light assembly. I could also work in a cafeteria." Darby changed the subject. "Gi-Gi, you mentioned the key. I found it lying on the floor of the nursery." She dug it out of her hip pocket and held it up.

I thought I put the key in my purse, the purse tucked into the back of the closet. It must have fallen out of the pocket of my pants when I draped my clothes over the side of the crib. I extended my hand to take it, but she closed her fingers around it.

"I was wondering (long pause), if you wouldn't mind, (another long pause) if I could look around for whatever the key opens. It may not open anything, but it would give me something to do rather than sit in the gazebo all day and read."

The key appeared to be a normal house key, unlike the skeleton keys that operated the locks on the doors throughout the house. To the best of my memory there wasn't a lock in the house it would fit.

I weighed the pros and cons of Darby exploring the entire house in her quest to find the lock the key fit. We hadn't found any personal papers belonging to Harold or any indication of his savings either in cash or through the bank. The trail to finding his assassin may be connected to the key and what it unlocked. Still I hesitated. "I don't know. The relatives like their privacy."

"I won't go into their rooms." Darby added, "unless I have their permission."

There was a glint in her eyes that told me she was excited to start exploring. I relented. "Go ahead and look for what the key fits, but I think you're going to be disappointed. From what you told me, the key isn't connected to Grant House. It's a random object Harold found in a parking lot."

When I placed the folded shirt I was holding onto the growing pile on the bed, Robert was gone. The reasonable explanation for his whereabouts was the bathroom. The toilet flushing and the water running in the sink confirmed my assessment.

He opened the door an inch and peeked out to see if Darby was still in the apartment before coming back into the bedroom. He walked over to the dresser and closed the drawer. "That key should be mine."

Robert was right. If he was legitimately Harold's brother, the key should be his. The 'if' was the big question. I took another garment from the closet, and trying to act nonchalant, I asked, "Have you filed your claim with the probate court yet?"

"You don't believe I am his brother, do you?"

I didn't answer his question. I didn't know what to think. I hadn't seen any proof of the relationship between the men and even if I did, I don't know if I was the person to determine the legalities of the situation.

Robert stomped out of the room like a spoiled little kid.

"Does this mean you don't want any of Harold's clothes?" I asked the empty space.

Alone in the butler's apartment I made quick work of emptying the closet. I didn't have to worry about the emotional outburst of Harold's (supposed) next of kin. I dumped the contents of the top drawer and sock drawer into a garbage bag. Robert was right about that, no one wants used underwear.

There was a layer of odds and ends type paperwork under the clothing, receipts and instructions for his television. (He paid cash.) Mostly it appeared to be travel brochures. Darby had told the truth. Harold was planning a trip of some sort, although the destinations appeared to be random. Mostly the brochures were to Caribbean Islands, although there were one or two booklets advertising exotic trips to countries in South America.

There was nothing in the drawers to indicate why Harold was killed or who the killer was. There was nothing in the apartment to disclose why someone hated our butler to the extent of wanting to murder him. Tears formed in the corners of my eyes.

It was sad. The earthly belongings of Harold's entire life were reduced to six garbage bags. Two of which were going straight to the trash.

I worked through the morning, ignoring the sounds of car doors opening and closing, and footsteps in the kitchen above, but when my stomach growled, I knew it was time for me to go upstairs and face the family.

CHAPTER 25

THE SCENE IN the kitchen could only be described as boisterous. I had never witnessed my relatives in such a state. The closest experience to the atmosphere I found was the night we dined at Hayden's Restaurant. Aunt Dorothy was telling Uncle Stewart about her day at work. Aunt Helen was waving shopping bags. Uncle Norman and Aunt Mildred were intently discussing something by the sink. Poor Connie was weaving in and out of the people trying to get from the refrigerator to the stove. I wanted to duck back to the peacefulness of Harold's apartment.

I quickly grabbed a banana from the bowl on the counter and turned to leave the room. Unfortunately, before I could make my escape, they noticed me. There was a split second of silence and then everyone started talking at once. The chaos of the room swirled around me.

I whistled sharply. "Whoa! One person at a time," I commanded.

It took another full second until everyone was quiet. I started with Aunt Dorothy. "How was work?"

Aunt Dorothy's hair hung lifeless, her complexion had the oily sheen from too much heat, her previously pristine apron was splattered with food, but her ear to ear smile told the true story. "I loved it. The restaurant owner assigned me to a cutting board and a knife and told me to julienne a carton of carrots." She drank an entire glass of water, wiping her mouth with the bottom edge of her apron.

Uncle Norman interjected, "He said he was surprised by how quickly she got through the box and how consistent the size of the pieces." During the ride home Dorothy must have given him a thorough accounting of her time at the restaurant.

"My finishing school education finally came to use."

"Tell Gi-Gi what else the owner said to you," Uncle Norman prompted.

"He said that chopping carrots was beneath my ability, so he moved me to the steam table."

Uncle Stewart beamed as if he was the person moved to the steam table. "That's the hot spot in a restaurant kitchen in more ways that one. Dorothy had to stand between the broiler and the serving trays, but what really makes it the hot spot is the fast pace. You have to dish up the food while cooking the to-order food. She did an excellent job keeping up. The chef only had to step in once to help, but that was because a large group of people arrived at the same time. He was very pleased with her work."

Aunt Dorothy added, "I had waitresses shouting new orders and others picking up their orders. I had a runner assigned to me to get the meats out of the cooler."

"Guess who the runner was." Uncle Norman didn't allow me time to guess. He lowered his voice, "It was the friend of Robert."

Everyone looked toward the back staircase as if Robert was standing there listening.

Even though she had denied it, Aunt Dorothy had sought

employment at Hayden's with the ulterior motive of trying to identify Robert's friend. I collapsed into a chair at the table. "There has to be more than one young man working in the kitchen. How do you know he was the friend of Robert?"

Aunt Dorothy took the chair opposite me. "He told me."

"Who told you?"

"Jimmy, that's the name of Robert's friend."

"Aunt Dorothy, did you ask him any other questions?"

"No, I was too busy, but I think tomorrow when I go to work, I'll ask Jimmy how he met Robert and how long he's known him."

"You can't do that. It's too dangerous."

"I work tomorrow. I'll protect her." Uncle Stewart's eyes glowed in anticipation.

"This isn't a game. What if Jimmy tells Robert you're asking questions about him? Robert may be the person who shot Harold. If he feels trapped, he may do something…." I paused, while I carefully chose my word. I wanted to convey to the group the danger of the situation without scaring them into heart attacks. "He may do something desperate."

Connie had been quietly listening while preparing food. "There's a killer in the house? You're just letting him live here, waiting for the right moment to kill us all?" She reached behind her back and started to untie her apron. "There are salads in the refrigerator. I think I need to go home early today."

A car horn beeped out front of the house and the clatter of feet on the staircase.

"I'll go," I offered.

I got to the door in time to ask the departing Robert, "Where are you going and what time will you be back?"

"You're not my mother."

"It's a common courtesy you extend to the people you live with so we can prepare meals. The question, *Where are you going?* lets me know whether you are going somewhere where you will be eating. The question, *What time will you be back?* lets me know whether to lock the door when I go to bed or whether you'll be out later than that."

"I won't be eating any meals here today and you can lock the door anytime you feel like it."

"Thank you." I don't know why I said thank you to the punk. I still didn't have any answers.

I tried to read the license plate on the car Robert got into, but the tires spun gravel and kicked up enough dust to obscure the numbers.

Five pairs of eyes were peering at me from different directions when I closed the door. They had strategically placed themselves to hear the conversation. There was no need for me to repeat what Robert had said.

From the slim opening of the door between the kitchen and the foyer, Connie was the first to speak, "Now that he's out of the house, I won't have to go home."

Aunt Helen vocalized what the others were thinking. "He's the killer. I knew it all the time."

Aunt Mildred had gone up the back staircase, used the top step as her vantage point, and was now coming down the front staircase. She squealed, "Oh, we have a killer living here. What should we do?"

The uncles emerged from the dining room. "We need to make a plan."

"Let's go into the kitchen and talk. Just because Robert is a wise guy doesn't make him a murderer. There could be a logical explanation for his friendship with Jimmy." I led the group back to the kitchen where Aunt Dorothy was snoring gently, her feet resting on the chair I had vacated.

Without saying a word, my little troop followed me to the parlor.

Aunt Helen, still holding her shopping bags, proposed that we call the police. I thought her suggestion had more to do with the contents of her bags and a certain police officer than the resolution of the murder and Robert's involvement. I did think she had a good idea. It was time to prod the police into action, if indeed we were living with a killer. Harold's murderer needed to be positively identified.

Uncle Stewart raised his hand in a halting gesture. "I think we need to wait one more day. I think Dorothy and I should go to the restaurant tomorrow and question this Jimmy character."

Uncle Norman nodded his head in agreement. "I'll have breakfast there, to provide backup to Dorothy and Stewart."

Helen shook her bags. "That's a good plan for tomorrow, but we could all be killed during the night."

Connie interjected, "I'm glad I'm not sleeping here tonight."

"Joel's ankle is improved. He was allowed to put some weight on it this morning. He moved back to his apartment." Aunt Helen's statement seemed random until she added, "The police could stay in that bedroom and keep surveillance on Robert."

Aunt Dorothy joined the group in the parlor, walking as if it took every ounce of energy she could muster to take a step. "I must have dozed off. What did I miss?"

Connie, sitting on the edge of the overstuffed recliner, recapped the conversation.

Aunt Dorothy yawned. "Why would Robert kill his own brother?"

"For the inheritance." Uncle Norman's three word statement was an 'aha' moment for me. Harold was a butler. He wasn't a millionaire with oodles of cash lying around, but he received a steady paycheck and had very few living expenses. He probably accumulated quite a bit of savings over the tenure of his employment, even after paying cash for his car. For someone who was out of work and didn't have any money at all, it would seem like a fortune. It would be motive for murder.

"But he didn't have opportunity."

Since when did my relatives become criminal experts, I asked myself.

"Is there any way we can prove or disprove Robert was on the bus from Philadelphia?" Uncle Norman asked. He had been giving the matter of Harold's murder and Robert's appearance a lot of thought. He offered us two valid points in a matter of two minutes.

There wasn't an answer to his question. Mary Ann and William entered the front door. One by one the relatives disappeared with barely a greeting to the betrothed couple, until I was the only person trapped in the room.

I cringed, waiting for the inevitable, obnoxious task Mary Ann would assign to me. I was surprised when Mary Ann reached into the shopping bag she was toting and pulled out a solitary plate. "Isn't this the most beautiful pattern? I'm going to take the old dishes out of the china cupboard and replace it with this. Of course, we'll be getting the full set as a wedding gift from my grandmother."

While Mary Ann gushed on and on about the china I tried to catch William's attention. He conveniently found a loose thread on one of his buttons and decided this was the crucial moment to pull it. I tried to listen to Mary Ann and share in her joy, but the issue of William marrying her for her family's money interfered.

"I'm going to take the center place setting out of the dining room cabinet and replace it right now."

"Maybe you should wait until your Grandmother sends the rest of the place settings. The impact on the room will be that much greater." I didn't want my Great-Grandmother's Wedgewood china packed, toted to the attic, carried back to the dining room, and unpacked after Mary Ann broke off the engagement. I was frantically thinking of ways to delay Mary Ann from putting even her one plate in the cabinet. "What about the new needlepoint seat covers? Are they going to match your china? The aunts are going to be disappointed when all the work they put into the new covers doesn't match the china."

Mary Ann studied her plate, and then smiled at William. "We'll have someone paint the dining room and we'll use the seat covers as throw pillows in another room. We'll need to purchase new furniture for the dining room, something more modern."

I tried mental telepathy to convey the message to William, "Tell her. Tell her now about your financial situation and that the house is really mine."

William avoided looking at me. Addressing his intended bride, he said, "Honey, I don't think there will be time before the wedding to do all that. Why don't you wait until after the honeymoon to repaint?"

I detected a hint of a pout on her lips, but Mary Ann agreed. "William, you are so practical. Of course there won't be enough time to select the paint color and purchase new furniture. What was I thinking? I barely have time to plan all the wedding details."

I felt a surge of relief. Great Grandmother's china wasn't going to be lugged up and down the stairs. It wasn't until later that I caught the irony of Mary Ann saying she was doing all the preparation for the wedding.

"But after the honeymoon, we'll be living in the townhouse close to your hospital. We won't have the opportunity to decorate this house," Mary Ann argued, but she did it such a way that it didn't seem like she was maneuvering William to get the mansion redone on her timetable.

I no longer felt relief. Panic was closer to what I felt. I waited for William to put his foot down on the issue.

"Whatever you want to do is fine with me, sweetheart." William was rewarded with a kiss.

I exited the room. I couldn't stand being in the same space as the two of them and I wanted to check on Darby. I wanted to find out if she had discovered the lock that the puzzling key opened.

CHAPTER 26

"Gi-Gi, do you have any magazines?" Uncle Stewart delayed me at the top of the stairs.

Magazines? With everything else going on in the house I had to stop for a moment and decipher the reason he was asking for something as mundane as magazines. Then I remembered his current passion for coupons. I imagined that within a week the house would be flooded with the small squares of paper offering ten or twenty cents off products we never use. "I don't have any. I threw them away when I moved from my apartment, but ask the aunts. They are always buying movie star and glamour magazines."

"Good idea." Satisfied, Uncle Stewart trotted along the hallway, tapping first on Aunt Helen's door.

I knocked on the nursery door and got no response. Darby was somewhere in the house trying to find the lock the key would fit. (I had a vision of Prince Charming trying to find the woman who fit the glass slipper.) I wanted to make sure she wasn't invading the privacy of the others with her search.

Behind me, I heard footsteps on the front staircase. Reluctant to encounter Mary Ann and the disgustingly wimpy William, I took the cowardly way out of the situation by going up the stairs to the third floor, Stewart's turret room – slash – study – slash – junk room.

As predicted, the space already showed signs of Uncle Stewart's new obsession. Scraps of paper were strewn around the desk area and filled the wastebasket, which surprised me, because I didn't think Uncle Stewart ever threw away anything. On the corner of the desk was a small pile of coupons. I imagined the pile growing until it reached the ceiling.

The short door to the attic was open and I found the subject of my search. Darby was currently occupied among the treasures in that space. The key jutted out of her left hand, in position ready to poke it into a lock. Her right hand was busy lifting the shrouds from the furnishings left behind by previous generations of Grants.

I couldn't figure out how to alert her to my presence without startling her, so I just said her name and waited for the shocked screech. I wasn't disappointed.

"Have you found a lock that matches the key?" I wiped the sweat, already forming, from my forehead.

"No, there are so many beautiful antiques up here, I haven't finished my search. I keep stopping to admire them." Darby, copying my action, wiped sweat from her forehead leaving a streak of grime. "I haven't given up."

"It's hot up here. Have you tried any of the other rooms?"

"Not yet. You told me not to go into any of the personal rooms without permission from the resident. I didn't see anyone to ask when I started the search. Are your relatives home now?"

"When I walked past, I saw Uncle Stewart knocking on Aunt Helen's door. Aunt Dorothy is in her room, but she is napping.

She's exhausted from her first day of work and I don't think you should disturb her."

"I should ask Helen and Stewart if I can search their rooms while they're here. I can come back to the attic later." She scooted her way to the child size door.

I looked around the attic. It didn't appear like Darby had searched very hard. Everything was exactly as I had left it. What would Harold be hiding that required a lock? The bigger question was: Why would he hide it in the attic?

When I heard car doors, I looked out the window in time to see Tony and Everet entering through the back door. I hurried out of the attic, closing the door, but not moving the boxes back to their original position. In the past few days, the attic had become a desirable destination and probably would remain a point of interest until Harold's murder was solved. I wasn't sure the solution to the murder was even in the house.

Connie was playing hostess, placing glasses of iced tea in front of the men when I took the last step. In a mock formal voice, she told them, "The lady of the manor has decreed that the meals today are salads. Would you care for some gelatin salad? It is very refreshing."

Both men looked at me like I was the ogre. They were accustomed to thick ham sandwiches slathered with mayonnaise, topped with slices of ripe tomato and crisp lettuce. The thought crossed my mind that Harold's murder wasn't going to get solved as long as the two officers were being fed. Maybe Mary Ann had the right idea; salads instead of sandwiches would hasten the resolution of the crime.

"Connie is referring to Mary Ann," I said, trying to get back in their good graces.

Everet accepted the offer of gelatin salad. Tony declined.

"How is the investigation coming?" I asked.

Neither of the men answered. They were staring at the opening to the staircase, mouths hanging open.

Aunt Helen was standing at the bottom of the steps, posed in a manner that would make a hooker proud. One arm snaked seductively high along the side of the door frame, the other hand shook the low neckline of an incredibly bright orange knit top with the word 'Sexy' printed on it. "I'm so hot," my aunt said, adding, "Connie, may I have a glass of iced tea?"

With her hips swaying in exaggerated motion, her entrance into the kitchen was reminiscent of a diva in a silent movie.

After the initial shock of Aunt Helen's appearance, I tried to keep from laughing out loud. Tony's expression indicated that he also saw the humor in the situation.

However, Everet's jaw continued to hang open. He swallowed hard. He stood up. His face was flushed. He forgot the gelatin salad and now had a different kind of hunger.

"Let's go out to the gazebo," Helen suggested to the older officer. She walked across the room, her hips swaying, and took his hand.

He followed her out the back door like a love sick puppy.

I bit my tongue to keep from laughing.

Connie was more practical. "If I'm not mistaken, all the preparations for a wedding aren't going to go to waste. There's going to be a wedding in this house soon and I don't mean Mary Ann and William."

I wished the couple much happiness, but I hoped that they would wait a while before they tied the knot.

"I believe you were asking about the investigation," Tony said, changing the subject. He reached across the table and slid Everet's untouched salad toward him and picked up the fork. "We got six weeks of call records from the pay phones at the bar. There weren't any calls made from the phones at eleven o'clock during that time."

"Maybe Darby meant Harold used a cell phone."

"Everet didn't find one among Harold's things."

There was a lag in the conversation as we weighed the implication of this discovery. "I bagged Harold's clothes. Is it okay to take them to the donation center?"

"Can you wait another day or two? Everet went through them for evidence, but I'm not sure his mind was one hundred percent on the task." Tony added a leer to remind me of the female distraction Everet had in the apartment while he was searching for evidence.

"Darby is searching the house for the lock the key, Harold gave her, fits."

"Darby? What key? Why is she still living here? We went by her place and there was nothing around her doorway to indicate someone tried to break in. We told her that this morning."

I put Darby's name on my list of people to be evicted. "She needs a day or two to calm her nerves."

I heard a "hmpf" from the direction of the cook. Obviously, Connie didn't agree with my assessment.

Tony ate the last bite of the strawberry gelatin and held his plate out toward Connie. She promptly slid another generous piece onto the plate. "Tell me about the key."

"A couple nights ago, Darby called and said she remembered a key Harold gave her for safekeeping. We went over to her apartment and got it. I intended to search the house for what it opened, but forgot about the key while I was dealing with all the other distractions. I dropped the key when I spent the night in the nursery. Darby picked it up and asked if she could look for what it opened. She thought it would be more entertaining than reading in the gazebo."

"What night was that?"

"The night Dorothy prepared the formal dinner for the family and guests."

"That long ago and you didn't tell me."

"Like I said, I had distractions."

"Where is the key now?"

"Darby has it."

"Let's go find her." Tony wiped his mouth and slid back his chair.

Uncle Stewart holding up a section of yellowed newspaper, blocked our way to the stairs. "Look what I found...."

"Not now Uncle Stewart. Tony wants to talk to Darby."

"But...."

"Not now." I immediately regretted the tone I used.

When we were standing in front of the door to the nursery, Tony asked, "What was that about?"

I explained, "Uncle Stewart has taken up a new hobby, clipping coupons. He probably found one for fifty cents off a can of peas or something."

"I'll talk to him later and make a fuss over his discovery. He seemed awfully excited about saving a little bit of money," Tony said.

My heart swelled thinking about the consideration he was showing toward my uncle. "He gets that way when he is involved in one of his pet projects."

Satisfied with my explanation of Stewart's behavior, Tony knocked on the door to Darby's temporary quarters.

When there wasn't any response, I turned the knob and pushed the door open.

Darby was lying on the bed in what appeared to be a sound sleep. I was skeptical. I saw this trick at the hospital numerous times when patients didn't want to be probed and prodded. "Darby, Tony wants to see the key Harold gave you."

"Huh?" (Good acting.)

I repeated my statement.

"It's on the dresser." She made her voice sound tired, like she was just waking up. She didn't bother lifting her head from the pillow.

"Did you find what the key fit?" Tony asked.

"No, but I didn't try very hard," she mumbled. "I searched the attic. When I saw all the antiques stored up there I got distracted and I lost track of what I was doing."

Tony picked the key up from the top of the chest of drawers and examined it. "Gi-Gi told me about the key but I would like you to tell me how and why Harold gave you the key."

"He said he found it in the parking lot at the supermarket. He gave it to me in a kidding manner, as a trinket. It didn't mean anything other than a joke. That's all I know."

"Why would he give it to you? You said you barely knew him." Tony turned the key over in his hand, examining it for marks that would help identify its use or the store where it was made.

Darby repeated the worn out phrase, "I don't know." She added, "I was convenient and he didn't want it in his pocket. I guess I knew him better than anyone else. The more I think about it, I don't think he found the key. I think he had the key made and gave it to me for safe keeping."

Tony rubbed the key like it was a magic bottle and a genie would appear explaining the mystery behind it. "Or he purposely gave it to someone who had only a loose connection to him, so the person searching for the key wouldn't associate the person with him."

Darby sat up and swung her legs over the side of the bed. "You make it sound like having the key puts me in danger."

"Possibly."

When Darby and I previously discussed the key and the attempted break in of her apartment, we had theorized about a connection to the murder. Tony's one word response made the connection real. I mentally erased Darby's name from the eviction list. If the key put her in danger, then she would use it as an excuse to stay until the case was resolved. Whoever killed Harold didn't know the key was now in the possession of the police.

"On the day of the murder there was a black metal box on the floor of Harold's closet. Maybe the key fits it," I recalled.

Tony's left eyebrow went up in a questioning manner. "I thought you didn't go through the apartment before we arrived at the crime scene."

I gave myself a mental slap in the head for letting the information slip that I had explored the apartment before the police arrived at the scene. "I didn't touch anything. I felt nervous standing beside the body, I had to move around."

Gone was the charming, understanding man I had visited the gazebo with, the man who tolerated the quirks of my relatives, the man who understood my crazy participation in the charade to help William. In his place was a no-nonsense police officer who said, "Tampering with evidence is a felony."

I stared at Tony. Even on the night of the murder, he hadn't threatened me with arrest. "I didn't tamper. I simply observed."

"Is the box still in the closet?"

"It's looks heavy to move."

"Let's go down to the apartment and test the key in the lock." Tony's words were suggesting we go, but the tone was insistent.

*****

Darby, Tony, and I stood in front of the closet, staring at the black metal box.

"The lid was open, but there wasn't anything in it when I first saw it," I explained. "There wasn't a need to touch it. I could see that it was empty." I bent over to try to lift the metal box.

"Don't touch it. There may be fingerprints on it."

In a little girl's voice, Darby said, "Mine."

"What do you mean?"

"Gi-Gi said that I could search any unoccupied room and look for the lock the key fit. Harold's apartment was unoccupied and I came in. I saw the lock on the box and tried the key in it."

Even though she made her actions seemed innocent enough, I wished Darby hadn't mentioned my name.

"Did it work?" Tony asked, removing the key from his pocket.

"No, but it was close. The key went into the lock but didn't turn the cylinder."

Tony gave the key another glance and knelt in front of the box. Carefully keeping his fingers away from the surfaces of the box, he inserted the key and tried to turn it. Like Darby said, the key slid smoothly into the lock but it wouldn't turn. He reinserted the key and tried again. "The mechanism may have been damaged when the lid was jimmied."

He stood up and pulled out his cell phone. I heard the ring tones come from the bathroom. "Everet, did you dust the box in the closet for prints?" Tony said into the phone, but he didn't need to.

Everet opened the bathroom door and answered, "No, I assumed the crime scene technicians dusted it."

Aunt Helen followed the police officer out of the bathroom. Her lips were swollen and she had the good manners to blush.

In full police mode, Tony said, "Dust the box for prints and take Darby's. She said she touched the box, but the killer's prints may be on it. And next time, hang a necktie on the bedroom door."

I was still recovering from the shock of seeing my aunt emerge from the bathroom, when Uncle Stewart entered the apartment carrying another small batch of coupons. "I found…."

"What are all you people doing in the basement?" Mary Ann stood at the door to the apartment, her hands on her hips. She would have made a good, old-fashioned school teacher.

Darby spoke up before Tony or I could stop her. "Harold gave me a key and we think we found what it fit."

"Police business." Tony stepped forward. "What are you doing down here?" he challenged. He tossed the key onto the bed.

"I wanted to check the apartment to see if it was ready for occupancy. We need to hire another butler." Mary Ann spoke as if hiring a new butler was one more tedious detail that needed to be done, like getting an oil change. Nothing about her demeanor indicated that she understood the human element behind the murder of Harold.

From the shadows beyond the doorway, William said, "Honey, it doesn't look like the police are finished with their investigation. We'll have to wait until after the wedding to advertise the position." William sounded like the mouse (or was it a rat?) that he was.

Mary Ann huffed, did an about face, and marched out the door. William lingered long enough for me to say, "When are you…?" before he scurried after his betrothed.

"Why do you need my fingerprints?" Darby asked. The whole vignette that had unfolded was lost on her.

In unison, Everet and Tony responded, "Because you handled the box."

"Oh." There was surprise and a little fear in her voice, then she visibly relaxed, "but I told you I touched it when I tried the key."

"You're not a suspect. We need your fingerprints to eliminate them. Then we can figure out if the killer handled the box. It was empty and open when we entered the apartment after the murder. There is a strong possibility the killer is the person who pried it open. He may have held the box to get leverage to open it."

Darby left the room like a teenager who hated her parents for not allowing her to stay out past eleven o'clock. I had a feeling Darby would be elusive when it came time to actually get her prints.

Uncle Stewart, sensing the tension in the room, quietly departed. "I'll show these coupons to you after dinner."

I looked around the apartment and was surprised to see that Tony and I were alone. He must have realized the same thing because the next moment the police officer persona was gone and I was wrapped in his arms and experiencing the most toe curling kiss I had ever had.

CHAPTER 27

WITHOUT MARY ANN and William at the table, dinner was a noisy affair. Connie had fried chicken to go along with the multitude of salads. Tony was seated in the coveted head of the table chair. Uncle Norman had given up his usual seat in favor of sitting beside Darby.

Most of the initial conversation centered on the contraband meat served with the salads.

"Her highness will fire Connie for disobeying her order to serve us only salads for our meal," Uncle Norman stated. "I'm going to smoke a cigar after dinner to mask the smell of the chicken."

"Maybe Connie should cook some cabbage. That smell always lingers in the house and should cover the smell of fried chicken nicely."

While the others talked about devious ways to hide the aroma of the chicken, I heard the front door open.

The others heard the arrival as well, quieted, thinking it was the engaged couple returning. I looked at the table and noticed the platter of chicken had disappeared, although I suspected Aunt Mildred was hiding it on her lap with the tablecloth covering the dish.

"Relax. It's Robert."

As I suspected, Aunt Mildred held the fried chicken on her lap. She carefully lifted the table cloth so none of the grease from the platter got on the fabric and scooted her chair away from the table. The chicken reappeared.

"Excuse me for a minute. I need to speak with Robert." I pushed my chair back and went into the foyer. Robert was already at the top of the stairs.

"Robert, there is plenty of food. Do want to join us?"

Robert stuck his head out where I could see him. "No, I'm not hungry."

"You need to be around people."

"No."

"Suit yourself, but if you decide you don't want to be alone, we are here." I thought it was going well. Robert hadn't slammed a door in my face or ignored me.

"Thanks."

I felt like someone had hit me with a lightning bolt. "Thanks" was a big improvement over his previous attitude towards me.

The front door opened. I sensed a coldness that had nothing to do with the temperature. From behind me, Mary Ann said, "Gi-Gi, there are packages on the back seat of the car. Could you be a sweetie and get them for me? And do be careful, there are breakables in the bags. You can put them in the bedroom where that gardener slept."

Mary Ann dropped her purse beside the sofa in the parlor and sat down. "Oh, before you get the packages, will you have Connie bring in two glasses of iced tea, sweetened and with lemon?"

Robert took one look at Mary Ann and William, trotted down

the stairs and in the longest burst of talk I ever heard him say, said, "Who do you think you are? You come in here and start giving orders as if you own the place. You're a guest. You should be carrying Gi-Gi's packages and you should certainly be going into the kitchen and getting your own iced tea."

"Young man," Mary Ann addressed Robert (even though they were probably the same age), "I think you should pack your bags and leave this house immediately."

"And I don't think you have the right to kick me out." He crossed his arms and leaned against the door molding.

"My fiancé owns this house and that gives me the authority to tell you to get out," Mary Ann countered. She was now standing, facing Robert.

"Can you read? What name is on the gate post? It isn't your fiancé's. It's Gi-Gi's name."

Mary Ann's posture changed as Robert's words sunk in. Her shoulders drooped forward. "William, is what he is telling me true?"

William paled. I waited for several seconds to see how he was going to worm his way out of this situation. I had to admit it took a lot of guts on his part, but he finally nodded. "Yes, it's true. The house isn't mine. It belongs to Gi-Gi."

"Oh, it belongs to one of your relatives?" The ingénue smile faded from her lips. She sunk onto the sofa.

"No." I took pity on my former boyfriend and answered her question. "It belongs to me. You are my guests."

"This house belongs to you?" Mary Ann wrinkled her nose as if she had caught a whiff of something that offended her.

Mary Ann stood up and faced William. "You lied to me." She twisted the diamond engagement ring on her finger. She couldn't get it off, which further humiliated her and ruined her grand exit. She spit out her next words, "The engagement is off. You'll get the ring back as soon as I get the dollar store diamond off my finger."

She disappeared from the parlor, followed by the sounds of her running up the steps and slamming the door to my old bedroom.

"But I love you," William said to the empty space where Mary Ann had stood. Tears glistened in the corners of his eyes.

Robert casually walked up the stairs as if a burden had been lifted from his shoulders. I could almost hear him whistle.

William dragged one foot in front of the other up the stairs. He opened and closed his bedroom door as if he didn't have enough strength to do more.

I knew my relatives heard everything because there was dead silence when I returned to the dining room and the chicken was on the table.

"It wasn't the way I would have handled it, but now she knows." I told the group.

"Perhaps it was the best way to tell her, like ripping off a Band-Aid. You have to do it quickly," Aunt Mildred stated. It was a fitting comment. It was the same analogy William had used to justify his manner of telling Robert about his brother's death.

Stewart summed up with the remark, "William got a taste of his own medicine. He callously told Robert about his brother's murder and Robert told Mary Ann the truth about the house in the same manner."

"She only knows that the house isn't his. She doesn't know William is marrying her for her money. She doesn't know the whole truth about his finances." Elbows on the table, I cupped my chin in my hands.

Uncle Norman broke the silence. He raised his glass and offered a toast. "The queen has lost her kingdom."

Iced tea glasses were raised. The others clinked them, with a merry *Hear, Hear!*

I refrained from joining the celebration. Mary Ann's reaction to the news was exactly as I imagined. What surprised me was how William had reacted to Mary Ann breaking off the engagement.

The others hadn't witnessed the tears in his eyes.

"I'm beginning to like Harold's brother," Aunt Dorothy said.

Tony took a more practical view of Mary Ann's and William's relationship. "Will she dump him when she finds out he doesn't have any money? He has the potential to earn millions as a doctor." It was the first time anyone had mentioned the possibility that Mary Ann was marrying William for his position or for his future earnings.

"I think the money factor is secondary to truthfulness and trust. If he had been honest about his finances, if he hadn't lied about this house being his, then I think the relationship would be on strong ground." I picked up my plate and utensils, preparing to do my part to clear the table. "I wouldn't take William back if he was the richest man in America."

The others stood and gathered their place settings. While we went into the kitchen, I noticed Uncle Norman and Uncle Stewart lagged behind. They were still deep in a whispered conversation when I returned to the dining room to carry the remains of the salads to the other room. I couldn't hear what they were saying, but I knew it would be trouble.

I had two bowls containing leftover salads in my hands, balancing a third bowl between them, and trying to open the swinging door with my hip, when Uncle Norman asked, "Gi-Gi, are we going bar hopping tonight?"

I almost dropped the bowls. "Why? We already found someone who knew Harold."

"There has to be more than one person locally who knew him," Uncle Stewart

argued. "Harold went out every night. He did the shopping and errands for the family. There has to be other people who can tell us about him."

I didn't know what the two men were up to, but I had other considerations to take into account. I had Tony. I didn't know how the local policeman felt about being seen with me in the community. I had Mary Ann and William with a broken engagement, emotionally distraught. And I had Robert, mourning his brother's death. Despite his protective attitude towards me when Mary Ann was giving orders, I didn't know if I trusted him totally. I also had Darby to entertain. I couldn't figure her out at all.

I shook my head. "I don't think I should go out tonight."

"In that case, Stewart and I are going to that little bar where the girls were playing music on the juke box."

Uncle Stewart tried to discreetly elbow Uncle Norman. The gesture reminded him to say, "Oh yeah. We thought we would ask Darby to go with us."

I could tell this wasn't his idea. I just had to figure out what they were trying to accomplish. Although, the way they were acting lately, the trip to the bar could be a case of sowing the wild oats they didn't sow when they were young. For one fleeting second, I had an idea it was some kind of set up to find Harold's killer, but the notion disappeared as soon as I thought it.

"Go. You don't have to ask my permission." They were, after all, adult men.

Stewart cleared his throat. "We weren't asking your permission, we were politely telling you where we were going and asking if you wanted to come too."

"In that case, thank you for the invitation, but I'm afraid I have to decline. Now go get dressed and have fun."

An hour later, Tony and I sat in the gazebo and watched Norman and Darby leave in the Mustang to go to the bars. Uncle Norman had mastered the gears (like riding a bicycle) of the muscle car during the last couple days.

Aunt Dorothy and Uncle Stewart had declined the invitation to accompany the two, pleading work early in the morning. Initially Aunt Mildred had accepted the invitation but Uncle Stewart had nudged her with a well placed elbow (He was getting good at elbowing people to get them to do what he wanted.) and she changed her mind with the excuse of washing her hair.

I don't know where Everet and Aunt Helen went, but I suspected there was more evidence in Harold's apartment that needed examined.

I was content to sit on the wicker bench, Tony's arm around my shoulders, my head leaning on his chest. Occasionally one of us would say something and the other would agree, but this wasn't the time for serious conversation.

Tony and I watched the lights in the house flick on and off as the members of the household went about their routines. Stewart was up in his study, I assumed he was working on his new pet project and tomorrow I would see a new stack of coupons. Aunt Dorothy's light went off shortly after she went upstairs. She had difficulty keeping her eyes open at the dinner table. She wasn't used to the rigors of working.

Robert's light was turned off. I thought he had gone to bed until I heard footsteps in the gravel. "Gi-Gi?"

"We're back here."

Robert followed the sound of my voice. "I wanted to let you know I won't be home tonight. You can lock up whenever you feel like."

"Thank you Robert. I'll feel much better with the doors locked." I controlled my temptation to ask him where he was going. He was old enough to take care of himself.

"Robert, I also want to thank you for coming to my defense this evening. It was kind of you."

There was silence, followed by footsteps in the gravel moving toward the front of the house.

"Excuse me," Tony whispered and he gently pulled his arm away from my shoulders. "I'll be back in a second."

My initial thought was that Tony needed to use the bathroom, but as soon as he left the gazebo, he took off running around the corner of the house opposite of the driveway.

He wasn't gone long. "You should have warned me about the rose bushes on that side of the house." He took out the ever present notebook and jotted down something I couldn't read. Then he settled down in the same position he had been in before his brief trip.

"Did you get the license number?" I asked lazily.

"How did you know that was what I was doing?"

"I'm beginning to figure out how you think." I snuggled closer to his chest.

The flood lights came on and the back door opened, spoiling the mood. Everet emerged from the house. "Tony, we got a call."

"I'm coming," Tony called out to his partner. Tony kissed the top of my head. Quieter, he said to me, "I'll call you tomorrow."

I sat alone in the gazebo for a few more minutes savoring the memory of his kisses and touch before I went back inside the house.

᠅

Thud. I heard some mumbling. Thud. I went to the front of the house to see what was going on. Thud.

"Mary Ann, what are you doing?" I whispered. The only light was coming from the nightlight on the foyer table, but I could still see the suitcase she was trying to maneuver down the steps.

"What does it look like I'm doing?" Judging from her tone, she was still angry at William.

"It looks like you're moving out." Mentally I cheered, one less guest.

"Can you help me with this suitcase?" Mary Ann asked. Remembering my status in the household, she added, "Please."

I argued with myself. As much as I wanted her out of the house, the romantic side of me won. "I'll help you carry it upstairs."

"No, I'm leaving."

"I don't think that's the right thing to do. It's late and you're not in a proper emotional state to drive."

"He doesn't love me." Mary Ann set her suitcase down on the step, using her leg to brace it in place.

"I think you're wrong. William loves you very much."

"And I love him."

"You know that's the reason why he didn't want to tell you the truth. He was afraid he would lose you." That, his ego, and her parents' fortune, but I didn't add those details to my argument.

"It's more than that, you know he's practically bankrupt and he's ashamed to tell me."

I was speechless. I didn't know how Mary Ann knew about William's finances, but I suspected that after spending a couple days in his company it would become obvious. I mean, after spending one evening with him I knew he was maxed out on his credit cards. "How do you feel about that?"

"I think he should have more faith in my love. I'm not marrying him for his money or the fact he's a doctor." Mary Ann looked up the stairs toward William's closed bedroom door. "If he loved me, he would be pounding on my door right now, begging me to stay."

"William is embarrassed. He pretends to have bravado, but I don't think he is confident enough to overcome his financial position." Personally I thought William wasn't man enough to do anything on his own, but that was the reason why I had to patch things up between Mary Ann and William. Otherwise I would have a permanent house guest. "Think about it overnight. In the morning we'll come up with a plan to get the two of you back together."

I picked up the suitcase using two hands and started to carry it up the steps. "What do you have in this thing? Maybe we should open it and carry some of your things up to your room loose and then come back down for the rest."

"I'll carry it."

I let her. I was carrying enough burdens without the added weight of a suitcase.

Lois Lamanna

CHAPTER 28

I GLANCED AT THE digital clock on the night stand, two o'clock in the morning. Who on earth was knocking on my bedroom door in the middle of the night? "Who's there?" If I gave it any thought, my guess would have been Mary Ann or William asking advice.

"It's me, Darby."

I fumbled around in the dark for my robe and was rewarded by stubbing my toe.

I was playing musical beds and was sleeping in the room Joel had used while recuperating from his sprained ankle. I managed to hop to the door putting my weight my my heel. I blinked as my eyes adjusted to the bright light from the hall. "What?"

"Your Uncle Norman followed me into my room." Darby was still wearing the clothes she had worn to the bar. Her hair was disheveled and her makeup worn, but she definitely had me at a grooming disadvantage.

227

"Why?" Somewhere in the back of mind, I thought I should be more articulate, but at that time of the night, an expanded vocabulary eluded me.

"I think he has dementia. He sat down on the side of the bed and started to make advances."

"Uncle Norman? Dementia? Advances? That doesn't sound like him. Lock your door. Go to bed. I'll talk to him in the morning." I started to close my door.

Darby put a hand on the door, preventing it from closing. She was surprisingly strong. "Please go talk to him now. Otherwise I won't be able to sleep."

I tightened the belt on my robe. It was better to get it over with, otherwise I would be sharing my twin bed with Darby. She slipped into my bedroom and shut the door as I hobbled down the hall to Uncle Norman's room.

I tapped on his door and twisted the knob. From my childhood, I remembered his room was more apartment than a single bed chamber. There was a living space, where Uncle Norman could sit and watch television or work at his desk in privacy. The furnishings were out of date, but still good quality. Further along was a bathroom and beyond that was the sleeping quarters. Add a hot plate and a young couple could live in the suite quite comfortably.

"Uncle Norman?" I said in my sweet nurse voice. "Uncle Norman, are you in here? Are you dressed?"

Uncle Norman, fully awake, attired in his pajamas and robe, came out of the back room. "What's up Gi-Gi? Why aren't you in bed?"

He seemed alert and in control of his faculties.

"How much did you have to drink tonight?"

"Nothing, I was driving the Mustang. Why?"

"Darby said you followed her into her bedroom." I didn't add the advances she claimed he made. It was too out of character for the man I knew.

"I was just checking on her. Robert is still in the house and I wanted to be certain she was in her room and there was no hanky panky going on."

"Hanky panky? I don't think they know each other."

"Stewart has…." Norman acted like he had said too much.

"Uncle Stewart has what?"

Uncle Norman sat in his recliner and put the foot rest up. "Uncle Stewart has a theory that Darby is lying about how well she knew Harold. He sent me to the bar to get her liquored up and see if I could get her to talk about Harold."

"Interesting. How did that go?" I hadn't seen any physical evidence that Darby was under the influence of alcohol.

Uncle Norman's next statement confirmed my opinion. "That girl can hold her liquor. She stuck to her story. Later in the evening she ignored my questions."

"So you cleared her as being the murderer?"

"Why would Harold give an almost stranger a key? He knew his brother was coming for a visit. Why not leave it hidden somewhere in the house and give it to his brother? It would be safe for a few more days. It would be impossible for the killer to search every square inch of this house and find one small key." I waited for Uncle Norman to light a pipe in the style of Sherlock Holmes.

My uncle continued, "Stewart thinks there isn't a lock in this house that the key will fit. She made up the key as an excuse so she could search the house."

I sat in the desk chair, staring at the blank television. In a crazy way, it fit. I didn't know Darby well enough to judge whether she would make up a story like that. There was one detail he was forgetting. I asked, "Do you think she knew the key would fit the black box in Harold's closet and is searching for a second one?"

"We don't know. If we figure out what she is searching for or if we determine how well she really knew Harold, we would be able to determine if she is the person who killed Harold."

"If this is Uncle Stewart's theory, why didn't he take Darby out to the bar?"

"Tomorrow is his first day at work and he wanted to get a good night's rest."

I realized I had been so wrapped up in my personal affairs that I hadn't listened to Uncle Stewart when he was trying to tell me about his theory. I would make a point of being more empathetic and hear what he had to say.

We were talking softly. The time of the night and our respect for the others sleeping in the house made this natural. The lateness of the hour also precipitated pauses, while we thought about the other's statements and weighed their significance.

It was during one of these pauses that we heard the squeak of a floorboard outside Uncle Norman's room. He held up his hand to silence me, but there wasn't any need. I was already alert to the movement in the corridor.

I heard it again. Had someone been listening to our conversation?

By silent agreement I got up and went to the door. (Uncle Norman's recliner would make a racket when he lowered the foot rest.) I listened for bathroom noises. Three of my guests, Mary Ann (even though William had offered to trade rooms he hadn't actually switched), Robert, and Darby shared the common bathroom in the hall. The squeaking floorboard could have been someone innocently taking a middle of the night constitutional.

I slowly turned the handle and when Uncle Norman nodded I swung open the door. Simultaneously, he lowered the footrest and jumped out of the chair to join me in the hall.

The doors were shut with the exception of the bathroom door. I looked at the small space at the bottom of each entrance. No lights were visible under the doors.

Tiptoeing, staying close to the wall to avoid the telltale floorboard creaks, I returned to my bedroom. When I opened the door, Darby was gone. I wanted to laugh at the fright I had given myself. Darby got tired of waiting for me to return from Uncle Norman's room and had gone to bed.

A second thought occurred to me, making me nervous. We had been talking about her possible involvement in the murder. Had she been listening outside Uncle Norman's door?

I removed my robe and crawled back in bed. In the morning I would worry about the person strolling the hall in middle of the night. I closed my eyes hoping to get some rest to fortify myself for the next day's drama.

Was it my imagination or was someone coming up the front staircase? Lacking a true weapon, I once again resorted to my hairbrush, thinking I could beat the intruder with it. In a repeat of the actions in Uncle Norman's room, I quietly went to the door and turned the knob. At the precise moment when the person was passing my door, I pulled it open with a loud, "Aha."

If I hadn't been so terrified, I would have laughed. Bread, ham, lettuce, and tomato went flying. Milk spilled to the floor. A loud curse hung in the air.

Robert stood there, bare-chested, bare footed, pants hanging low from his hips, hair tousled.

"Sorry." I grabbed two towels from the linen closet, handing one to Robert to dry the milk from his chest, while I tackled the floor. "I didn't realize you were in the kitchen making a sandwich."

"I missed dinner."

"Did you see anyone else while you were down there?"

"No."

I realized Robert wasn't about to become the most articulate person and expand on what he had experienced. It would be up to me to ask the right questions if I was going to get the answers I wanted. "Robert, I thought you weren't coming home this evening. The doors were locked. How did you get in?"

"The old guy and the chick."

I interpreted his comment to mean when Uncle Norman and Darby had returned from the bar, he entered the house along with them. Neither of them had mentioned Robert's return.

"What woke you?"

"I heard the chick talking."

"Do you mean Darby?"

"Yeah, her."

"Who was she talking to?"

"Him." Robert pointed to Uncle Norman who was standing in the hall.

"Is that when you decided you were hungry?"

"I tried to go back to sleep, but then I heard another door opening and someone tapping on a door."

"That must have been me trying to get Uncle Norman to open his door."

"No."

"No?"

"It was a man's voice. I think it was that crazy guy who has been following that uppity dame all week. He kept saying, 'Mary Ann, open up. I want to talk to you.'"

Ah, William was trying in his own way to apologize to Mary Ann. He could have chosen a more appropriate time, like nine o'clock in the morning instead of the middle of the night. William was going to have to do better if he expected Mary Ann to return to his arms.

"Did you hear me go to Uncle Norman's room and knock on his door?"

"No, that's when I decided you have a bunch of crazy people living here and went down to the kitchen to get a sandwich."

I still didn't know exactly who had been walking along the hall while Norman and I were talking. "Come on, let's go to the kitchen and I'll fix a sandwich for you. I'm feeling hungry myself."

Another door opened and Aunt Mildred stuck her head out. (I wished she hadn't.) She had some kind of green goop spread over her skin and curlers in her hair. She smelled like avocado and looked liked a creature from a fifties horror movie. "What's going on? Don't you know what time it is?"

I skipped the highlights of the last hour and got to the end. "Robert and I are going to get a snack. Go back to bed."

I heard her famous "tsk" and the door close. Norman went back to his room, closing his door without so much as a click.

Perhaps Robert was a better judge of people than I was. Maybe the residents of Grant House, including myself, were a little crazy. I was going to be alone in the kitchen with a suspect in a murder investigation. All sorts of deadly utensils were there. I felt my hair brush dig into my leg as a reminder of how ill prepared I was to meet the murderer.

As a result of my nervousness and my lack of judgment, I seated Robert as far from the knife drawer as possible and fixed two sandwiches. When I sat at the opposite end of the table, I asked him, "What do you remember about your brother from when you were growing up?"

Something about the late hour usually inspires the exchange of confidences. This wasn't the case with Robert. Upstairs, while cleaning up the spilled milk and the sandwich on the floor, he had been positively verbose. Now in the light of the kitchen, he took another bite of his ham sandwich and with his mouth full of food, said, "I don't want to talk about him."

I tried again. "Was Harold a good student?"

"I said I don't want to talk about him."

"What would you like to talk about?"

"I'm going to bed." Robert picked up his empty plate and placed it in the sink.

I lost my appetite. I dumped my half eaten sandwich in the trash and followed him up the stairs.

CHAPTER 29

AT FIRST IT sounded like rain drops hitting against the window. Rainy days are perfect for sleeping late. Then I thought it was puppy paws traveling on the wood floor outside the bedroom door. When I took the pillow from my eyes and listened carefully, I discerned the sound was tapping on the door. There had been a lot of tapping on doors during the night. I should have identified the source of the noise on my first guess. "Who's there?"

"Oh, thank heaven you're awake." The door opened without a proper invitation. "I thought you were going to sleep all day. I wanted to talk to you earlier, but the shrew in the kitchen wouldn't let me come upstairs. She said she would use a dull kitchen knife. Well that isn't important. You're awake now and I know you'll tell me what I should do."

"William, get out of my room."

"Do you mean this one or the one I've been sleeping in because I can sleep in another room. I'll move my things today, although I would really like to stay in that room." I never heard William speak so indecisively.

"I meant this one. I don't think it's a good idea for you to be in a woman's bedroom when you are trying to get Mary Ann to marry you."

"That's why I came to see you. You think of everything. I'll wait in the hall."

"Shut the door on your way out." William wasn't making much sense and he was talking too fast. I wondered if the stress of his love life and financial situation was driving him over the brink.

"You'll hurry? You won't go anywhere without talking to me first?"

"Only to the bathroom. Now get out."

I caught a glimpse of myself in the mirror and was tempted to go back to bed. I didn't have bags under my eyes before I moved back to the family home. I thought longingly of my clothes. I had slept in so many bedrooms and moved my things so many times; I couldn't remember where my clothes were being stored. I picked up the clothes from the day before and trying not to think about their condition, put them on.

"William, I'm only going to say this once and then I won't say it again. *I told you to tell her about the money.*"

"I deserved that," he said, but he didn't appear to mean it.

"How can a brilliant man, a doctor, be so stupid?" Why did I care one wit about his feelings?

"I was socially repressed as a child. My parents made me study instead of participating in sports and social events."

"Don't blame it on your parents. Admit you are selfish."

"Gi-Gi, are you going to help me?"

"I don't know. What do you want me to do?" I asked. I didn't feel the need to get involved in his relationship with Mary Ann. I was merely a bystander, who could watch the situation and not care one way or the other how it turned out.

"I need you to explain the situation to Mary Ann and convince her to marry me."

"I can't talk to her for you. I don't know the situation. You're going to have to do that yourself."

His voice cracked. "I don't know what to say."

I didn't know the depth of his feelings for Mary Ann. I felt myself caving. "Yes I'll help you, but I'm going to make you grovel a little first."

"What does that mean?"

I pretended to think, going as far as touching the side of my head with my fingertip for effect. "I seem to recall a man lying on his bed while I cleaned his bathroom."

"Will cleaning the toilets get Mary Ann to forgive me?"

"No, but it will make me more inclined to help you get her back." I had a long list of tasks that needed done. "While you're cleaning the bathrooms, Mary Ann and I will get our nails done."

"You'll talk to her?"

"No, you are the one who has to talk to her, but the manicure will soften her for when you speak with her." I merrily trotted down the steps to the kitchen. My middle of the night snack wasn't a replacement for breakfast.

⁂

The kitchen was in the midst of confusion. Uncle Stewart and Aunt Dorothy entered from the direction of the port cochere. They had decided to give up the convenience of the back door in favor of staying dry. They both had bags from the grocery store in each hand.

Uncle Norman was like a lion waiting for its prey. He pounced on Uncle Stewart as soon as he pushed open the swinging door. "What did you find out?"

Connie rushed to take the bags as if there wasn't a scrap of food left in the refrigerator and this was the only food we would see for the next month.

"I met this character, Jimmy, who claims to be BFF with Robert." Uncle Stewart shrugged off Connie's attempt to take

236

the bags, in favor of placing them on the counter himself.

Connie moved to take the bags from Aunt Dorothy, who gratefully handed them to the cook.

"BFF?" Aunt Helen asked.

"Get with it. BFF is text message shorthand. It means *best friends forever*." Stewart bounced with pride as he imparted his new knowledge to the rest of us.

I wondered how Uncle Stewart found out the acronym and its definition. As far as I knew, he didn't have a BFF, unless it was Uncle Norman.

"Forget about the cell phone and text message jargon." Uncle Norman was getting inpatient (or was it jealous?). "Tell me about Jimmy."

"He's a busboy," Aunt Dorothy said, twisting her mouth as if she tasted something sour when she uttered the word busboy.

With my limited knowledge, I inferred that a busboy was a lowly position in the restaurant hierarchy.

"I didn't get much chance to talk with him, but I did get a good look at the time cards. There is a R. Petrick who is a busboy at the restaurant and he hasn't worked there all week. I heard the boss say that if this character doesn't show up for his shift tonight, he was going to be fired, and someone else hired to take his place."

"I see what you're saying," Uncle Norman mumbled.

"I'm sorry. I don't see what you're saying," Aunt Mildred said.

Stewart sat down at the table. In a low voice, he said, "I think Harold's brother didn't come from Philadelphia. I think he's been in town all along, working at the restaurant."

"So Harold's real last name was Petrick or Robert's real last name is Peters. Either way Robert didn't come all the way from Philadelphia to visit his brother. He only had to come from Hayden's," Uncle Norman said, summarizing the situation.

"If Harold knew his brother was living in town, why didn't he visit him?" Aunt Mildred asked.

Norman explained, "We don't know that he didn't. I mean, Harold may have checked on Robert while he was out doing errands."

"I have to tell Everet." Aunt Helen hurried from the room, pulling her cell phone out of her pocket in the same manner a gunslinger pulled his weapon from his holster.

"She is behaving like a love sick teenager. Any excuse to talk with that man and she's rushing off to call him." Aunt Mildred added a "tsk" for emphasis.

I lowered myself back into the chair, hoping no one noticed that I started to get up to call Tony. I planned to tell him the last name the busboy used. Maybe Petrick was Harold's real last name and Tony would finally be able to find some background information about our deceased butler.

"What am I supposed to do with this?" Connie held up a can as if it was a dead bug. She puckered her mouth, expressing the same sentiment.

"I thought you could serve it for breakfast," Uncle Stewart said, as if the repugnant can was a delicacy.

"You can eat it for breakfast."

"What is it?" I asked.

"It's a can, mind you, a full size can of pureed mushrooms. I have never, in all the years I've been cooking, needed or wanted to use an entire can of mashed fungus. I don't even know what to do with it. I use fresh or canned sliced mushrooms, but never have I seen a recipe calling for pureed mushrooms."

The rest of us stared at Connie.

"I had a coupon," Uncle Stewart said, as if the word 'coupon' exonerated him from buying things the household didn't need.

Connie set the can on the counter and selected another product from the bag. In a calmer voice she explained to Stewart, "We don't use this stuff either. This is for households that have cats. The cost of the product even with the coupon wipes out the savings on the products we do use. From now on show me the coupons before you grocery shop and I'll decide whether to use them, then we'll start saving money."

Out of the corner of my eye I saw the dining room door open a crack and was gently closed. The visitor from the other room had decided against joining us in the kitchen. If my guess was correct, Connie's tirade wasn't the reason the person had retreated.

I went looking for William's ex-fiancée. I found her in the entry. "Did you get any rest last night?"

One look at Mary Ann's bloodshot eyes told me the answer. She didn't have on any makeup and her hair looked like she had dragged a brush through it, but hadn't attempted to style it.

"Oh Gi-Gi, I think I made the biggest mistake of my life." Tears formed in the corners of her eyes. I wondered how much of her appearance was due to regret over her decision to break off the engagement and how much could be attributed to William knocking on her door every half hour begging her to open the door.

"Shh, he'll hear you." William and Mary Ann deserved each other, but I wasn't willing for them to reconcile yet. I had bathrooms that needed cleaned and a slew of other chores I could convince my former boyfriend to do for the sake of getting Mary Ann back.

"I told William we were going for manicures this afternoon and I think we should stick to the plan."

Mary Ann nodded. She looked younger than her age.

Uncle Stewart pushed open the door, holding out my cell phone. "Tony wants to speak with you."

To Mary Ann I said, "Go on upstairs and grab your purse. I need to speak with the officer in charge of the murder investigation." I had more to say to Mary Ann but it could wait until our nails were drying.

"Tony, did you figure out who killed Harold?" I asked without the usual preamble to the conversation.

"Let's say we're getting closer to finding the killer."

I interpreted his statement to mean, he was having no luck finding the killer. "Did Everet talk to Aunt Helen?"

"Which call do you mean? I think they have called each other three times already today."

"Uncle Stewart started his job today at Hayden's Restaurant. I'm worried about him. He met a busboy by the name of Jimmy." My thoughts were as jumbled as my conversation.

"That should be good news. Uncle Stewart is getting out and meeting new people."

I almost made the 'tsk' sound Aunt Mildred used to express disapproval, but I caught myself in time. "You don't get it. Jimmy may be the link to Harold's true identity."

I heard Tony adjust his phone. "I'll question him later. What else is going on at the house?"

"Uncle Norman tried putting the moves on Darby, which led to some middle of the night activity. She came into my bedroom …."

"You actually had a bedroom last night?" I heard Tony chuckle.

I ignored his comment and told him about the drama that had interrupted my sleep.

"So you had a bed to sleep in but you didn't get any sleep."

"I may not get enough rest until some of my guests leave and they aren't leaving until you find out who killed Harold."

Tony made some empathetic comments then turned his attention to the more serious matter going on in the house. "What do you make of all the activity?"

I heard Mary Ann coming down the steps. "I don't have time to explain it now. I'm going to get a manicure."

"Gi-Gi, before you hang up, I actually called you for a purpose other than to talk about the murder and all the people living in your house." Tony paused. "I wanted to ask if you would like to go out to dinner and a movie tonight, just the two of us."

I didn't have to think about my answer. I couldn't wait to

escape the bedlam my house had turned into. I wanted to show off my nails. But the main reason I wanted to accept was that I would be able to spend some quality time with Tony. "That would be an excellent idea."

CHAPTER 30

Mary Ann seemed happier when we returned from our manicures. She had a clearer understanding of her emotions and how she felt about William.

I detected true love and thought they were back on track for a wedding, but she needed to talk with William to make it clear that she expected total honesty in the future.

With one problem settled, I was feeling a bit smug. I would have buffed my fingernails on my chest, but I wanted to preserve their freshly polished appearance for my date. I wasn't concerned about the aunts and uncles huddled around the dining room table. A telephone book, newspapers, tablets, and pencils were strewn across the surface. Their conversation stopped when I circled the table to open the drapes.

"I'm going out with Tony tonight. I won't be here for dinner."

"That's lovely," Aunt Mildred said, without even glancing in my direction. "Have a good time."

The others nodded their heads in approval.

I had prepared for disappointment and pouting when I made my announcement. I thought my five relatives would want to go with us like they had the previous time Tony and I tried to have dinner alone.

I lingered in the tub, admiring the surgically clean bathroom. William had proven himself worthy of my advice. I made a mental note to allow him to cut some flowers from the garden to place in Mary Ann's room.

Waiting alone in the parlor, I felt like a teenage girl waiting for her first date. I actually wished my aunts and uncles would join me as a distraction. I kept smoothing imaginary wrinkles in my clothes and touching my hair to make sure it was still tidy. It was silly because Tony and I had gone to dinner before.

Tony knocked on the front door. Using that entrance added a degree of formality to the visit and defined it as a date rather than a police assignment.

When he entered the foyer he complimented my outfit and then there was an awkward silence. I wasn't the only one nervous about the evening.

I giggled.

Tony commented on the rain we had that day, said it had cleared up, and the evening was going to be pleasant. I didn't know if he was referring to the weather or if he was predicting a good meal and an entertaining movie without the company of my relatives.

As if reading my thoughts, Tony commented, "I thought we would stop and pick up a newspaper to see what movies are playing."

"I saw a newspaper lying on the dining room table." This would also give me the opportunity to tell my relatives I was leaving and say good night.

When no one was in the dining room, I continued to the kitchen. Connie was alone, wiping the counters and hanging the tea towel over the oven handle.

"Where is everyone?"

The question became rhetorical when I heard the engine of the Mustang roar down the driveway. I caught a glimpse of Uncle Norman driving, Uncle Stewart in the front passenger seat and the aunts in the back seat. All of them were wearing sunglasses and hats or scarves. "Where are they going?"

"They said something about Robert and following." Connie threw out the comment as if it were a recipe for a peanut butter sandwich. She picked up her purse and headed for the door.

It was Tony who verbalized what I was thinking. "This can't be good."

My brain played a rerun of the havoc the aunts and uncles had created at Darby's apartment the night we went for the key. "I think we should follow them and see what they are up to."

Tony pulled the keys from his pocket. He didn't need to ask me to explain. Even though he had only known my relatives for a short time he knew what to expect.

I barely had time to snap my seat belt before Tony had the car in gear and we turned onto the highway on two wheels. I kept my eyes on the traffic ahead looking for the Mustang's distinctive rear end.

"We've lost them," Tony said, admitting defeat.

"I think we should try Hayden's Restaurant."

"Why?"

"Uncle Stewart mentioned a busboy by the name of R. Petrick."

"What's R. Petrick got to do with anything?"

I hadn't listened as closely to Uncle Stewart as I should have and for the second time in two days, I promised myself that from now on I would pay more attention to what he had to say. I strained my brain. "I think he said R. Petrick was a busboy who hadn't showed up for work this week and the boss was going to fire him if he didn't report for work tonight."

Tony slowed the car and turned onto a side street, meandering through a residential area. It served the purpose of distancing us from the drama at Grant House. I felt more relaxed. "Are you telling me that we are chasing your relatives on the chance that there is a job opening at the restaurant?"

"There was more. Uncle Stewart thinks R. Petrick is Robert Peters, Harold's brother. If that's the case, Robert has been living in the vicinity for some time. He didn't come from Philadelphia like he said."

"Aha, so we are getting somewhere."

"It was just a hunch and Aunt Helen did tell Everet about the busboy."

"He didn't tell me." Tony increased the speed of the car. "He's so love sick that he would forget to wear his shoes."

"Love sick?"

"Yeah, don't be surprised if there is another wedding to plan in the near future."

"Connie said something like that also, but…." I found it ridiculous that two people their age would consider getting married.

"I know what you are thinking. They haven't known each other long enough for their feelings to be true love, but I have a feeling that when two people meet and the chemistry is there, it's there. It doesn't take months and years to discover it."

I shamed myself. I had only thought about the age factor. I hadn't even considered the length of their courtship.

Tony continued his marriage discussion. "Look at William and Mary Ann. They have only known each other for three months and they're getting married."

"I don't know if love is William's only motivation for a quick marriage. There is a large financial reward for marrying Mary Ann."

"You think money is the reason why he proposed?"

I wanted to scream, *Yes, why else would he break it off with me?* I kept my mouth shut. It wasn't my business if William and Mary Ann were or were not in love. We pulled into the parking lot for the restaurant.

I spotted the Mustang in the far corner. In the dim light I could make out two people slumped low in the seat. A quiver of fear ran down my spine. Where were the others? "Tony, stop the car."

I was out of the car before it came to a halt. In spite of their amateurish disguises and their feeble attempt to hide, I instantly recognized Uncle Stewart and Aunt Dorothy. "What are you doing?" I sounded like a mother who had discovered her children out after curfew.

"Shh." Uncle Stewart looked toward the back door of the restaurant. "It's almost time for the busboys to take their breaks."

As if on cue, the kitchen door opened and two men came out and immediately I saw lighters flick on. I dove into the back seat of the Mustang.

"Stay down," Uncle Stewart ordered.

Aunt Dorothy shifted in her seat, peeked over the dashboard, and said, "I don't recognize them."

"That's because these guys work dinners and we work the breakfast shift. There are different people working this shift."

"Robert isn't with them."

"Where's everyone else?" I whispered to the occupants of the front seat.

"We decided to have Norman and Mildred eat dinner inside."

"Where's Aunt Helen?"

"She's working the bar area."

"Working?"

"She insisted."

"How can she just walk into a restaurant, apply for a job, and start working the same night? Don't they have to check her references? Doesn't she need training?" I sat straighter in the seat, eyes elevated to a height to see over the dashboard.

"Gi-Gi, I didn't mean employed. I meant she was talking to the bartender and flirting with some of the male customers. You have to admit, Helen has turned into a real looker. She'll get a lot of attention." Uncle Stewart sounded like he approved of his transformed relative.

"What's going on?" Tony's voice whispered from behind the dumpster.

This time I sat up and was pushed back down by Uncle Stewart's hand stretched between the bucket seats. "Don't let them see you," he commanded.

Aunt Dorothy pointed. "There's Helen now."

"She wasn't in there very long," Uncle Stewart observed.

I lifted my head long enough to see Helen, hips swaying, walk around to where the smokers were relaxing, and start talking to the men. Uncle Stewart's long arm pushed my head down again.

"This isn't part of the plan," Aunt Dorothy mumbled. "She was supposed to go into the bar area and find out if R. Petrick was working tonight."

"She was supposed to find out how long he's been employed there," Uncle Stewart corrected Dorothy.

I kept my eyes on Aunt Helen, worrying about her safety. Tony startled me by hopping into the backseat next to me. "I couldn't see what was happening from behind the dumpster," he explained.

Helen giggled with the busboys. What was she doing?

"What happens if Robert is working as a busboy tonight? Won't he recognize Norman and Mildred?" Tony asked.

"We have that covered. They wore disguises," Dorothy answered from the front seat.

"Mildred and Norman both have their cell phones with them," Uncle Stewart contributed, "They won't have to pay full price. I had a coupon."

"I'm still thinking about their disguises. What did they do to change their appearance?" Robert lived in the house for almost a week. During that time he had seen Aunt Mildred and Uncle Norman many times. He would recognize them easily if their appearances were not changed significantly and professionally. I recognized them as they drove down the driveway or did I recognize them because they were the only people who would be riding in the Mustang?

No one answered my question. At that moment, Helen turned away from the smokers and started walking toward the car.

"Quick, Dorothy, plan B," Uncle Stewart whispered.

Immediately, Aunt Dorothy slid closer to Stewart and wrapped her arms around his neck, positioning herself as if she was about to kiss him, hiding his face with hers. To the guys watching from the back door of the restaurant, they were a couple seeking a secluded area for a passionate moment.

Still in shock over their behavior, I felt Tony lunge toward me and similarly wrap his arms around my shoulders. The difference was Tony started kissing me for real - bone melting kisses.

"The busboys went inside," Stewart reported. I heard the rustle of movement as Dorothy returned to her original position.

Tony didn't release me and I didn't want him to.

Helen opened the passenger door and tried to shimmy around the seat to get in the back with Tony and me.

"What happened?" Uncle Stewart asked.

"Nothing. I waited in the bar as long as I could without causing suspicion and kept an eye on the service door between the kitchen and the dining area. I didn't see anyone who looked like Robert. I asked the bartender if he knew a busboy by the name of Robert Peters and he told me he had never heard of him."

"Did you ask about R. Petrick?" Stewart asked.

"I didn't get a chance, not without arousing suspicion about why I was there."

"I wonder if he decided not to show up for work. That keeping his identity as Robert Peters was more important than the job," Tony said. "Robert is still under the illusion that he will be getting Harold's car and money. To him that is a fortune."

"Let's hope Mildred and Norman have better luck."

During this exchange I studied Aunt Helen. There were subtle changes to her features that took decades from her appearance. I could see why the men didn't laugh at her flirtation, especially in the fading light.

"They were finishing their meal when I came out. All they had to do was pay their bill."

On cue, the couple came racing around the corner of the restaurant. Norman kept looking over his shoulder as if he expected someone to come after him with a gun. When they were half way across the parking lot Norman called out, "Start the car!"

This time I asked the question, "What happened?"

"The coupon was expired!" Norman explained. "I didn't realize how expensive that place is. I didn't have enough money to pay the whole bill. Let's get out of here."

Without regard for the fact that the backseat was already fully occupied, Norman and Mildred climbed in, causing me to sit on Tony's lap, squeezed against the leather interior panel.

Stewart turned the key and shifted into drive, grinding the gears in the process. Tires spun on the pavement as he steered the Mustang out of the parking lot, miraculously not hitting any parked cars.

With their voices carried away by the wind blowing into the convertible, I had a hard time hearing what happened in the restaurant regarding Robert and the missing busboy.

When we were several blocks from the restaurant, Tony calmly said, "We have a couple problems here. Stewart you need to pull over and stop the car."

Uncle Stewart applied his selective hearing and kept going.

Tony repeated his statement, this time with more vehemence.

Uncle Stewart shifted gears and again the grinding occurred.

"Stop the car or I'm going to give you a ticket."

This time Uncle Stewart complied, pulling into a retailer's parking lot. "What's wrong?"

"The list is long. Let me start with the fact that Norman left the restaurant without paying his bill. That's the equivalent of shoplifting. Petty theft."

"I plan to go back and pay it," Norman explained.

"Then there is the matter of you driving without a license."

"I let it expire years ago. I didn't need it." Stewart didn't sound like he was sorry. "Driving is like riding a bike. Once you learn how, you always remember."

"A judge wouldn't see it like that," Tony countered. "Then there is the matter of you having too many passengers for the number of seatbelts in the car."

"A detail."

"But the main reason I wanted you to stop is because my car is still in the restaurant parking lot. I was trying to get you to stop so that Gi-Gi and I didn't have as far to walk to get the car."

"Oh."

"But now that you are stopped, I think Norman should drive since he has a valid driver's license and when Gi-Gi and I get out, the seatbelt issue will be corrected."

What occurred next was the equivalent to an elderly person's version of a Chinese fire drill. Norman took Stewart's place, Stewart took Dorothy's place and Dorothy climbed into the back seat of the Mustang. Tony and I started walking back to Hayden's to retrieve Tony's vehicle.

"How do you know Stewart doesn't have a valid driver's license?" I was hurrying to keep up with Tony's long strides.

"I checked."

"You checked? When?" I stopped. I couldn't believe that Tony had so little faith in his own instincts that he had background checks done on the members of my family.

"I'm in the middle of a murder investigation. I did a background check on all the parties involved." Tony stopped, allowing me to catch up and walk beside him. He didn't apologize.

"Even me?"

"Especially you."

This time it was me who stopped. "Why me? I'm the one who discovered the body and reported the murder to the police."

"Don't you watch television? Reporting the murder is one of the ways the killer misleads the police into thinking he's innocent."

"But me?"

"I had other reasons." Tony took my hand and took a step toward me.

I took a step back. "What other reasons?"

"I thought you were beautiful and I wanted to know if you were single."

I blushed and was thankful that the sun had set. This time when Tony took a step toward me, I didn't move. I turned my face upward and was rewarded with another of his soul wrenching kisses.

"Come on, I promised you dinner and a movie."

CHAPTER 31

I FLOATED DOWN THE back staircase, basking in the afterglow of a fabulous date with Tony. It had started weird, with the relatives staking out Hayden's Restaurant, but had ended with the late show at the movies and pancakes at the all night diner. There were some details of the date I wanted to keep to myself, but Tony was proving to be a wonderful man who I could easily fall in love with if I was in the market for a new boyfriend.

"Darby is gone."

Connie's comment quickly brought me back to reality.

"What do you mean, *Darby is gone?* Is she gone for a couple hours, the whole day, or has she moved back to her apartment?" There was no sense getting excited about the news that one of my bedrooms was vacated until I knew for sure that it was permanent. I had been burnt twice thinking William had moved out, only to be disappointed later.

"Stella said Darby's bed wasn't slept in and all her things were out of the room."

"It sounds like she went back to her own apartment." I reached for a slice of toast. Not only did it free up another room, it also eliminated one suspect in Harold's murder case from being on the premises.

"There is one other thing."

I set the toast on my plate. I hoped the news was as good as having Darby gone, but I didn't like the tone in Connie's voice. "Yes?"

"Come look at this." Connie led the way to the foyer. She pointed. "See the two straight lines coming down the steps."

"Yes." A blind person could see the two deep scratches, about sixteen inches apart, running the length of the staircase. I ran a finger along the scratches.

"They weren't there yesterday."

So Stella had dragged the vacuum cleaner up the front stairs instead of lifting it. "I won't fire Stella over a couple scratches in the floor. I'll have Joel apply a little stain and they will hardly be noticeable."

"Stella didn't make them." Connie didn't say anything more, waiting for me to draw my own conclusions.

It took several seconds for me to come to another realization, based on the conversation. "Are you saying that Darby made the scratches and felt so bad she left? I'm not that callous. Like I said, Joel will apply a little stain to the marks and no one will notice them.

"What I think is she stole something that was too heavy for her to lift and she had to slide it down the stairs."

"What did she borrow?"

"Borrow? If she was borrowing something she would have left a note. She wouldn't have felt the need to do it when everyone was out of the house." Connie leaned against the newel post, still looking at the marks in the wood. "Stella is searching the house now to see what is missing."

"Darby went through every room yesterday hunting for a lock that the key, Harold gave her, fit. Maybe she found the lock and it was attached to a large, heavy item."

I was getting a bad vibe from the situation. The key fit the metal box in Harold's closet, but what if she found a second box, identical to the first one. "It had to be extremely heavy if it made those scratches in the wood. If Harold had brought something into the house that big, someone would have noticed it."

Connie corrected me. "They would not have noticed. The relatives weren't expecting Harold to bring something that size into the house. They rarely left the front parlor. He could have carried it in the back door or waited until after they were in their rooms."

Connie was correct. I had seen the way the aunts and uncles had fallen into a comfortable lifestyle. They hadn't noticed the addition of a car in the stables. Harold could have had a party in the parlor after their bedtime and they would not have noticed.

I followed the lines up the stairs, trying to determine where they originated. At the landing on the second floor, the Persian rug was out of position, turned so that the pattern in the carpet was opposite its usual direction.

"She didn't try to hide what she did," I commented. "I'm calling Tony."

Connie smirked. "Now you sound like your Aunt Helen, calling your boyfriend at the first sign of trouble."

"What exactly do you want me to do? There are a lot of valuable furnishings in this house and Darby took one without permission. She may have taken more. That's stealing and it's a police matter. Tony happens to be the police and he is familiar with the people involved as well as the murder investigation." To strengthen my argument, I added, "The insurance company will want a formal report as well."

I placed the call, using the house phone. I kept the tone as professional as possible since Connie (smiling smugly) was listening.

Ten minutes later, a car pulled into the driveway and Aunt Helen appeared at the top of the steps. "Is that Everet?" She stopped. Her attention diverted to the hideous scars. "Who made the marks in the wood?" she asked.

"That's what we are trying to find out. That's why I called the police."

"I don't think the police repair wood."

I ignored Helen's comment. "We think Darby stole something that was too heavy for her to lift. I called the police to report the theft."

"So Everet is coming." Aunt Helen dashed back to her room, presumably to tidy her hair, reapply her lipstick, and change into one of her new outfits intended to capture the officer's attention.

I waited at the top of the stairs. Connie went back to the kitchen to open the door for the officers.

I heard the latch on the front door, a slight screech from the hinges, and saw the light in the foyer brighten as the door opened. I peered over the banister to view the person in the foyer. "Darby? What are you doing here?"

"I'm staying with you until Harold's murderer is found, remember?"

I descended the stairs so that I could confront her face to face. "But your things are gone and you didn't sleep in your bed last night."

Darby's cheeks reddened. "I got bored and lonely. The house was too quiet. I decided to go out last night and I met a man."

"That explains why your bed wasn't slept in but where are your clothes?" I joined her in the foyer.

"I didn't bring that many clothes with me. They were all dirty from searching the attic and the other unused parts of the house. I decided to wash them, but when I went to take them to the laundry room I couldn't carry them all, so I put them in the tote to transport them to the cellar."

In an attempt at full disclosure, Darby went on. "I don't have laundry facilities in my apartment complex. I went home and gathered all my dirty clothes, sheets, and towels."

That made sense.

"What happened to the steps?" Darby asked. She was either truly surprised by the marks in the wood or she was a good actress.

"We don't know. We were hoping you knew what caused the scrapes."

Darby didn't get a chance to answer. Tony and Everet entered the foyer by way of the dining room, followed by a frowning Connie. Aunt Helen was standing at the top of the stairs, waiting for her beau. She descended, nodding, and waving by rotating her wrist in the same manner as the Royals. She acted as if she had no previous knowledge of the older policeman's intended arrival.

In the midst of the greetings being exchanged, I heard a faint call from Stella. When I turned to find out what she had discovered, I felt a hand on my arm. "I'll go," Connie said. She cast a suspicious look towards Darby before placing her foot on the first riser.

"If you'll excuse me for one minute, I'll fix a pot of coffee." I hurried away before anyone could protest. I dumped coffee grounds into the filter without measuring them and hurried down the stairs. My final destination wasn't the kitchen, but the laundry area to verify that part of Darby's alibi.

I found a load of wet clothes in the washer and there was a duffel bag on top of the dryer. Darby told at least part of the truth. She still had time last evening, while she was alone in the house, to steal something. I checked Harold's apartment while I was in the basement. Nothing seemed to have been touched since the last time I was there.

If Darby was innocent of stealing something, then who had caused the scrapes in the wood? I quickly eliminated the family members and staff.

Mary Ann's suitcase was heavy when she attempted to leave. It had been so heavy she had asked me to help her with it. Maybe she got so fed up with William's lack of romance that she departed while the rest of us were out and slid the suitcase down the stairs, scarring the wood in the process.

I breathed a sigh of relief. I had figured out the cause of the marks on the stairs and got rid of one more of my house guests.

"Gi-Gi, come up here please. Stella discovered what is missing," Connie called down to the basement.

I felt smug as I complied with her request. The news Connie was going to tell me was about Mary Ann's suitcase and I already figured it out.

"It's the Chinese cabinet that is used as a nightstand in the master bedroom."

"What about it?" I asked, not putting two and two together. I had solved the scratches on the stairs mystery and the Chinese cabinet didn't fit the format.

"It's missing."

"Why would anyone steal that old thing?"

"Gi-Gi, you have lived here all your life and you take for granted all the antiques and treasures in this house. That cabinet, with the lacquered finish and hand painted details, is worth more than most people, including yours truly, make in a year. It can easily be sold to a collector."

"Who do you think stole the cabinet?"

Connie didn't have to think about her answer. "William."

"William? Why would he steal the Chinese cabinet?"

"It was in his room. He's broke. You told me that yourself. He's reached the limit on his credit cards. He can't even pay for the detailing he had done to his car. He can't afford to fill his gas tank. He needs money. He has a woman, with expensive tastes, who he needs to win back. He probably stole the cabinet, sold it, and bought something pretty for Mary Ann."

I had to admit Connie had a point. The next question was

whether to press charges against William if he was the culprit who stole the cabinet. I sat down on the nearest chair. I had to decide quickly. I had two police officers waiting in the foyer.

I resented William for dumping me in favor of his rich patient's daughter, but having him arrested seemed a little over the top when it came to revenge. He probably didn't see it as stealing. He only thought of it as a means to get Mary Ann to marry him. On the other hand he did take the cabinet without permission, that was stealing and stealing was a crime. I decided on a compromise.

I slipped up the back staircase. I intended to confront William and have him return the Chinese cabinet. It wouldn't make him less of a thief, but at least I would have my valuable antique.

Yesterday, he seemed sincere when he talked to me about winning Mary Ann back. He needed to understand he couldn't do it at my expense.

I was on the landing at the top of the steps when a thought occurred to me. In all of the discussion since finding the scrapes in the wood, no one had suggested Robert as the mastermind behind the missing night stand. I returned to the kitchen to talk to Connie about the possibility. There was no need to cause a scene with William if Robert had done the deed.

Connie seriously considered my theory. "I never thought it could be Robert who caused the marks. I haven't seen enough of the young man to realize he's even in the house. He doesn't come to meals. If he eats, he makes a sandwich after everyone goes to bed. He sleeps most of the day. As soon as he wakes up he goes out with his friend." Connie shook her head. "It could have been him, but when did he see the cabinet and would he know how valuable it is? He appears to be strong enough to carry the cabinet down the stairs instead of dragging it."

Having four strangers in the house was causing difficulties. The sooner they moved out the better I would feel. How to extract them from my home was the problem.

This time when I left the kitchen I headed toward the foyer where I found Aunt Helen so close to Everet that a piece of paper wouldn't fit between them. Subtle body language on the part of the older police officer indicated that the embrace was initiated by Aunt Helen, but he was definitely enjoying the moment. Tony studied a painting on the wall, trying to ignore the intimate behavior of the couple.

I coughed as I entered the space hoping the noise would alert my aunt and her boyfriend to my presence and they would put a couple inches between their lips.

"What did you find?" Tony asked, obviously relieved to have a distraction from the physical closeness of the other two. He walked toward me.

"Darby has laundry in the washer and dryer. That part of her story was the truth. Stella discovered a Chinese cabinet is missing from William's room. I think Robert took it."

"What's a Chinese cabinet?"

"It's a black nightstand with pictures of birds, a dragon, and some lotus blossoms painted on it. It's old, originally purchased by my great grandmother. Supposedly the cabinet is very expensive."

"Why would Robert take a night stand from William's room? The whole house is furnished with valuable antiques." Tony pointed toward the artwork on the wall. "Why would he take one that was too heavy to carry? There are plenty of things that are lighter and more portable and more salable than a piece of furniture. If he was determined to steal antique furniture, why didn't he take something from the parlor?"

Tony made some excellent points. I could only counter with one comment, "Thieves aren't smart. If they were smart they wouldn't get caught."

"That's true." Tony conceded my point. "We'll go talk to Robert." Seeing his partner still engaged in kissy face with Aunt Helen, Tony amended his statement, "I'll go talk to him."

Left with the two love birds, I understood why Tony felt

awkward. I had limited choices. I could stare at the pictures on the wall like Tony did, or I could say something that would put a temporary end to their romantic interlude. I chose the latter, after all I had seen the paintings before. "Excuse me. There are other people in the foyer."

Everet adjusted his tie. "Where's Tony?" Everet asked when he turned his attention away from Helen.

"He's upstairs talking to the suspect in the Chinese cabinet robbery."

"Alone? Why didn't he ask me to go with him?"

Everet's question was rhetorical. I didn't bother spelling out the reason for Tony going upstairs by himself.

"Where did Darby go?" I asked, but Everet was already pulling his self up the flight of stairs to find his partner.

"Aunt Helen, I think…." I was about to give my relative a short lecture on the proprieties of kissing in a public place when the reason for Tony's and Everet's trip to the second floor walked in the front door. "Robert?"

My house guest mumbled a greeting, but kept his head down, studying the messages on his cell phone, fingers flying as he responded in length to a text message. (I wondered if the police would have more success getting answers from Robert if they texted him.)

"Those are some ugly scratches on the wood. They spoil the entrance. You need to get a professional to fix them," he said without lifting his head, as if I hadn't seen the scratches myself or reached the same conclusion.

"Do you know how they got there?"

"Nope."

"The police are upstairs, questioning everyone about them."

Robert, who hadn't committed himself to going upstairs, veered to the right. "I think I'll get a ham sandwich and a glass of milk."

I remembered I hadn't had my morning coffee and followed

him to the kitchen. "Robert, where were you last night?" I tried to keep the tone of my question casual as I poured the brew into a mug.

I waited. I had tolerated the young man's insolence and disrespect, but this time I was going to get an answer from him.

When Robert realized I wasn't going to walk away without an answer, he said, "I stayed with a friend."

"Who?"

Robert ignored Connie, opened the refrigerator, and inspected the contents.

"Who did you stay with?"

"I said I stayed with a friend."

"You'll have to give me an answer. A valuable piece of antique furniture was stolen from the house and right now you are the prime suspect. If you don't want to go to jail, you may want to give me a specific name."

The mention of jail got his attention. Robert closed the refrigerator door and looked at me. "I only know him by the name of Too Tall."

"No last name?"

"No."

"Do you know his address?"

"No."

"Do you really expect me to believe that you slept at this guy's house last night and you don't know where he lives?" I couldn't believe Robert didn't know where his alibi lived.

"I didn't drive and I didn't pay attention to where we were going."

"How did you meet this fellow?"

"Gas station."

"What were you doing there? You don't have a car."

"Hanging out."

"There was a murder in this house last week." The reminder was heartless on my part. I was talking to the young fellow who claimed to be the brother of the victim. "You are the person who benefits the most from his death. That makes you a prime suspect for that crime as well. You need to be squeaky clean or else you will not only go to jail for stealing the cabinet, but also for murder."

"I didn't kill your butler."

"You haven't told the police any information that would prove where you were on the night of the murder."

"I'm going out." Robert took two steps in the direction of the front door.

Connie blocked his way. "I think you should stay here and talk to the police."

Robert spun around and hurried toward the back door.

I blocked his way.

Trapped, Robert sat down at the table. "I didn't kill Harold and I didn't take your whatchamacallit."

"Saying it doesn't make it true. There are plenty of people in prison who say they are innocent. You have to be able to prove where you were the night of the murder and where you were last night."

"This is America. I don't have to tell you anything. You have to prove I was here the night Harold was murdered."

"And I think you should answer Gi-Gi's questions," Tony said from the bottom step.

Tony studied Robert. Robert had been living in my house for almost a week and Tony had been a frequent visitor during that same time, but, except for the first night when everyone went to Hayden's for dinner, the two of them hadn't had any face to face time. As I waited, I recalled Robert's body language at the restaurant. He had hidden behind the menu. While Robert ate, he had kept his face down and had purposely sat in a position where Tony didn't have a clear view of his features. To the best of my knowledge, this was the first time Tony got a good look at my houseguest.

"Don't I know you?" Tony asked. He squinted his eyes and took a step closer to Robert as he tried to recall where he had seen the younger man.

"No, not unless you're from Philadelphia." Robert didn't look directly at Tony.

I admired the cocky attitude Robert displayed.

Tony shook his head. "Repeat what you told Gi-Gi about your activities last night. I want to hear it directly from you."

"I stayed with a friend." Robert responded like a belligerent teenager instead of the twenty something year old he was. "His name is Too Tall. I don't know his last name or where he lives."

A light went on in Tony's head. "I know Too Tall. His last name is Samuels and he lives on Third Street. You stay here, in the kitchen, where Connie and Gi-Gi can keep an eye on you and don't use your cell phone until I come back. If you leave the kitchen before I return, I'll throw your butt in jail." He addressed his next comment to me. "Too Tall is not someone I would want my son to hang out with. He doesn't have a police record, but he always seems to be on the fringes of whatever trouble is happening."

Tony started toward the front door and turned back. He called up the stairs, "Everet, come on. We're going to check out a lead."

I heard thundering footsteps on the front stairs and the door open and shut, then silence. Robert stared at his cell phone.

"Keep it on the table where I can see it." I had enough patients hide their cell phones under their blankets and text well into the night instead of getting the rest they needed. I knew if I didn't see Robert's phone, he was probably using it.

Connie started preparing a sandwich for Robert. I noticed she pulled the longest knife she owned from the drawer to cut the ham. It wasn't her usual utensil of choice. I figured she was keeping it handy in case she needed to persuade Robert to stay in the kitchen.

CHAPTER 32

CONNIE WAS PLACING the Dagwood-style sandwich in front of Robert and pouring cups of coffee for herself and me when we heard Darby's shriek from the basement. It was her equivalent of "Eureka!"

I looked at Connie, in a silent exchange she agreed to stay in the kitchen guarding Robert while I investigated what had caused the exclamation.

I called to Darby from the landing. "Darby, are you okay? What are you doing in the basement?"

"I'm fine. I'm waiting for my clothes to dry."

Her voice increased in volume as I descended to the basement. "There's no need to shout. I'm right behind you. Now start over. What are you doing in the basement?"

"I was waiting for the dryer to buzz and decided to explore the butler's apartment." She added, as an aside, "It sure is small."

"He didn't need much space. He used the upstairs kitchen." I

264

Lois Lamanna

wanted to get to the reason for her screech of delight.

"I told you I tried the key in the black box in Harold's apartment and it wouldn't turn the lock mechanism. Then that cop tried the key in the lock and the same thing happened." While Darby waited for me to recall the incident, she reached into the dryer, pulled out a knit top, and folded it precisely. Earlier, Darby mentioned she had work experience in a laundry. She told me the truth if the manner she used to fold the top was any indication.

"I remember, but why did you call out?"

"I recalled seeing another box exactly like it somewhere in the house. I got distracted by a painting or something else and forgot to try the key in it. It must have been before I tried the key in the empty box in the butler's quarters. I need the key. I want to search the house again."

A second box? The possibility had crossed my mind.

I could understand her excitement because I was feeling it too. Since the original metal box was empty, it indicated to me that the killer was after the contents. Harold must have known he was in danger, emptied the one in his room, hid a second box somewhere else in the house, and gave the key to Darby. When we found the second box, we would know who the killer was and what the killer was searching for, something important enough, valuable enough, or incriminating enough to be the motive for murdering Harold.

I watched Darby pull another shirt from the dryer. This one she hung on a hanger and ran her hands down the front to smooth the wrinkles.

I tried to play it cool. "You are aware that the contents of the box may be the reason Harold was murdered. When you find the box, you'll be in danger also."

"No one outside of this house even knows about the key. That one cop took it away from me. Why would I still be in danger?"

My mind went to Robert sitting in the kitchen, while the police talked to Too Tall regarding his alibi for his activities last evening.

Robert felt strongly that Harold's possessions belonged to him. If there were valuables in the second metal box, then he would want them. Maybe Harold told the close mouthed Robert about the contents of the box and that was the reason he continued to stay.

The sound of a car on the gravel driveway alerted me to the arrival of guests. Perhaps Tony and Everet were back from talking with Too Tall. We would finally get some information.

"The last time I saw the key, Tony dropped in on the bed in Harold's apartment." I left Darby to her laundry. I was anxious to have the matter of the missing chest cleared up.

"No." Uncle Stewart was adamant. "I was doing a quality job. The restaurant needs to have more than one dishwasher working in the morning."

Aunt Dorothy had her hands on her hips and an equally stubborn expression on her face. "You were not working fast enough. I ran out of knives before I ran out of orders." Her voice was so loud, Joel in his apartment over the garage, could hear her.

Stewart glared at Dorothy and in an equally loud volume, said, "You could have gone over to the sink and rinsed the knife you were using. You didn't need a clean knife for each tomato you slice."

I stared at my aunt and uncle. Aunt Dorothy never had a bad word to say to anyone and never in my life had I heard a shouting (bickering - yes, shouting - no) match between the relatives.

I wasn't the only one staring at the two. Aunt Helen, Aunt Mildred and Connie were watching, interested in the discussion taking place. Robert was gone.

I interrupted the heated debate on the number and frequency of washing knives at the restaurant. "Where's Robert?"

Silence, if there were crickets in the house, I would have been able to hear them chirp.

"Robert?" Connie asked, as if she had never heard of the

person before. She spun around.

"Yes, you were supposed to be watching him and now he's gone." I didn't wait for the excuse for shirking her duty. I hurried out to the foyer in time to see the young man casually opening the front door, his cell phone in his hand. In my most proper nurse tone, I ordered, "Get back in here. You're not supposed to leave the kitchen or use your cell phone until the police get back."

"But Too Tall texted me. He told the police that I was with him all night playing video games. I'm innocent. I didn't take the piece of old furniture."

"Until I hear it from Tony myself, you will wait in the kitchen." I held out my hand for the cell phone.

My mind fast forwarded to the various scenarios involving the Chinese cabinet removed from the master bedroom. Was it possible that William had taken it? I knew he was desperate for cash, but would he stoop to stealing in order to get some money?

Reasonably certain Connie would keep a watchful eye on Robert, the not-so-juvenile, juvenile delinquent. I decided to approach William directly. I waited only long enough to confirm Robert went into the kitchen before I rushed to the master bedroom and pounded on the door. "William, I need to speak to you now."

Across the hall, the door to my childhood bedroom opened. William was buttoning his shirt. "What's the emergency?"

I spun around. "What are you...?" It didn't take a college education to figure out that Mary Ann and William had sorted out their differences.

"Shh, Mary Ann is packing. I don't want her to get any wrong ideas about your visit."

I recalled that less than twenty four hours earlier I had tried to make the same point to William when he had entered the bedroom I was using. I didn't waste time calling his attention to the fact. "I need to speak to you."

"Go ahead." My former boyfriend neatly tucked his shirt into the waistband of his pants. He stepped into the hall, closing the door behind him.

"The Chinese cabinet that was in the master bedroom is missing."

"Missing? I didn't take it. I don't even know what a Chinese cabinet looks like."

William sounded surprised. I tried to read his expression. "It is a black lacquered nightstand with pictures of flowering trees and dragons painted on it."

William still looked puzzled.

"It was right beside the bed. When was the last time you saw it?"

"Saw it?"

"Yeah, the piece of furniture you put your watch on at night." I remembered he had traded in his watch and didn't feel the slightest remorse for reminding him of it. "When was the last time you were in the master bedroom?"

This time he had the gentlemanly grace to pale. "I took Mary Ann out to eat. We went to a restaurant on the other side of town and got back late. I didn't sleep in my room last night." As an afterthought he added, "I had my wallet and the keys to her car on it. When we left, I put those items in my pocket. I guess that's the last time I saw the cabinet."

Mary Ann opened the door fully. "I can vouch for William. He was with me all evening." She was smiling broadly.

William draped his arm around Mary Ann's shoulder. "You should be the first to know, the wedding is back on."

Mary Ann extended her hand to display the diamond ring, the same ring she had proclaimed as coming from a dollar store. "Of course, this time, we're going to have a longer engagement and a big church wedding." Mary Ann giggled.

I was almost blinded by the light reflecting from the ring on her finger. I congratulated the happy couple, but didn't linger. I only gave a brief thought to all the wedding preparations going to waste. I had other issues I needed to think about. If Robert's alibi was solid and William and Mary Ann could vouch for each other's whereabouts all evening, there was only one other person in the house who could have stolen the cabinet – Darby.

I wanted to call Tony and tell him what I had found out. I reached for my cell phone. Of course, Uncle Stewart, the hoarder still had it. I considered using the phone in the hall, but Tony would be arriving momentarily to personally confront Robert and I would tell him my suspicions then. I could wait.

It didn't matter that in the past hour or so I had accused each of my house guests of stealing the Chinese nightstand. This time I had it right.

CHAPTER 33

A S IF ON cue, I heard a car door slam and tires crunch on the driveway. Tony had arrived. No, that wasn't right. That was the wrong order for someone arriving. Someone was leaving! I rushed to the closest window and saw the taillights of Darby's car disappearing onto the highway. Through the hatchback's rear window I could make out the square shape of the cabinet, covered with a towel. Her car almost clipped the fender of the Mustang as Uncle Norman turned into the driveway.

I raced out the front door to meet him. "Uncle Norman, follow that car!" I knew the words sounded trite. I didn't bother opening the car door, instead I tried to vault into the front seat like the good guys always did on television. (After one failed attempt, I settled for the standard method of entering the car and promised myself I would get into better shape.)

Uncle Norman ground the gears as he released the clutch. The tires spun in the gravel. The car jerked forward. We were off, following Darby's hatchback.

Uncle Norman didn't slow for approaching traffic. The Mustang fishtailed as he turned in the direction of town.

I fumbled for the seatbelt as we entered the highway. I braced myself against the dashboard, positive I was on a suicide mission. With the top down, traveling at the speed Uncle Norman was doing, I felt like an astronaut experiencing G-forces. My face was blown back by the wind and the pull of my hair.

It didn't take long for the Mustang to catch up to Darby's four-cylinder compact. She was traveling at the posted speed, unaware we were in pursuit.

Uncle Norman shouted over the engine noise, "Do you want me to ram the rear of her car?"

I looked at my uncle. He had an expression of determination on his face and if I wasn't mistaken he was enjoying the chase experience. As for ramming the back of Darby's car, I hadn't thought about what we would do once we were behind her. I only saw the rectangular shape, draped with fabric in the back of her car. I assumed it was the Chinese nightstand.

At the moment, Darby didn't seem to be aware of the Mustang following her.

A siren in the background seemed to be getting closer. I glanced at the speedometer and hoped the dealership had put a new license plate on the back of the car and that Uncle Norman's driver's license was truly up to date. Otherwise, the cop was going to get writer's cramp issuing citations for one traffic stop.

"Pull over to the side of the road," I advised my relative.

He complied with the verbal asterisk, "We're going to lose Darby."

"If you don't, you'll lose your license." I was jolted forward by the sudden braking, happy I had my hand against the dashboard and happier still when the police cruiser whizzed past us.

I didn't have time to recover from my near death experience. Directly in front of us, inches from the Mustang's front bumper,

Darby had also pulled over to allow the emergency vehicle to pass. I had a new appreciation for Uncle Norman's driving skill. If he hadn't stopped in the manner he had, we would have run into the rear of Darby's hatchback.

Hurriedly, I got out of the Mustang. I didn't want Darby to pull back into traffic before I confronted her about the missing Chinese cabinet in the back of her vehicle. I ran up to her window and tapped.

Darby gave away her guilt by checking the load in the rear of her car.

"I want to see what you have in the back."

She had the good grace to blush. "It's my laundry."

"Yeah, and I'm the queen of England."

"Take a look." She reached into her glove box and pushed a button. The hatch was released.

I lifted the rear door to reveal a large laundry basket. filled with towels and under garments. I had been mistaken. I visually inspected the contents and pushed down on the towels. It wasn't a Chinese cabinet covered by a towel. It was exactly what Darby had said it was - laundry.

I apologized with a "Sorry," and went back to the Mustang.

"I was wrong. We chased her for no reason at all. It was her laundry not the missing cabinet," I explained to Uncle Norman. I was a little disappointed. Between the murder, too many guests, and the missing cabinet there were too many loose ends in my life. I wanted, no, I needed something resolved.

Norman politely waved Darby to pull into traffic first, allowed several cars to pass before sedately doing the same. Compared to the way he had driven trying to catch up to Darby, Norman was lollygagging along like the proverbial Sunday driver.

I was kicking myself for being paranoid about the woman. She had been doing her laundry. I had seen her take shirts out of the dryer. I should have figured that she would take it back to her apartment. It wasn't until the Mustang stopped at the opposite end of the block, away from Darby's apartment building, that I quit chastising myself for my foolishness and paid attention to where we were. "What are you doing?"

"Surveillance."

I watched Darby remove the hangers from the back seat. "Uncle Norman, She's innocent. She had laundry in the back of her car."

"She has a bad suspension."

"You're following Darby because she needs her suspension replaced?" I didn't know what a suspension was, but it didn't seem like a reason to follow a person and then stop a couple hundred feet away. If her suspension was bad, logically, why wasn't Uncle Norman pulling up beside Darby's car and telling her?

He explained, "She has something in the back that is heavy enough to cause the car to tilt. A single basket of laundry doesn't weigh enough to do that."

"What do you mean? I checked the basket."

"She has something hidden among her clothes, something heavier than some women's underwear."

"Towels?"

"Heavier."

"How heavy? Should I call Tony?" I asked. My internal alarms were going off. If Darby had stolen the Chinese cabinet, what else had she taken from the house and what would she do if she was confronted?

"Not yet. I want to be sure I'm correct before we call in the police. I want to watch Darby carry the basket into her apartment."

"It is a large basket for laundry and I didn't check it thoroughly," I admitted. Uncle Norman had sharp eyes. I couldn't even detect the slightest tilt of Darby's car. The weight in the back of the car had to be less than a passenger would have been. Then I realized something more important. "What if she sees the Mustang? It is a distinctive car and there isn't another one like it."

Uncle Norman looked up and down the street as if he was

only now aware of the unique quality of his vehicle. "I need to move the car. Get out."

"Get out? Why?"

"You're going to watch the apartment while I hide the car."

"What if she sees me?"

"Hide. Wait inside that little grocery store, but keep an eye on the building where Darby lives. Watch what she does."

Uncle Norman was exhibiting strange behavior, but I got out and crossed the street. He took off around the corner. I didn't know what he was going to do and we hadn't discussed when he was going to come back to get me. We hadn't discussed what I should do if Darby did come back to her car. Furthermore I didn't have my cell phone and felt vulnerable without it.

Inside the store the aroma of Indian spices tickled my nose and made my mouth water. I tried to focus my attention on Darby's apartment building, but the clerk's insistent chatter about purchasing something and the tantalizing aromas pulled me further into the little shop. I casually strolled along the aisles, perusing the shelves and reading the labels, while watching the front of the apartment building and Darby's car. Finally I couldn't stand the pressure of the clerk's gaze and selected a spice from the shelf.

I placed a small can of curry powder on the counter, reached for my purse, and realized I didn't have it with me. I searched my pockets for money and came up empty.

The clerk watched my actions with increased interest. "No money, no curry." She snatched the spice container from the counter and hugged it to her chest. "Get out." She pointed toward the door.

Humiliated, I weighed my options. I didn't have any excuse to linger in the food store, but I didn't want to stand on the sidewalk in clear view of Darby's apartment either. A produce van pulled up to the sidewalk in front of the shop. Without thinking about what I was doing, I took advantage of the visual barricade and scurried out the door with the intention of hiding at the side of the store.

"Gi-Gi." I heard someone call. It sounded like Uncle Norman. I spun around, looking for the source of the voice.

Uncle Norman was leaning out the passenger window of the panel van. "Get in," he ordered.

I pulled open the sliding side door of the truck and was greeted by the solemn faces of the aunts and uncles. "What are you doing here?" I asked.

Like puppets on a common thread, the aunts and uncles held up their cell phones. "Norman called."

That answered one question. I didn't have time to contemplate the irony of everyone having a cell phone except me. I had a different question. "Uncle Norman, where did you get the truck?"

"Gi-Gi, I'd like you to meet a friend of mine, Augie. It's his van." I glanced at the driver. The gray haired man looked familiar but given the circumstance how I knew him didn't seem important. I sat on an empty fruit crate surrounded by the smells and sights of decaying lettuce leaves and other discarded pieces of fruit and vegetables.

"Isn't this exciting? We're on a real stake out," Aunt Dorothy said. "When Norman called and asked if we wanted to come, we didn't even have time to comb our hair. We just hurried down to the driveway and jumped into the back of the van. I've never ridden in the back of a produce truck before."

"We don't know if the Chinese cabinet is in Darby's car." I tried to lower the group's expectations. I didn't want them to be too disappointed when the content of the hatchback was laundry with nothing hidden amongst it.

"I guess no one told you. We found that fancy nightstand. The exterior didn't appear to be harmed, but it did have a couple screw holes inside. I don't think the holes will hurt the value too much," Uncle Stewart said.

Aunt Mildred contributed, "It's made out of balsam wood. It

was so light; I could pick it up. I don't know why the scratches on the stairs were so deep."

Things were starting to add up. Darby's search of the house, her questions earlier about the key and the possibility of a second black metal box, the indication of heavy content in the Chinese cabinet which was now light as a feather. Uncle Norman was correct. Darby had something in the back of her car that she didn't want us to know about.

"Uncle Stewart, I need my cell phone back."

"I bought a new phone. I put yours in the junk drawer."

"Aunt Helen, let me use your cell phone."

"I'm expecting a call from Evvie." She hugged the little electronic device to her chest.

"He'll call you back." I reached for the phone.

"Here, use mine." Aunt Mildred offered her phone and I accepted it, rapidly punching in the numbers for Tony.

"Mildred, I don't have time to talk right now, police business," Tony answered.

I hesitated for a second while I thought about the officer having Aunt Mildred's cell phone number programmed into his phone. "Tony, it's me, not Aunt Mildred."

"Gi-Gi, I don't have time to talk. I have to go."

"Tony, don't hang up," I said to the dead phone. I tried again, but this time when the phone rang it went straight to his voice mail. I felt like curling up in a fetal position and crying.

"Trouble in paradise?" Aunt Mildred asked.

"I don't think there ever was a paradise in this case, at least not one including Tony and me," I replied. The occupants of the produce van fell silent.

"Is that the woman, you are waiting for, coming out of the building?" Augie asked. We all turned to look, but only Uncle Norman had the perspective of actually seeing out the window.

"Yep, that's Darby. Now watch as she lifts the laundry to see if the basket is heavier than a bunch of folded towels would normally be," Uncle Norman instructed.

I wiggled forward on the crate. I was anxious to watch Darby's movements, to see if she was struggling to lift the laundry basket or if it was a normal weight.

Uncle Norman gripped the door handle. "As soon as she lifts the basket, I'm going to go chat with her. She won't be able to run with her arms full of clothes."

"I'm going with you." Uncle Stewart crouched toward the side panel of the truck.

"So am I," Augie volunteered.

I didn't say anything because I didn't want to place the aunts in danger, but I also planned to confront Darby.

If I strained forward and closed one eye I could see Darby. She looked up and down the street, as if she was checking to see if anyone was watching. Then she moved toward her car, opened the hatchback, and rearranged some of the laundry. I watched as she struggled to slide the basket closer to the edge, where she could lift it.

"I'd say the basket is heavier than a bunch of gutchies," Augie said.

"I have to agree." Uncle Norman pushed his door open.

Uncle Stewart and I exited by way of the sliding side panel of the produce truck. Augie waited until we were in front of the truck, then he joined us.

Darby didn't notice us until we were behind her. She had the laundry basket in her arms. Without any experience in these matters, I had to agree with Augie's assessment. There was something in the basket heavier than the towels that were visible.

Now that we were confronting Darby with the evidence of her theft, I was speechless. Uncle Stewart, ever the gentleman, took the matter into his own hands. "Can I carry that upstairs for you?"

Darby's arms tightened around the basket. "No thank you. I can manage."

"I insist." Uncle Stewart reached for the basket and pulled.

Darby's grasp wasn't strong enough. In spite of her intentions, she allowed it to slip from her arms.

Uncle Stewart wasn't prepared for the weight.

The laundry spilled to the pavement - with a crash.

If I hadn't seen it in the attic only days before, I would not have recognized the shattered urn, the gift I intended to give William and Mary Ann for their wedding.

Aunt Mildred also recognized the large ceramic piece. "Isn't that the urn Grandmother Grant received as a wedding gift from an English duke? It was worth a fortune when she got it and is probably worth more now."

"Personally I'm glad it's broken. It was ugly with all the frogs and bugs painted on it." Aunt Helen shuttered.

While they were analyzing the debris, I watched Harold's girlfriend, waiting for her to run. To my surprise, she did the opposite. Darby collapsed onto the curb and started to weep. "I only wanted to clean it up, repair the one little chip, and give it back to you as a present for allowing me to stay with you."

"You knew the vase's value?"

"Of course, anyone who studied antiques and collectables would recognize the design. That's why I selected that particular piece to restore to its former condition." Darby wiped the tears from her eyes with a towel she picked up from the sidewalk.

I looked at my relatives to see if they believed her version of what had occurred. They were divided fifty-fifty, if my intuition was accurate. I remained skeptical. "Why didn't you ask permission? I would have allowed you to restore it."

"I wanted to surprise you." Darby sounded sorry.

The aunts were picking up the laundry from the sidewalk, the men were standing around discussing the poor suspension on Darby's car.

Aunt Mildred's cell phone rang. We all turned to face her and listen to the conversation. "It's Tony."

"Tell him I don't want to talk to him."

"He didn't ask for you. He wants to know if anyone has seen Everet?"

Aunt Helen dramatically raised the back of her hand to her forehead, appearing to swoon. "Oh no. What's happened to Evvie?"

Aunt Dorothy tapped her on the arm. "Knock it off. Nothing's happened to him. He just hasn't reported in and Tony wants to know where he is."

Aunt Helen threw her arms in the air and started to wail. "He hasn't called me since this morning."

This pronouncement didn't alarm me. It was only three hours. Men were likely to spend that amount of time in a hardware store staring at gadgets. I politely asked Helen, "Did he say what he was going to do?"

"He had some personal errands," she replied. In addition to the arms in the air and the wailing, Aunt Helen started to rock back and forth.

Mildred relayed the message to Tony.

Uncle Norman, Uncle Stewart and Augie finished their discussion. Norman, acting as spokesperson for the trio, said, "We've discussed the matter and we feel Darby should continue to stay at Grant House."

I hurriedly pulled Uncle Norman aside. "Are you crazy? This could be the only thing we caught her taking. She may have stolen a lot more."

"Trust me, kiddo. I can read people and this girl is innocent."

"But she could be Harold's killer," I whispered.

Apparently Uncle Norman needed his hearing checked, because he smiled, walked over to Darby, and invited her back to the house.

I felt Uncle Stewart's hand on my shoulder. "It will be alright," he said, and he gently led me back to the produce truck.

CHAPTER 34

I WENT STRAIGHT TO my room, the one formerly assigned to Joel. Someone, probably Stella had gathered my belongings from the nursery and placed the boxes on the floor beside the bed. There was comfort derived from having my personal belongings surrounding me and at the moment I needed the comfort. Tony was more anxious to talk to Aunt Mildred or anyone else than me. I didn't realize how important he had become and I wasn't confident the feeling was mutual.

I looked out the window and saw the gazebo. No one had bothered to remove the decorations intended for William and Mary Ann's wedding. There was an altar-like pedestal in the center of the platform and folding chairs under a tarp. Sections of the white net garland, draped between the posts, fluttered in the breeze. Yard debris was beginning to accumulate on the wicker furniture. I would ask Joel to remove the reminders of the postponed ceremony.

Somehow I felt sorry for the couple. They had a multitude of problems facing them in their married life. Mary Ann had made the proper decision, to delay the wedding until William could be honest with her. At least for the moment they knew they cared for one another.

As I thought about the couple and continued to view the scene of what should have been their wedding, I noticed Everet coming out of the garage. I opened the window and called out to him, "Tony is looking for you."

It took him a second to locate the source of my voice. "Gi-Gi, is that you? I didn't know you were back." He shielded his eyes against the sun.

"What were you doing in the stables?"

"I'm still trying to find some piece of evidence to link Harold's murder to the killer. I was examining the Chinese cabinet. I can't figure out why after going through the trouble to lug it down the stairs and out to the garage, the thief didn't take it."

"Tony said you were a workaholic and that you enjoyed trying to solve cold cases."

Everet nodded his head. "I don't think we can classify this one as cold, at least not yet."

From a window three away from the one I was leaning out, Aunt Helen joined the awkward conversation. "Everet, is that you?" She didn't wait for an answer. She continued, "I texted you and I'm waiting for you to call me."

"I had my cell phone turned off," he explained. "I needed to concentrate."

"I'll be right down," Aunt Helen called. At least one romance was going in the right direction.

I closed the window and stared at the boxes surrounding the bed. There was no sense unpacking until I resumed residence in the master bedroom.

I sat on the edge of the bed and pondered my situation. I wouldn't be able to take my rightful place in the master bedroom until William and Mary Ann moved out, Harold's killer was caught, and my other house guests moved out. I added the disappearance of the Chinese nightstand and the cause of the scrapes on the stairs as matters that needed to be resolved.

I had part of the house guest issue solved and then Uncle Norman invited Darby to come back to the house to stay. I felt strongly that one of my guests killed my butler and I had them staying with me waiting to kill one of us.

Footsteps in the hall provided a diversion. Anything was better than the maudlin thoughts I had. "Hi, Uncle Stewart, what are you doing?"

"I thought I would clip coupons. I've saved a lot of money. Do you want to help? I have a large pile of magazines I want to go through."

It wasn't my first choice for entertainment and I was about to make up an excuse when I remembered my resolve to show more interest in the lives of my aunts and uncles. I followed Uncle Stewart along the hall like I did when I was a kid, chatting about the weather and the local baseball team.

I stopped at the door, stunned by the appearance of the room. It looked like it snowed. Drifts of scrap paper were scattered on every surface of the room and if anything the stacks on the floor appeared to have grown. The carpet was covered with the scraps from his endeavor. The only glimmer of hope was an overflowing wastebasket and a large garbage bag sitting in the middle of the space.

Uncle Stewart chuckled. "I know it looks bad, but I'm thinning out and compacting my collections." He walked over to the desk and took two pair of scissors from under a magazine. I blinked. I couldn't believe he could find anything in the mess.

"What do you want me to do?" I asked. I hoped he would say, throw everything away.

"Start on that pile of old newspapers. Most of the coupons aren't any good, but every once in a while there's one with no expiration date."

With those basic instructions, I sat on the floor and started with the top section of the paper. Several minutes later I looked up to see Uncle Stewart in full concentration mode. His glasses were perched halfway down his nose and the tip of his tongue protruded. He flipped through a newspaper section, hunting for the elusive coupon that would save fifteen cents. Every couple minutes he would say, "Bingo," and then I would hear the scissors snipping the paper.

I wasn't quite as enthusiastic about the task as Uncle Stewart. I did find a few coupons of value, but mostly I found ones that had expired in a previous decade or were for products we didn't use. My mind wandered and I found myself reading the articles and not searching for the coupons. When I finished one section, I shoved the scraps into the bag and reached for the next section.

Mechanically reaching for the next section, my brain on auto pilot, I stared at the artist rendering the family had discussed when we were searching for Harold's resume. This time when I saw the picture, I had a vision. "Uncle Stewart, hand to me a pen."

"Why do you need a pen?" He really didn't care, he was making conversation.

"Who do you think this looks like?" I asked, holding up the paper.

He glanced up from his newest hobby. "I always thought the guy looked familiar, but I couldn't figure it out."

I drew glasses on the picture and darkened the character's hair. It was a childish addition to the sketch, but it served the purpose. I repeated my question.

"By golly, it looks like Harold!"

I read the caption. *Suspect in the bank robbery*, I said out loud. *Story on page three.*

"We're mistaken. Our Harold didn't seem like the bank robber type."

"What exactly is a bank robber type?" I challenged.

"Sinister?" Uncle Stewart stared at the picture.

"Do you have the rest of the article?" I started flipping through the stack of newspapers.

Uncle Stewart didn't answer my question.

"Think about it. This is the perfect place for someone to hide," I said.

"Yeah."

"Harold purposely blocked every avenue to his past. His previous life has been completely wiped out. The police tried to trace him but every time they thought they had a lead to his past, they met a dead end."

"Yeah."

"There's no one local who can link him with his roots."

"Yeah."

"He told Darby that he was coming into money."

I waited for the "Yeah," but it didn't come.

"Harold was murdered," I said. "Based on a fifteen year old sketch drawn from witnesses' descriptions, he may have been a bank robber. But he didn't kill himself."

"And the killer may be living in our house." Uncle Stewart delivered the statement in a flat tone, but I felt the whole range of emotions.

"Do you think I should call Tony?"

"I definitely feel he should know about the sketch." Uncle Stewart reached into his pocket and pulled out his new cell phone.

I punched in the numbers and listened to the phone ring. I didn't feel the butterflies in my stomach I usually got when I anticipated talking to Tony. This was serious business.

While I waited for Tony to answer, I thought about the possibility of Harold, our live-in, long tenured butler, being a bank robber. It didn't make sense. He had lived the life of a perfect domestic employee for fifteen years. He spent within his means including the purchase of a new car and a couple of beers.

Why had he waited before he spent his ill-gotten gains? I examined the picture again. Was it our imagination interpreting the artist's rendering as Harold?

I closed the phone.

"Why did you hang up?" Uncle Stewart asked.

I was confused. I couldn't formulate my thoughts into words. I started to cry.

Uncle Stewart reached over and awkwardly patted my shoulder, "There, there, it isn't so bad."

His gesture made me cry harder, chest heaving sobs.

My relative gently pried the phone from my fingers and started tapping the keypad. I recovered long enough to ask him what he was doing. "Texting the others."

*****

Aunt Mildred was the first to arrive in the study, quickly followed by Uncle Norman and Aunt Dorothy. Aunt Helen was the last to enter, jingling a charm bracelet on her wrist.

Uncle Stewart waited until everyone was seated. "We have a situation. Gi-Gi and I found something among my collections and we need your opinions." Without any further preamble he held up the sketch from the newspaper.

"Zowie." Uncle Norman added a whistle to emphasize his point. "Where did you get the sketch of Harold?"

Uncle Stewart drew his self to his full height, straightening his back and his shoulders. "This is the same picture we found in the stack a couple days ago and everyone agreed that the person looked familiar, but no one could figure out who it was. Gi-Gi added the hair color and glasses. The only problem is the caption to the picture indicates the person was a suspect in a bank robbery."

Aunt Mildred picked up a magazine and started to fan herself. "The sketch can't be Harold. Harold was such a nice person."

Aunt Dorothy commented, "We have valuables sitting everywhere in the house and nothing ever disappeared."

Aunt Mildred nodded her head in agreement.

Uncle Stewart repeated the earlier comments I made.

Aunt Helen squinted her eyes and stared at the picture. "It certainly appears to be Harold. I never thought he was handsome, but he is in the picture."

Uncle Stewart pointed at the newspaper's banner. "The date is consistent with when he applied for the position."

I was in better control of my emotions when I asked, "What are we going to do?"

After clearing his throat, Uncle Norman suggested, "I think we should find out more about the picture. We need to find out the details of the bank robbery."

"How are we going to do that?" Aunt Dorothy asked.

"We could spend hours in the library reading old newspapers or we could do an internet search," I suggested.

"An internet search?" I could hear the shock in Aunt Helen's voice. "I don't know how to use a computer."

"The police should have a report of some sort about a bank robbery fifteen years ago," Uncle Norman offered.

The relatives were planning their strategy, trying to decide how best to prove (or disprove) the person in the picture was Harold, when Robert casually strolled into the study. "I'm leaving." He had his small suitcase in his hand.

"Why aren't you in the kitchen where Connie can keep an eye on you?."

This wasn't my day to get answers. Robert attention was focused on the paper Uncle Stewart held. "Who's the guy in the picture?"

"You should know. It's a picture of Harold," Uncle Stewart answered. "Your brother."

"I was just fooling around. I thought I could get your butler's money or maybe his job." Robert was downplaying the scam he committed. "Why is there a picture of Darby on the other corner?"

"Darby?" Six pairs of eyes turned toward the lower portion of the newspaper and examined the other photo on the page. Some of the relatives stood up to get a closer look. We had been studying the sketch of Harold so intently, that none of us had glanced at the other picture.

Uncle Stewart, who was still holding the front page, read the caption. "Bank robbery suspect captured."

It was difficult to see the face of the suspect the police had arrested. Her hair was hanging in front of half her face, her head tilted downward, but the body was the same and there was a definite similarity between my house guest and the person in the fifteen year old picture.

"Fifteen years." The occupants of the room spun toward the voice. Darby grabbed our attention. She was holding a gun.

My mind was racing, trying to figure out what Darby meant by her comment and what I could do to get my relatives out of harm's way. I chose the easy way. "What do you mean fifteen years?"

"That's how long I spent in prison for the bank robbery. I was doing other prisoners' filthy laundry and cooking slop in the cafeteria while Hal walked around without getting caught. I kept my mouth shut and what did I get for it. Two, three minutes phone calls a week. Not one single visit."

"Oh I think you got even when you shot him."

"He was holding onto my share of the money. He was going to give it to me in little installments, like an allowance." I was hoping her comment would stand up in court as a confession to murdering Harold.

"And you wanted it all."

"That's right. I did my time. I want to get out of the country and live the good life on one of the Caribbean islands. I need all the money to do that." Darby waved the gun.

"Why are you still here?" I asked. I tried to look Darby in the eye, but all I could do was stare at the barrel of the gun.

"He tried to trick me. The metal box in his apartment was empty, but the money has to be hidden somewhere in the house." She slowly turned, stopping to point the gun at each person. "I haven't found the money, but that's going to change. You're going to help me look for it."

"How are we going to do that?" Aunt Helen asked.

"I think." Again she looked at the individuals in the room. "I will keep Gi-Gi here with me while the rest of you search the house. If anyone tries anything, I'll shoot her."

My eyes stayed focused on the gun, but my ears were alert to footsteps on the stairs.

Mary Ann entered the room, pushing past Darby. William followed closely. She held out her left hand. "Look everybody. We got married this morning at the magistrate's office. Isn't it romantic?" Mary Ann circled the room making sure everyone saw her wedding ring, including stopping in front of Darby to display her trophy. Inches away from the gun, the new bride didn't even notice the weapon.

I remained frozen. If Darby panicked and pulled the trigger, the result would be a point blank shot. William would become a widower within hours of becoming a husband.

Fortunately Darby stepped back, to get the ring out of her face and to watch the occupants of the room. Unfortunately, Uncle Stewart's hoarding ways tripped her, causing the woman to lose her balance. Everything happened quickly after that.

The gun went off, firing into the ceiling.

Surprisingly, William acted first. He pulled Mary Ann away from where Darby fell.

Uncle Norman kicked the gun out of Darby's hand.

But it was Robert who jumped on top of Darby and wrestled with her. His hundred and twenty pounds were no match for a woman who survived prison life for the past fifteen years.

Darby easily pushed him off and ran from the room. She took the stairs two at a time. Seconds later I saw her emerge from the house and race toward her hatchback.

"Call the police. Call 9-1-1," I shouted. No one moved. I grabbed Stewart's cell phone from the desk and punched in the numbers. I yelled, "Quick! She's getting away." I looked around the room and everyone was gone. I watched out the window while I answered the emergency operator's painfully precise questions.

Robert was the first to exit the house, followed by Uncle Stewart. There was a pause and surprisingly Aunt Helen was the next person I saw sprinting from the porch.

I was supposed to be taking care of the relatives. They were supposed to be frail. They were supposed to be sedate. I worried about blood pressures and arthritis, bone fractures and heart attacks. They were catching a murderer.

The police car turned into the driveway. Siren blaring. Lights flashing. Tony and Everet opened their doors and took protective crouch positions, weapons drawn. Their actions were a little too late. Darby was being tied up with the cord from the hedge trimmers.

In the middle of the confusion, William sedately escorted Mary Ann to his car, a car I hadn't seen since the night he had arrived. Mary Ann's hand rested on his arm. In his other hand was a small suitcase.

A small suitcase? In a flash, the answer came to me. I knew where the money from the bank robbery was. Mary Ann had a suitcase so large she couldn't carry it by herself. William also arrived with a large suitcase. The busboy from the restaurant carried it to his room the night he arrived, William too intoxicated to carry it himself.

William had found the safe hidden in the night stand in the master bedroom. He had dragged it to the garage. Using the tools available, he managed to open the safe and get the money. The money was the reason Mary Ann had changed her mind and decided to marry him.

I didn't know what he had done with the safe.

He proved he could afford the life style she wanted. In the midst of all the activity, the irony hit me. Mary Ann married William for his money.

I pounded on the glass. When I couldn't get anyone's attention, I unlatched the window and opened it. "Don't let William leave." I didn't wait to see if anyone heard me. I hurried down the steps.

"Tony! Stop William."

For once Tony listened to me. He pointed the gun at my former boyfriend.

CHAPTER 35

I WALKED INTO THE parlor and opened the drapes. No one commented. Daylight wouldn't change the gloomy atmosphere in the room, but other than murdering another staff member, I didn't have many options. I tried talking the relatives into going shopping at the mall, or dining at restaurants with foreign foods. I even tempted them with bar hopping. Nothing I suggested had motivated them to leave the parlor.

In the brief time since the arrest of Harold's killer, the return of the money, and the exodus of the houseguests, my relatives had reverted to their former dormant lifestyle. Uncle Norman had covered the Mustang with a tarp. Uncle Stewart and Aunt Dorothy had taken leaves from their jobs.

Needlepoint seat covers, in various stages of completion, rested on the laps of the women. Aunt Helen jabbed her needle into the mesh as if it were a voodoo doll and she had hexes she wanted to bestow. (I hoped I wasn't the subject of her curses.) Officer Everet Swanson had not returned her calls in the past two days.

291

Room for Murder

Uncle Norman and Uncle Stewart were bent over the daily crossword, bickering about the interpretation of the clue for seventeen down.

I joined the others, sitting sedately on the upholstered chair, trying to appear relaxed. I had one more trick up my sleeve to restore their vigor. It was my last resort, a secret phone call. I hope it worked.

I only had to wait a few minutes. On cue there was a knock on the front door.

"I'll get it." I was barely able to contain my excitement, but I didn't rush to greet my guest. I was certain that before long, the household would be in full wedding preparation mode (again).